Heaven
A Novel by
75,00

HEAVENS SHAKEN

First edition. February 26, 2024.

Copyright © 2024 E Arlo Sharp.

ISBN: 979-8224099078

Written by E Arlo Sharp.

If you're reading this, that means I made it. I couldn't have done it without you guys.

EAS

PART I

A^{WAKENING}

CHAPTER 1

Tav knew his eyes were open, and yet he couldn't see anything. Several feet away from him lay his father's body. He could no longer hear him struggling to breathe. All he could hear now were his own breaths, deep and heaving against the muggy air that hung in the kitchen. He was rocking back and forth rhythmically, his dark red hair swaying with every motion.

Moments later, footsteps—*click, clack, click, clack,* stopping just feet away from him. Rysha Barlett now loomed over the scene, taking in every gruesome detail with pinpoint precision. He was well dressed in a black suit with a red tie, paired with black work boots. His dark hair was in a low ponytail, with a well-kept goatee on his chin. Behind his glasses, his dark brown eyes were carefully scanning the scene. Working as a homicide detective had presented him with the harsh reality of death many times, but this seemed... Different. Something was off.

Rysha turned to the body. The man looked to be in his 40's, perhaps older. He was lying face up, eyes stuck in a position that perpetually elicited true fear. His face looked relatively intact, but such could not be said for the rest of him; It looked as though an explosive blew up mere feet from him, invisible shrapnel riddling his body. Beneath the body, a blackened muddle swirled like cream in coffee amongst the blood. In the man's hand, there was a pistol. Rysha put his latex-gloved fingertips against the barrel. It was cold.

Rysha returned his attention to the young man. He was still breathing, however he appeared to be in a trance state. As he rocked back and forth, Rysha caught a glimpse of his shirt; blood had just begun to soak through. If he had been shot in the heart, his chances of survival dwindled by the second.

"I need a paramedic!"

At this exact moment, Tav collapsed.

By now, several other investigators had made their way into the home. Some were taking pictures, others were talking amongst themselves. Rysha still couldn't shake the feeling that something was unusual here. Within seconds, the paramedics arrived to take care of the person that was still alive, and the coroner to take care of the person that was not. He decided that once the young man was released from the hospital, he'd talk to him. There had to be something he didn't know.

• • • •

Tav blinked awake in the dimly lit hospital room. Everything felt fuzzy, as if his brain had been numbed. He slowly turned his head to his left and saw an IV protruding from his arm. There was also a device attached to his finger that displayed his pulse and other vital signs on a monitor nearby. To his right, his arm was pointed slightly more outward from his body, and a pair of handcuffs attached his wrist to the handle of the bed.

As his consciousness slowly came around, Tav could hear the conversation that was taking place just outside of the room. He could only detect one half of it; a deeper voice. Every once in a while, he could pick out a key bit of information.

"Well, with his father being dead,"

"Legal guardianship,"

"Trial,"

Tav was now incredibly curious as to who was speaking. Soon enough, a nurse walked in, followed by a tall man with a black ponytail.

"Hi, honey, how are you feeling?" The nurse asked.

Tav had to remember how to speak.

"I..."

Tav closed his eyes. Truth be told, he wasn't sure exactly how he was feeling.

"It's okay, honey. Someone is here to talk to you. Is that okay?"

Tav opened his eyes to see that the nurse and the man were now standing on either side of him. The man flashed him a weak yet genuine smile. The nurse turned to him and then to Tav.

"I'll let you two talk a moment, but I'll be back to check on you soon, okay?"

Tav nodded, and with that, the nurse quickly walked out of the room, shutting the curtain almost all the way as she left.

Now, Tav was alone with this mysterious man. The man sat down in the chair adjacent to the hospital bed, and pulled out a notepad.

"Tav, right?"

Tav nodded again. That's all he felt like doing, but telling by the notepad in the man's hand, he was going to have to say something more than that.

"I'm Detective Barlett, but you can call me Rysha. Pleasure to meet you, Tav."

Something about Rysha's voice was somehow calming. Tav felt that he could let his guard down a little bit.

Rysha continued, "I'd like to ask you some questions, if that's okay?"

"Sure," Tav stammered. His voice was gravelly and deeper than usual.

"Great, I'll start off easy," Rysha began. "What's your last name?"

"Segol."

"Tav Segol, gotcha... And your father, Joseph, right?"

"Yeah, Joseph."

Rysha scribbled down some notes. "And how old are you, Tav?"

"16."

"Alright, and are you in school right now?"

Tav hesitated a moment, then replied,

"No, I dropped out last year."

"I see, I see..." Rysha made some more notes. "May I ask why you dropped out?"

Great. Tav was not at all in the mood to talk about this. But, he figured that it was in his best interest to cooperate.

"My mom died last year. She had been homeschooling me, and my dad didn't want to do it, so I just..." Tav didn't know how to finish the thought. "Dropped out, I guess."

"Right," Rysha said reassuringly, "I can understand how that would be hard for you. I'm sorry for your loss."

Tav stayed silent. He never knew how to respond to that. "It's okay" would be a blatant lie, but to say "It shattered the very earth I stood on" was a little much, especially for a complete stranger to hear.

Rysha continued on.

"And your father, what did he do for a living?"

"He was a firefighter, before he retired. He..."

Bam. It felt like a flashbang went off in Tav's mind. He remembered everything; the shot, the blood. Panic quickly set in, and he went to sit up to no avail. The handcuffs made a loud *clank*.

"Easy, easy," Rysha stood and put up his hands as if preventing a growling dog from getting any closer. Tav's breaths quickened, and he began to hyperventilate.

"Hey, it's okay," Rysha said, trying his best to calm him down. "You're not in trouble or anything, we're just going to talk about what happened, okay? You can relax."

Tav shook his head. He couldn't relax.

"*I... Killed... Him...*" Tav whimpered between breaths.

"Just lay back down, okay? We're going to talk about it." Rysha gently put his hand against Tav's shoulder and guided him back down onto the bed. Tav's breathing steadied, and he looked over to Rysha, who was once again sitting in the chair.

"Were you there?" Tav asked.

Rysha nodded. "First person there, actually. That's why I'd like to know what happened. What do you remember?"

"Well, my dad..." Tav hardly knew where to start. "We were having dinner. I saw an article online about something called the 'Anomaly Project Scandal.' So, I asked him if he knew anything about it."

Rysha was listening attentively.

"Then he got mad, and..." Tav took in a deep breath. "He got the gun. From the drawer."

Rysha scribbled away in his notes.

"What happened after that, Tav?"

"He... Shot me? I guess? But..."

Tav looked down for the first time since waking up. He saw that his once-white t-shirt had a couple holes in it, dried blood crusted around the holes.

"I don't... Feel... Where he shot me, though."

"Well, that's another reason I'm here to talk to you." He flipped a couple pages in the notebook. "The circumstances surrounding this entire situation are... Interesting? Unusual? Understand what I'm saying?"

Tav looked at him blankly, which was answer enough.

"Your father's death was abnormal. It seemed like he was hit with some kind of an energy blast. Know anything about that?"

Tav's brow furrowed, and he shook his head.

Rysha decided to press a little bit.

"Did your father have any special powers or anything? Or your mother?"

Tav became increasingly incredulous, and shook his head once again.

"We're just trying to figure out where that blast of energy came from, that's all," Rysha reassured.

"Does that make me a criminal now?"

"Well, technically-"

"Technically I killed him, so that makes me a murderer," Tav interrupted him with just a twinge of fear in his voice, cleverly disguised as anger. "But, *he* was attacking *me*."

Rysha didn't waver. "That's why we need all the details we can get. If the event was truly in self-defense, your chances of getting jail time significantly decrease."

Tav backed off now. *Jail?* He thought.

"Do you remember anything that your father said to you before he got the gun?"

Tav thought back to it. His father had gotten defensive when he asked about the article. He had stood up, thrown the chair backwards, and headed for the living room.

"He said something like, 'You were never supposed to know about this,' or something. I don't remember exactly what it was."

"I see..." Rysha was buried deep in his notes, scribbling along with Tav's every word. Then, he looked up. "Well, here's the situation for now: Since you're under 18, you're going to be temporarily put into my custody. You'll be under my jurisdiction until the trial."

Tav looked Rysha straight in the eyes with a certain hopelessness that Rysha couldn't help but empathize with.

"I didn't want you going straight to jail and not having a fair trial, so I did everything I could."

Tav understood. Things could definitely be a lot worse.

"Why are you being so nice to me?" Tav asked.

Rysha now had a genuine smile on his face.

"Because I feel everyone is deserving of kindness, no matter their past."

• • • •

CHAPTER 2

Something awakened that day, and it did not go unnoticed.

Far off in a world unknown to humanity, V's eyes snapped open. Without moving an inch in her bed, she shifted her eyes to the window. It was night, which was hardly distinguishable from the day here. A dense fog partially obscured the trees that stood not 50 feet from the window.

V shuffled herself to the other side of the bed. Why had she awoken so suddenly? She listened carefully, and not a single noise alerted her ears to anything peculiar. Something was telling her she needed to move, and quickly.

Eyes still blurry, V removed the covers and sat up. The cold of her room sent a shiver up her protruding spine as she stood. It was as if her movements were now controlled by an external force; Every step she took felt like it had a purpose. She quickly draped a shawl over herself and walked towards the front door.

As she did, she caught a glimpse of herself in the mirror and paused. She was lanky, borderline gangly. In the dark her pale blue skin reflected what little light filtered into the room. She looked into her own wide-set, amber eyes—All four of them. She blinked a few times. It was humbling to be reminded of her own existence.

However, she had more important things to worry about right now.

V opened the heavy wooden door, then carefully shut it behind her. She looked to her left, then to her right. No one was awake, so no one would see her. She began to briskly walk down the street, away from town. She knew now in her alert clear-headedness what she needed to do: She needed to look into the lake.

V reached the pier, taking note of the dense fog hanging over the lake. Through it she could barely make out the three moons forming a perfect triangle in the sky. She looked back down into the still, black water. She crouched, now touching the water with her hand. As she did, an image appeared: A teenage boy, hunched over mere feet from a dead man, presumably his father, whose body was surrounded by nefarious energy.

She knew now what had happened. It was him.

He came back.

V could hardly believe what she saw. She hadn't seen energy like this since the attempted takeover of the Heavenrealm. There wasn't a single soul in this realm, let alone any of them, that could emit energy exactly like this.

Except for Wrath.

But, V thought, *there's no way it could be him. Is there?* Wrath was supposedly wiped out by God, and everyone thought he was dead, or at the very least sealed away somewhere that would never again see the light of day.

She withdrew her hand from the water, and the image disappeared. She had to talk to Elias about this. As she got up to head back for town, she was met with Elias' singular electric blue eye staring her down. His tall, looming figure was covered by a cloak, concealing his otherworldly body. V jumped backwards, startled.

"What did you need to talk to me about?" Elias asked calmly.

V was certain that he already knew the answer.

"Well... I was alerted to the lake. And..."

"And you saw something."

"Yeah..." There was no point in trying to hide anything from Elias. This was *his* realm, after all. He knew everything.

"Well," said Elias, his eye now looking beyond V and out to the lake. "Tell me what you saw."

"I had a vision of a boy," V started, "With who I assume to be his father, who was dead. It looked as though the boy killed him. But something was strange."

"There was energy there that seemed awfully similar to Wrath's, am I correct?"

V nodded, then looked down at the ground.

"You know that is a very bold claim to make, V."

V's four eyes looked up at Elias. "I know. But I also know what I saw."

Elias sighed. "Well, do you suppose we should gather the others?"

"I think so," V replied. She knew what to do. She turned away from Elias and faced the three moons, closing her lower two eyes and looking up to the moons with the remaining two. She pressed her palms together, and a ring of light pulsated in the sky. The others would be here soon.

Sure enough, she was right. Mere moments later, Azriel strode onto the pier with Rukii sleepily ambling behind them.

Azriel and Rukii could not be more polar of opposites. Azriel was considerably shorter than Rukii, and considerably more well put together. Their blonde hair was at a reasonable length, and their sparkling green eyes reflected the few street lamps lighting the pier. They arrived in their typical uniform, an all-black jacket with a grey shirt and black slacks. Overall, they were the type to be "ready," any time, anywhere. The only thing about them that would tell you they weren't exactly human was their teeth, which were jagged and razor sharp. For this reason, when not in their own realm, they would wear a mask, as even their human form retained this detail.

Rukii, on the other hand, was a different story. As he walked up the pier he let out a loud yawn, stretching one arm up and running the other through his messy, silver hair. He had a white t-shirt draped over his almost skeletal structure, with black sweatpants to match. He generally didn't wear shoes, either. Not to mention, he had three eyes, two regular pale green ones and a vertical red eye on his forehead. In his human form, he would cover this eye with a headband,

and only take the headband off if he were to use his tracking arrow abilities. However, even with that specific skill set, if laid-back and aloof were an entity, it would be Rukii.

"Morning, crew," Rukii said through another yawn as he and Azriel approached V and Elias. No one else returned a word.

"What's this about?" Azriel asked, not very well concealing their bitterness at having been woken up at this odd hour.

"V had a vision in the lake," Elias began, as if giving a businessman's debriefing. "There's a pretty good chance something big is happening, and it's our duty to do something about it."

"Oh?" Rukii asked with genuine curiosity. "What's going on?"

Elias looked over to V.

"Do you want to tell them?" he asked.

"S-sure," V stammered. "I... I had a vision of a human that had killed his father. But... It seemed like he didn't do it alone. Like Wrath's energy possessed him."

There was a moment of silent contemplation amongst Azriel and Rukii. After a moment, Azriel decided to start asking their own questions.

"And what makes you so sure?"

"This energy looked like nothing I've seen before. Nothing, except what Wrath was capable of producing," V replied calmly.

Azriel was not satisfied.

"And why do you think Wrath would possess a human? He has no reason to do that."

"Ooo," Rukii piped up, "I have a theory! Maybe Wrath saw this kid kill his dad and thought 'Hey, this kid will make a good vessel.' All things considered, it would make sense."

"He has a point," Elias added, "Perhaps Wrath found his ideals to be of a similar caliber."

"Regardless, he's up to something," Rukii continued, heavily paraphrasing the same thing Elias had just said moments ago, "And it's our job to do something about it before he does anything stupid." Rukii's face twisted into a smirk as he punched his hand into his palm. "Let's kill him."

"No," said Elias, "We will capture him for questioning first, *then* kill him, if the situation calls for it. We don't want to kill a potentially innocent human without knowing for certain if he is truly the vessel of Wrath."

"I'd hardly call him innocent," Azriel scoffed. "Regardless, he *did* kill his own father." They pulled out their dagger and began twirling it between their fingers.

"So," Rukii began, ignoring Azriel's acidity. "When do we start?"

"Well," said Elias, "Let's wait a day and see if anything interesting happens. Then, tomorrow: Rukii, V, I am assigning you two the task of capturing the boy. Azriel and I will set up base somewhere in the city. Once you capture him, you'll bring him to us and we'll do the talking." Elias looked over at Azriel, who was half-listening but mostly idly fidgeting with their dagger. They looked up for a brief moment before returning their attention to the blade.

V and Rukii nodded. Rukii suddenly looked as though he had sprung to life and was more than ready to go. V, however, looked mildly apprehensive. She looked at Elias.

"How are we supposed to capture him?"

Elias turned his head to her, and replied softly yet sternly, "You'll figure it out."

• • • •

CHAPTER 3

It was the next morning. This time, Tav woke up in a bedroom. This was the first time in the past few days where he woke up and didn't immediately feel like death.

He was alone with his thoughts for a moment. That man, Rysha; didn't he say something about being his new legal guardian? He assumed he was in his house right now. It was a nice bed— huge, actually. The covers were plain grey and white, with a soft comforter that had a geometric pattern on it. There was art on the walls of the room, also geometric in nature. In the corner, there was a desk with a single light atop its dark grey surface.

As he took in his surroundings, he looked through the slit in the curtains and out the window. Huge skyscrapers stood above the city below, with smaller buildings scattered between them. He must have been several stories up, because from this angle he couldn't even see the street.

Just then, Rysha knocked on the door.

"Can I come in?"

Tav looked towards the door.

"Yeah," he called out.

The door carefully opened and Rysha stepped inside.

"Hey," he started, "How are you feeling?"

"Fine, I guess," Tav responded as he sat up, "all things considered."

Rysha smiled. "Good. I'm glad to hear it."

Tav looked around again. "So, this is your house?"

Rysha nodded. "Yep, sure is."

"Well, I like the art," Tav began, "Looks like stuff I'd draw."

"Oh?" Rysha asked. "You're an artist?"

Tav nodded. "I mostly draw swords, though, that's kinda my thing."

"Ah," Rysha replied. "Well that's pretty cool. Have you ever used a sword?"

"Nah, I just draw them from this game I play, *Brawler 7*."

"Oh yeah, I've heard of that." Rysha smiled again. "How would you like to learn?"

"Learn...?" Tav carefully inquired.

"Y'know, learn how to use a sword." Rysha made a swinging motion with his arms as if he was hitting a baseball with a bat.

"Yeah, that would be... Really cool. Why?"

"Well, I figured we should do something enriching to pass the time until your trial. We train at a complex in town and I figured I'd take you down there today and show you the ropes. How does that sound?"

Tav was truly excited now. The thought of using an actual sword woke up the childish part of his brain. But, he remained cool on the exterior.

"Yeah, definitely," Tav answered. For the first time in a while, he himself smiled.

"Good! Well, get ready, and we'll head down there. But first, you probably need a different shirt."

Rysha tossed a white t-shirt to Tav, and Tav completely missed it so it landed on the bed just out of arm's reach. Tav looked at the shirt and then at Rysha.

"Thank you."

"Of course."

With that, Rysha stepped out of the room and shut the door. Tav stood up and swapped his bullet-hole riddled and blood-stained shirt for the new one. It was about two sizes too big, but that was okay. It smelled like fancy laundry soap.

While Tav was changing, Rysha had stepped out onto the balcony porch for a cigarette. He dug one out of the pack, lit it, and stuck the lighter back in his pocket. He had a phone call to make, unfortunately, so he figured he'd get that taken care of first thing in the morning. He scrolled through his contacts until he found "Allen Wilson," and pressed it to call. It rang a few times before Rysha heard,

"Aim is Up, this is Allen, how can I assist you?"

"Hey. It's Rysha Barlett."

"Rysha! How are you doing, my good sir? It's been a minute since I've heard from you."

Rysha took a drag off his cigarette. "Yeah, I know. I've been busy."

"Oh, I imagine," Allen replied, "Being a cop and all. That'll do you in one day, y'know?"

Rysha just chuckled. "Nature of the beast."

Allen chuckled back, then after a moment asked, "So, what's new on the agenda for you?"

"Well," Rysha started, "Something... Interesting, happened with a case I'm working." He looked back into the glass doors to see if Tav was still in his room, then continued, "A kid killed his dad, but it wasn't under 'normal' circumstances. I'm pretty sure he has some kind of powers."

Rysha could hear Allen's tone harden through the phone.

"What kind of powers are we talking?"

"My guess is healing and some kind of an energy blast," Rysha answered. "The kid got shot three times in the chest and lived. He woke up this morning like nothing happened."

"Is he with you?"

"Yeah, I have temporary custody until the trial. I think, considering the circumstances, I have the best shot at getting him out of trouble."

"I'd say you're right," Allen responded, "You're probably the only guy in the NYPD with your own set of powers, right?"

Rysha sighed. "As far as I know."

"Well," Allen began, "If that's the case, swing by sometime this week and we'll see what we can do for him. Alright?"

Rysha realized his cigarette was all smoked, and he tossed the butt into the ashtray on the adjacent table.

"You sure? I've kinda been..."

"Absent? Yeah, you have," Allen said, finishing Rysha's sentence for him. "But hey, he's just a kid, we gotta do what we can to help him out. When's the trial?"

"June 10th, in three days," Rysha replied.

"Well, what are you doing in the meantime to keep him busy?" Allen asked.

"I don't know, I figured I'd take him to spar, get him into a healthy outlet for any, er, residual emotional problems. But that way, I can also figure out if he has any other powers."

"Smart, smart," Allen responded, "I also have another suggestion."

"Oh?" Rysha asked. "What's that?"

"Take him over to Dr. Todd's office and let her run the test on him. That will give you some more definitive answers."

Dr. Todd, more specifically Doctor Angela Todd. That was a name Rysha hadn't heard in years.

"You really think I can get an appointment with her?"

"Rysha, of course she'll remember you, you'll have no trouble," Allen reassured, despite that not being exactly what Rysha had asked. "Her office should be open now, and if you tell her what's going on, she might even be able to squeeze you in today."

Rysha thought about this for a moment. Even though it had been 20 years since they last saw each other, Dr. Todd really did well by him when they briefly worked together.

"Well, it's worth a shot," Rysha finally said. "Thanks, Allen, you're really doing me a solid here."

Allen replied, "Don't mention it. I'll see you this week."

That was over. Now, Rysha needed to call Dr. Todd's office. Did he even have the number in his contacts? He once again glanced behind him to see if Tav was still in his room. He was. Rysha decided to just search for the office phone number on the internet, and after finding it, he pressed it and dialed.

"Thank you for calling Medical One's New York City office, we will be with you shortly."

Then, hold music. Great, just enough time to light another cigarette. He perched the cigarette between his lips and cupped his hand that wasn't holding the phone to protect the flame from the light wind.

"Hi, you've reached Medical One, how can I help you?"

Rysha, in the middle of lighting up, grabbed the now-lit cigarette and put it in his off hand.

"Yes, hello," he started nervously, "Can you put me through to Dr. Todd?"

"Sure. She's with a patient right now, but you can leave a message."

"Great, thank you." More hold music. Rysha took a long drag, relieved he wouldn't have to talk directly to her right now. Rysha was sincerely afraid she had forgotten about him, after all these years. He was one of her first patients, back when the Anomaly Experiment first took place. He was 18 back then, and she was 23; She was a young, budding scientist with a particular interest in molecular biology, who became part of a rag-tag team of scientists that were conducting experiments with DNA that would supposedly yield special powers. Rysha, freshly graduated from high school, was tantalized by the proposition that he could be given superpowers "simply" by letting a scientist inject him with "weird stuff", so, naturally, his name was one of the first on the list.

"Hi, you've reached the voicemail box of Dr. Angela Todd, please leave your name and a brief message and I'll get back with you as soon as possible." *BEEP.*

"Hey, this is Rysha Barlett, I'm calling to see if you could, uh, help me out. Thanks, bye."

With that, he hung up. *That went terribly,* he thought. He didn't even tell her what he needed help with. Oh well; hopefully, she would understand and call him back soon.

Rysha finished off his cigarette and stepped back inside. Tav was still in his room. Strange, did he think he had to stay in there?

Rysha walked over to Tav's door and knocked again. "You can come out whenever you're ready."

Tav, meanwhile, had been keeping himself busy. He had done a quick look-through of the desk and found a notebook and pen, and had started a drawing not dissimilar to the art on the walls of the bedroom. He was just about done with it when Rysha knocked.

"Okay," Tav called back in response. He hurriedly stuffed the notebook back into the desk drawer and shut off the light.

Moments later, he stepped out and saw Rysha standing in the kitchen. Tav waved to him, and Rysha smiled and waved back.

"Once I get this coffee brewed up, we'll get going, okay?"

• • • •

The training facility was two stories tall, and chock full of every piece of equipment imaginable. The first story looked like an average gym, and most people only used that floor. The second story was more geared towards training for mixed martial arts, with punching bags and practice weapons lining the walls. In the middle, there were two separate arenas, one larger than the other.

Tav and Rysha walked in through the glass revolving door, and Tav was immediately awestruck. He had never seen a facility like this before; even the concept of a public gym was foreign to him. Music was blasting at an appropriate volume, and the place smelled like generic cleaning supplies.

Better than sweat, though, Tav thought.

"Come on, this way," Rysha directed.

Tav followed closely behind. Some of the people here seemed pretty intimidating, giving the duo sideways glances as they walked by. Others offered a friendly wave, with Rysha occasionally responding with a "Hey! How are you?"

As they stepped onto the escalator, Rysha decided to strike up conversation.

"Do homeschooled kids do sports?"

"Hm?" Tav snapped his attention back to Rysha. "Oh, some kids did, I never did though."

"Oh? Did it just not interest you?"

"I guess not. I was always more into the Arts."

"Ah, I see. Well don't worry, it's never too late to start something new." Rysha flashed a smile.

Tav reciprocated. "You're right on that. I'm actually really looking forward to this."

"Really? Great!"

The two stepped off the escalator and onto the second floor. Almost directly in front of them, two men were sparring in the larger of the two arenas. It was a good old fashioned hand-to-hand match. Another man was throwing punches at a punching bag in the corner, grunting a bit each time his fists made contact.

"Since they're using that one," Rysha began, "We'll use the smaller arena for now. Sound good?"

Tav nodded. While Rysha had a confident yet refined air about him, Tav himself couldn't help but feel tiny and skittish in such a new environment. Yet, he had every bit of faith that Rysha wouldn't let anything bad happen.

Rysha walked over to the practice weapons and picked up two kendo sticks of similar size. He turned around and made a tossing motion to Tav, without actually throwing the weapon. Tav flinched. Rysha just chuckled quietly.

"Don't worry, I wouldn't actually throw it." Rysha walked over to Tav and handed him the stick. Tav examined it; It was made of bamboo, with several joints where the pieces came together. It had a white handle made of leather and matching string. Tav swung it in a circle a few times, getting a feel for the weapon's weight. It was light, maybe? Tav had nothing to compare that to, so it was just a guess.

Rysha headed for the available arena and motioned to where Tav should stand. Tav walked over to it and Rysha stood in front of him.

"Alright, let's start easy." Rysha readied himself into a stance, with the kendo stick stuck out directly in front of him.

"There are eight main angles of strike: Down, up, left, right, diagonal down left, diagonal down right, and then diagonal up left and diagonal up right." With each stroke, Rysha carefully swung the stick in the respective direction.

"Mmhm," Tav hummed. He carefully eyeballed each of Rysha's movements.

"Then, there are the defensive positions to counter these strikes: Overhead," Rysha extended the stick upwards and across his body, then similarly on the opposite side.

"The up sides," Rysha pointed the stick vertically on his left, then on his right.

"And the down sides," Rysha flipped the stick downwards on each side.

Tav nodded in understanding. This seemed relatively easy, so far, which wasn't surprising. In the fighting games he had played before, each button on the controller corresponded to a certain type of move. Instead of buttons, though, he would have to literally make the corresponding motion, which could potentially prove difficult.

"So," Rysha stepped forward. "If I do this..." He went for a very slow diagonal strike from the right. "What would you do?"

Entirely reflexively, Tav went into a defensive position and successfully blocked the strike.

"Eh?" Tav said, now somewhat doubting himself.

"Right! Yes!" Rysha affirmed. The two reset to neutral positions.

"How about this?" Rysha now came at him from the left side, straight down the middle. Tav parried the move perfectly.

"Well," Rysha started while stepping backwards. "I'd say you have a pretty good grasp on that much. Now, *you* come at *me*."

"Oh, okay." Tav shuffled his feet to get into a better striking position.

"Dominant foot forward," Rysha corrected him, noticing the conflict between his footwork and striking stance.

"Right." Tav put his right foot in front now. He then went in for a strike. The sticks made a *clack* as they made contact, and the duo reset themselves.

"Great! Try it again."

Tav thought about it for a moment, then decided to go in for a lower strike for the knees. Rysha blocked it with ease.

"Good job!" Rysha exclaimed.

Tav smiled. He was surprised by Rysha's affirmations. He was interesting in that in any other situation, he may have come across as condescending. But somehow, he wasn't. He was entirely genuine, and came from a place of true compassion and understanding.

"Now," Rysha started, "Let's try it for real. Ready?"

Tav grunted and nodded. He readied himself to parry whatever strike Rysha was about to throw at him. *Dominant foot forward,* he remembered. He mentally ran through each of the striking positions and their respective blocks. He was ready for anything.

Or, so he thought.

Quick as lighting, Rysha struck Tav squarely in his side, sending Tav toppling over onto the mat beneath their feet. Rysha really knocked the breath out of him. Tav, surprised, looked up at Rysha from the ground.

"What the hell!" he exclaimed.

Rysha just laughed.

"See, it's easy when it's slow, but when you're as quick as me..." Rysha slashed the air with the stick. "You have to do more intuitive thinking than *actual* thinking. Let yourself do what comes naturally." Rysha made a beckoning motion for Tav to stand up.

Tav very carefully stood up and got ready once again. This time, though, when Rysha went in for a strike, he didn't follow through. Tav flinched instead of blocking.

"It's okay," Rysha reassured, "I won't hit as hard this time. Promise. Ready?"

Tav nodded and gulped down some air, and got himself into a defensive position. This time, Rysha did actually go for the hit, and Tav successfully blocked it. He went in for another, and Tav blocked it once again. The two went on for a few minutes before Tav decided to switch it up. This time, *he* went in for the attack. Rysha blocked it. He went in for another. Blocked. Rysha smirked.

"You gotta be quicker than that," he chided playfully.

Tav did his best to only huff internally. But, he was pretty sure he did it on the outside, too. Tav went in for several more strikes, each better than the last, and Rysha blocked every single one of them. Tav just wanted to get him one time, *one time,* and have him not block it.

Suddenly, Rysha's phone started ringing in his pocket. He stopped. Tav, not realizing this, went in for a strike, and the stick made perfect contact with Rysha's shoulder. Rysha put his hand up, and Tav finally realized what was happening. He gasped.

"Are you okay?" Tav quickly asked.

Rysha, while digging his phone out of his pocket, nodded. He answered it.

"Detective Barlett." Rysha looked at Tav and silently mouthed, "Don't worry about it."

Tav still felt bad, though, and brought the stick down to his side.

"Hey, Rysha, It's Angela."

Rysha immediately recognized her voice. "Dr. Todd! Hey! Give me one second," Rysha set down the stick and headed for the locker room. Tav was left to himself in the arena.

Rysha got to the locker room and holed up in one of the stalls. "Sorry, I was teaching a student. Erm... Yeah, student."

"Uh huh," Dr. Todd said through the phone. "What can I help you out with?"

"Well," Rysha looked around, silently hoping there wasn't anyone else in the locker room. "I have this, kid, well, teenager, that..." Rysha sighed. "I'll give it to you straight. I'm pretty sure he has powers and I want to know for sure."

"A kid, you say?" Dr. Todd asked inquisitively. "How old?"

"16."

"Well, that is certainly interesting. Do his parents have powers? Are they around the age to where that would make sense?"

"See, I don't know," Rysha replied. "Both of his parents are dead. His mom died several years ago and his dad... Well, his dad died like two days ago. And he did it."

"*Ohh...*" Dr. Todd said, choosing her next question carefully. "By he, you mean the kid?"

"Yeah. In self defense. His dad had shot him three times, and he lived. We've been practicing striking techniques, so I think it's safe to assume that he's fine."

"Interesting," Dr. Todd remarked. "Well, swing by my office around 3:00 today, and I'll run the test. Sound good?"

Rysha looked at his phone. It was 2:00. If they left now, and Tav was willing, they would make it there just in time.

"Yep, I can do that. Hey..."

"Yeah?"

"Thank you. I really appreciate it."

Rysha thought he could feel Dr. Todd smile through the phone. "Of course, don't worry about it. I'm happy to help where I can. By the way, what's the kid's name?"

"Tav. Tav Segol," Rysha responded.

"Got it. See you at 3:00, then?"

"See you at 3:00."

With that, Rysha hung up the phone. It had been all these years, and she still was willing to help him out. So, Rysha headed back out to the floor.

Tav, meanwhile, had been standing in the exact same spot where Rysha had left him.

"Y'know you could've sat down or something," Rysha said to him.

Tav whipped his head around. "Well, I wasn't sure."

Rysha cleared his throat. "Unfortunately we'll have to call it quits for now. We have an appointment."

"We?" Tav asked.

"Yes. We. I'm taking you to a doctor that specializes in..." Rysha lowered his voice. "... Powers and such."

Tav's eyes widened. "Doctor?"

"Yeah, but don't worry, she's just going to run an easy test. No big deal."

Tav looked to his side and sighed. He then looked up at Rysha. "Sure, I'll go."

"Good," Rysha said as he motioned for Tav to give him the kendo stick. Tav handed it over.

"I think this will help a lot in your case, I'm not just doing it out of personal curiosity," Rysha told Tav.

Tav nodded. "I know."

Rysha walked the sticks back over to the rack. When he returned, he looked at Tav.

"Well, let's get going."

• • • •

CHAPTER 4

The car ride was anything but comfortable. Tav and Rysha were both nervous, and for different reasons: Tav due to the thought of a medical test, Rysha because he'd be seeing a... *Friend? Colleague? Doctor?* At this point in time, he wasn't entirely sure where they stood. Classical music from the radio quietly attempted to make the space more palpable; Rysha's comfort music, and completely foreign to Tav.

"We're almost there," Rysha stated, adjusting his glasses.

"Cool cool," replied Tav.

Rysha took a hit off his cigarette, and did his best to blow the smoke out the window.

"Smoke doesn't bother you, does it?"

"Nah, nah," Tav waved his hand in the air nonchalantly, simultaneously waving away the mentholated cloud. "My dad smoked too."

"Ah, okay." That was a relief, be it a strange one. Rysha threw on his turn signal and got over into the turn lane, then maneuvered into the Medical One parking lot. He chose a spot and shut off the car, sighing as he set the butt of the cigarette in the ashtray.

"Well," Rysha said, turning to Tav, "Let's get this over with, right?"

Tav smiled a little and nodded.

"It won't be too bad."

Rysha smiled back and opened his car door, Tav doing the same. *WHAM!* Both doors shut at almost the same time. The two walked up to the doors and opened them simultaneously.

As they walked in, the receptionist greeted them with a hopefully-not-forced friendliness.

"Hi! Do you have an appointment?"

"Yes, with Dr. Todd," Rysha told her, walking closer to the desk. Tav followed suit.

"Great, and your name?"

"Barlett, B-A-R-L-E-T-T."

"Barlett, gotcha..." The receptionist clicked away on her keyboard before finally saying, "Alright, I've got you all checked in."

"Thanks," Rysha said with a smile. He and Tav made their way over to the waiting room, picking chairs across from each other.

Tav looked around at the art on the walls: It was what those in the art community would refer to as "Dentist's Office Chique": Drab corporate art with the intention of making you feel more comfortable in a naturally uncomfortable space. It was oftentimes abstract, but sometimes loosely depicting scenery or something similar. It was an interesting style and not necessarily a bad one, just...

Flavourless, Tav thought. Oh well.

Rysha, on the other hand, had some different thoughts going on. What kind of results were they going to get? And if Tav *does* have powers, what are either of them supposed to do about it?

"Barlett?"

This snapped them both out of their heads and back into the present. Rysha looked at the nurse and nodded, then the two got up and walked over to the door.

"Right this way," the nurse guided. They walked back through the maze of rooms and offices before eventually arriving at a large patient room.

"She'll be with you shortly."

The nurse left, and Tav and Rysha were on their own. Tav hopped up onto the exam table, and Rysha took a regular seat on the other end of the room. Tav was finally starting to feel *actually* nervous.

"You okay, bud?" Rysha asked Tav. Tav looked down and realized his entire body was shaking ever so slightly.

"Yeah, yeah," Tav reassured. He gave Rysha a half-hearted thumbs up. Rysha returned it, using both thumbs.

Then, a knock on the door. After a moment, Dr. Todd stepped through the doorway. She was short of stature, with dark red hair and brown eyes magnified by very strong prescription glasses. She was dressed in a white coat over a green blouse with khaki pants, and was carrying a laptop with some papers. She smiled.

"Hey, friends, how are we doing today?"

"Hey," Tav and Rysha replied at the same time. They looked at each other, then back to the doctor.

"You must be Tav, right?" She extended her hand out to Tav, and Tav shook it.

"That's me," Tav said with a cheeky smile.

"Great, we're off to a great start. My name's Dr. Todd, I'll be administering the test today."

Dr. Todd then looked over to Rysha. She took on a mildly playful tone.

"And I assume you're Mr. Barlett?"

"Yup yup," Rysha said with a chuckle. He stuck out his hand and the two had a nice, formal handshake.

"So," Dr. Todd sat down on the doctor's stool. "Before we do *anything,* tell me what the heck happened."

"Well, uh," Tav started off. "My dad, uh, shot me? And then I... Y'know..."

"Uh huh," Dr. Todd said, typing on her laptop. She stopped typing and looked up at Tav, encouraging him to say more.

"I... Fought back. Hard. And I guess besides that there's a pretty good chance I have powers, since I healed so quickly."

Dr. Todd nodded, and kept typing. After a moment, she looked over to Rysha.

"Can you attest to this? You don't have to tell me details," she asked.

Rysha nodded.

"Definitely. It looked as though some kind of an energy blast went off at some point. And, obviously, he's sitting upright mere days after being shot in the chest three times."

"Good point, good point," Dr. Todd said.

Tav looked between them as they spoke.

"Well, the Genetic Anomaly Locator Test will tell us with pretty good certainty whether or not you have the thing in your DNA that allows for powers," Dr. Todd told Tav. "We'll have to give you an injection. Is that okay?"

Tav nodded confidently.

"Shots don't scare me."

Dr. Todd smiled wide.

"Good, we don't hear that too often!" She closed up the laptop and set it on the table. She then stood up. "Let me go get the supplies, and we'll get started."

Tav nodded, and with that, Dr. Todd left the room.

"Wow, you're not scared of shots?" Rysha asked Tav once Dr. Todd had fully shut the door.

"Nope," Tav replied. "Never have been. It's really not that bad."

"Huh." Rysha made more of a noise of amusement than a standalone statement.

Within moments, Dr. Todd knocked once again. This time, she had a cart with medical supplies on top of it. She wheeled in the cart and parked it next to the exam table where Tav was sitting.

"Alright," Dr. Todd began. "Here's how this works: We give you this shot, and if you test positive for the genetic abnormality, certain parts of your skin will turn black and swirly." Dr. Todd made a swooping motion with her hands. "Like tattoo ink, but it's temporary. Only lasts three to four hours. Do you have a preference for which arm I do the shot in?"

Tav shook his head.

"Either is fine."

"Alrighty." Dr. Todd readied the syringe, drew out the substance from the vial, and tapped the syringe a few times. "Ready?" she asked.

"Ready," Tav replied.

Dr. Todd swiftly plunged the needle into his right arm, and pushed down the plunger. Tav watched the serum leave the syringe, fascinated. Dr. Todd took out the needle and stopped the bleeding with a gauze pad and a piece of medical tape.

"See? Not too bad," Dr. Todd said with a smile.

Just then, Tav began to feel quite strange. It was as though he could feel the contents of the syringe coursing through his blood in his arm. He looked down; sure enough, black swirls began to appear on his skin. They traveled down towards his hand before stopping at his wrist.

"Well, that's pretty definitive," Dr. Todd remarked.

However, it didn't stop there. Suddenly, a mark started to crawl across Tav's hand that was entirely different from the rest. It was a triangle, much like a *triquetra*, or as some would call a Celtic Knot. A dragon wove through the left side of the triangle.

Dr. Todd couldn't help but furrow her brow.

"That's... Let me see that."

Tav, unsure of what she meant, stuck out his hand. Dr. Todd gently took a hold of it and looked it over, turning his hand to each side to get a better look.

"Well," Dr. Todd started, "I have... never seen a reaction like this, if I'm honest."

"Neither have I," Rysha concurred, peering over Dr. Todd's shoulder.

"I... Have no idea what this means, um..." Dr. Todd was rather flustered. She let go of Tav's hand and rolled backwards with the stool.

"Really?" Tav asked. He looked down at his arm and hand, his concern growing by the second after hearing their reactions.

"Well, what I *can* tell you is this: You have powers, that's for certain, I just can't tell you exactly what they are. I do have a guess, though," Dr. Todd opened up her laptop. She typed something in, scrolled for a moment, and clicked on something. "Genetic Abnormality Class C, Self-Healing."

Rysha looked at her. "Class C?"

"Yup, that's what it says here," Dr. Todd said. "You would think something that powerful would be in a higher class, but normally Classes B and A are reserved for the... *Really* wild stuff, y'know?"

Rysha thought about this. "My own personal powers are all Class B, right?"

"If nothing has changed since 20 years ago, yes," Dr. Todd replied.

Tav piped up. "What exactly *are* your powers, Rysha?"

Rysha and Dr. Todd looked at each other, and came to a mutual conclusion.

"Classified," Rysha responded, looking back at Tav.

"Fair enough," Tav replied dryly.

Rysha looked back to Dr. Todd.

"So, what now?" he asked.

"Well, while we don't have specific answers, we can put it in his chart that he has the presence of the anomaly in his genetics," Dr. Todd said. "And, it will look favorable in the trial. As for the symbol on your hand..." Dr. Todd now looked Tav straight in the eyes. "Keep an eye on that. Got it?"

Tav nodded enthusiastically.

"Good. If anything, er, 'untoward' happens, don't hesitate to reach out. That goes for both of you." Dr. Todd scrambled for a piece of paper and quickly wrote down her number, then handed it to Rysha. "Call my personal, it's easier to reach me that way."

"Thank you, Dr. Todd," Rysha told her gratefully as he took the paper.

"Please," Dr. Todd replied, smiling. "Call me Angie."

. . . .

Rukii and V walked the streets of New York City. They looked significantly more normal now, being in their human forms. V had her deep blue hair tied up in a ponytail, as well as sunglasses to hide the one set of amber eyes she now had. Rukii towered over her still, and looked especially tall in the sweatshirt and long pants he was wearing. He hadn't yet perfected getting into a human form, so to hide the weirdness of his limbs he decided to cover up as much as he could. As well as this, he had the headband to hide his third eye.

V suddenly stopped.

"What?" Rukii asked.

V closed her eyes.

"He's close..." She opened them. "I can sense it."

Rukii nodded slowly, unsure as to whether or not he should believe her. Were they on a wild goose chase right now? Or was V actually going to be right this time?

Then, a car pulled up not 100 feet from them. Out stepped a tall man in a suit, and on the other side, a similarly tall boy in a black zip-up hoodie and jeans. The man silently walked up to the building, the boy trailing behind him. V pushed her sunglasses down her nose to get a better look. As she did this, the boy pushed his dark red hair out of his eyes. On his hand, a symbol, and not just any symbol; It was Wrath's crest.

YES! V thought to herself. *I was right!*

Rukii grabbed V by the back of her shirt and yanked her into the adjacent alleyway.

"Are you crazy?" Rukii whispered very loudly. "We can't just stand out in the open like that. We gotta be strategic about this."

"Right, right, but... You saw his hand, right?"

"Yeah, you were right, *blah blah blah*, let's just capture him and get this over with."

V nodded. "How do you suppose we'll do that?"

"Remember the plan?" Rukii asked rhetorically. "I go in, I kill anyone that isn't the boy, the boy will run out, and you'll meet him at the door. Right?"

"Right," V replied. "Well, better head in there before they get to the apartment."

"Right. I got this." Rukii winked at V and "very-not-suspicious-ly" walked around to the front of the building. V peeked from the alley and watched him enter.

Now, V thought, *I just have to wait for the boy to come out. Easy. There's no way we'll mess this up...*

• • • •

"Are you doing okay?"

Rysha and Tav were walking down the long hallway to Rysha's apartment. It had been several minutes since either of them had said anything, so Rysha had decided to break the silence.

"What do you mean?" Tav asked.

"I mean, physically, emotionally, y'know. Stuff like that."

"Hmm..." Tav thought out loud. "I... I guess I'm okay. I don't hurt anywhere."

Tav looked down at the symbol on his hand.

"I'm a little confused about all of this."

"Is there anything I can do to help?"

Tav looked back up at Rysha. In a matter of days, this man had taken him in, advocated for him, and helped him when most people would have left him to rot in prison. Rysha seemed to see a different side to him, one that wasn't a cold blooded killer and was still a teenager that had no idea how to navigate life.

Suddenly, Rysha stopped dead in his tracks. He put his arm out to stop Tav from walking any further. The hallway was silent.

Rysha's eyes darted left, then right, then left again, then right again. There was one place he didn't look, though, and that was above. Rukii dropped from his position on the ceiling and came down on top of Rysha with a mighty thud. Tav jumped backwards, startled. Before he could even blink, Rysha had Rukii in a headlock.

"Eh!" Rukii exclaimed. He struggled against Rysha, but Rysha's grip did not falter.

"That's enough of that," Rysha said between breaths. Rukii was fighting hard, but Rysha was not about to let him loose.

"Nice job... With that one, at least."

That voice came from behind where Tav was standing. He then heard the sound of an arrow being drawn back in a bow. As he heard this, the clone struggling against Rysha disappeared into thin air.

"Now, hand over the kid, and there won't be any problems."

Rysha, still laying on the ground, looked up at the looming figure that was the real Rukii.

"What for?" Rysha snarled.

"The fate of the universe, or something, I don't know." Rukii shrugged casually, all the while pointing the arrow directly at Rysha's forehead. "Regardless, it's important, so hand him over."

Tav looked at Rysha, whose eye contact with Rukii had yet to be broken. In one swift motion, he drew his gun before Rukii even had the chance to fire an arrow.

"No way." Rysha's hands were steady and unfaltering, pointing the gun at Rukii's knees.

"Fine, you want it to end this way? Then let's end this."

With that, Rukii fired. Flames erupted in front of Rysha, blocking the arrow and sending bits of fire directly back at Rukii. Rukii yelled with a combination of surprise and annoyance.

"Come on! This way!" Rysha was now standing behind the wall of flames. Tav and Rysha quickly started running down the hall in the opposite direction of the chaos.

"Do you know that guy?" Rysha yelled.

"No!" Tav replied. He had never seen him before in his life. He had looked strange, though, like something about him was slightly off. But, in truth, he hadn't really gotten a good look at him.

They approached a joint in the hallway and turned left. They could both run pretty fast, and were quickly clearing the distance between themselves and the attacker. Now, down the stairs. Not much farther to go, and they'd be out of the building, where Rysha could call for backup. Except, there was one problem. As they approached the doors, a woman with blue hair stood in their way, wielding a staff and looking for a fight.

• • • •

CHAPTER 5

Tav and Rysha screeched to a halt.

"Wow," V said with a scoff, "You both made it out? *That nitwit.*" The last part, she muttered to herself.

"What do you want?" Rysha asked sternly.

"Not you, obviously. You're in the way." V directed her attention to Tav, who was quivering ever so slightly.

"Listen, honey," V began. "You're the vessel of someone very important, and the only way to get rid of him is to kill you. But, we don't want to do that just yet, do we? We want to ask him some questions first."

Tav's heart leapt through his throat. A *vessel?* What did she mean by that?

"So, either you come with us..." Within the blink of an eye, V had her staff pressed to Rysha's throat. "... Or he dies. Your choice."

"Hey! I was supposed to do that part!"

Rukii came sprinting down the hallway, looking a bit singed from the flame shield Rysha had created earlier.

V snapped her neck around to yell at Rukii, giving Rysha just enough time to escape her grip. He slid backwards and put out his hand. Soon enough, he was holding a sword made of flames and steel. The metal looked white hot, and cooler red and orange flames circled the blade.

"You dumbass!" V yelled, getting herself into a new defensive stance. "You made me lose my concentration!"

"I didn't make you do shit," Rukii yelled back as he approached the scene.

"ENOUGH." Rysha readied himself in a position to strike. "Nobody moves, nobody gets hurt. Care to explain what the hell you're doing here?"

"Hmm..." V and Rukii hummed in unison. They each got a smirk on their face before turning back to Rysha.

"No."

All hell broke loose. Rysha and V began to duke it out right in the lobby of the apartment complex. All standerby's in the large room had promptly evacuated. For a moment, Tav just stood back and watched. The fluidity of the fight, the natural progression of ebb and flow; Suddenly, it all made so much sense to him.

"Go," Tav heard a voice say. Was it in his head?

"Fight her. Don't let them win. Take them down." The voice continued. It was definitely in his head. It almost felt like intuition, but louder and more in the present-mind than the subconscious. Tav looked down at the mark on his hand. It was glowing slightly red.

"Concentrate. Create a weapon," the voice coached him. Tav put all of his thought into his right hand, and before long, a silver longsword extended from it.

"Good. Now, fight!"

Tav charged into the fight from behind V and struck her shoulder. Surprised, she turned around. She now had Rysha coming at her from one side, and Tav from the other.

During all of this, Rukii had jumped up onto a high surface and uncovered his third eye. It blinked a few times as the pupil darted around the room, tracking each movement of the two members of opposition. Rukii closed his main two eyes and readied the arrow. He fired, and the arrow flew towards the fight like a guided missile.

Tav caught a glimpse of the arrow as it whizzed past his head. *That's headed for Rysha,* he realized. In a moment he could only describe as slow motion, Tav vaulted over V and struck the arrow from the side with his sword, before it could make contact. The arrow deflected momentarily, but quickly circled back around and headed straight for them once again. This time, Rysha was ready. He swung his sword straight through the arrow, splitting it down the middle. It landed on the ground in a ball of flames.

"Damn it," Rukii scoffed at himself. He could only use one tracking arrow during a certain period of time, as it had a cool-down before he could use it again. He loaded up a regular arrow and began to shoot steadily at Rysha.

Rysha, however, was dodging or blocking every single arrow, and V was now preoccupied with Tav. As they fought, Tav started to notice a pattern with V's attacks and defenses; Much like a CPU player in a fighting game, her motions were predictable and easy to parry. Tav gritted his teeth and met the next strike with a perfect block. Sparks flew as their weapons collided squarely with one another. V was surprised; It seemed like Tav was getting ready to push the offensive. Tav's strikes became twice as fast, like a newfound battlesense had kicked in. She was struggling to keep up at this point. She looked over to Rukii, who was still shooting arrows from his perch, but... Wait a minute.

Did he make another clone? V asked herself as she realized that there was another Rukii fighting with Rysha directly. The clone was going hand-to-hand with Rysha, their swords clashing in big booms. V knew that Rukii couldn't keep this up for long, as he had to concentrate on both himself and the clone, and that was another thing he hadn't quite perfected. She had to intervene.

V darted out of Tav's line of attack and over to Rysha, going for a strike on the other side. Rysha deflected it.

"Really?" Rysha exclaimed, now exasperated. He was fighting three different entities at once, two up close and one with a bow.

Tav realized what was happening and decided to strategize: If he took out the main body, the clone would disappear, right? Tav sprinted over to where Rukii was perched. Rukii realized that Tav was headed for him and crouched down, pointing an arrow directly at him.

"Don't come any closer!" Rukii warned. "I didn't want to have to shoot you, but I will!"

Tav stood steadfast in front of the arrow. It looked razor sharp, and would fly directly through his heart if fired.

"Seriously, if you just come with us, this will all be over," Rukii continued. "Just put down the sword and go easy."

With that, Tav ran at Rukii full speed, and went in for an overhead strike. Rukii used his bow to block it, but Tav was coming down hard, and the bow was beginning to bend backwards.

"V!" Rukii yelled.

V stopped fighting for a moment and turned to Rukii.

"Let's get out of here!"

V, despite agreeing completely with that notion, replied,

"But what about the kid?"

"Forget the kid, we need a better plan!"

V nodded, more to herself than Rukii. She reached into her pocket and grabbed a smoke grenade that Elias had given her, throwing it down forcefully as the two made their escape. Tav coughed and coughed. He couldn't see anything. He frantically looked around for Rysha.

"Tav!"

Tav ran towards the sound of Rysha's voice, and eventually the two met in the middle of the smoky lobby.

"Are they gone?" Tav asked, breathing heavily.

"I certainly hope so," Rysha replied with a huff.

The smoke slowly cleared, and the lobby was completely empty. The two stood there for a moment, gathering their thoughts.

That was intense. Is this going to be my new normal? Tav wondered to himself.

Rysha wiped his forehead and laughed a little bit.

"You know, I haven't had a fight like that in years."

Tav looked at Rysha; He was beaming, like he had enjoyed himself despite having been in immediate peril. Tav, on the other hand, was still looking around the lobby for any trace the two attackers could have left behind. Surprisingly enough, not much was damaged. A few chairs were tipped over, and where Rysha had been throwing fire attacks had some black ash marks on the floor. All of Rukii's arrows had dissipated as well.

"What do we do now?" Tav asked.

"Well, I think we should be okay for now. You're not hurt, right?"

Tav looked down at himself, and not even his clothes were damaged. He shook his head. "Are you?"

"Nah, I'm good. Great, actually." Rysha circled his arms, as if limbering himself up. "Let's head upstairs."

· · · ·

Later that night, Rysha was out smoking a cigarette and talking to Allen on the phone.

"So far, the working theory is that he has healing powers and some kind of energy blast." Rysha deliberately failed to mention the weapon creation, in case the battle that had ensued earlier that day had been a fluke.

"Interesting," Allen replied. "And Dr. Todd ran the test on him?"

"Yes, and he tested positive for the gene abnormality for powers. But... Something weird happened."

"Which was?"

"A symbol appeared on his hand, too, as well as the regular marks that appear after the test. It was a triangle of sorts with what looked like a dragon running through the left side."

There was a pause.

"Any idea what that means?" Rysha asked.

"No, haven't the faintest, honestly," Allen replied, with a sudden seriousness that was uncharacteristic.

"Me neither, but someone that's neither Tav nor myself knows something about it."

"And who would that be?"

"We fell under attack today by two entities that also had powers, but I didn't recognize either of them from the organization."

"Different chapter, perhaps?"

"Maybe," Rysha paused to hit his cigarette. "Regardless, they were after Tav. The woman said something about him being the vessel of someone important? And in order to get rid of the possession they were eventually going to kill him?"

"Hmm..." Allen didn't know what to make of this information, but he did have a theory. "You know, some people who had the genetic modification ended up... Y'know. Going off the deep end."

"Yeah..." Rysha thought back to the times they had lost someone in the organization due to them being hospitalized, or worse, taking their own life, due to the side effects of the injection. It wasn't common, but it happened frequently enough that it was worth mentioning.

"So," Allen continued, "I would personally chalk it up to something along those lines. But if it happens again, don't hesitate to use deadly force. We can deal with the repercussions."

"Right..." Rysha was barely listening at this point, and Allen could sense this.

"Well, keep me updated, okay?"

"Will do, chief, thanks again." Rysha hung up the phone. He let out a heavy sigh that he had been waiting to breathe. He closed his eyes...

• • • •

It was the summer of 2002. Rysha was 22 at the time, and on vacation with a friend. Ronan, with his larger-than-life personality, had decided that the two would skip state and head for the beaches of North Carolina.

"I'll pay for all of it! I make too much money anyways!" Ronan had exclaimed after initially proposing the idea to Rysha the week before. Ronan's short blonde hair bounced a little as he spoke, his light green eyes beaming with a huge smile.

Rysha, never the type to get overly excited, returned Ronan's enthusiasm with a firm "Fine"; not without a little bit of a smile, though.

And now, here they were. Rysha could feel the fading warmth of the sunset radiate through the sand beneath his bare feet, the smell of the ocean permeating the air with a fresh breath of relief. It was nice to have a break from the Academy. He took a sip of his beer, savouring the cool, sweet, mint that cascaded across his taste buds.

Ronan was already inching towards the water, more ready than ever to get his feet wet.

"This is my first time at the ocean, y'know?" Ronan turned to Rysha and smiled wide.

Rysha returned his smile and replied,

"Same here."

"Come on! Come feel the water with me."

Rysha shook his head. If the water was anything like the lakes back home, there'd be sticks and mud and all kinds of squishy stuff beneath the surface.

Ronan knew exactly what Rysha was thinking.

"Ah c'mon, it's soft sand, I promise." Ronan was already ankle deep in the water at this point.

Rysha thought about it, then ultimately decided to give in. He set down his beer and walked over to where Ronan was standing. Carefully, he stepped off the shore and into the water. It was cold at first, but it felt nice after a couple of seconds. He took a few more sloshing steps over to Ronan.

"Tada," he said, making a jazz-hands gesture with his hands.

Ronan just laughed.

"Dweeb."

He stepped even closer to Rysha, and took his hands into his own.

"You know, we should do this every year. Make it a tradition."

Rysha was taken by surprise, not only due to the act itself, but because he could feel the softness of Ronan's small hands within his own. He couldn't help but give him a cheeky smile.

"We should, you're right."

Ronan looked out into the expansive ocean, and Rysha did the same. It seemed endless, the ocean did. Rysha took it as an allegory for the future: Endless, ever-expansive, and full of mystery.

• • • •

That night, Tav was laying in bed, staring at the ceiling. Today had been quite eventful, so he had a lot to think about. He definitely had powers, but what was up with the weird symbol on his hand? Tav raised his right arm up and faced the top of his hand towards himself to get a better look. It was a cool symbol; it looked like a tattoo he would unironically get. The rest of the lines were mostly gone by now, but the mark on his hand looked just as dark as when it first appeared.

Tav put his arm down, and looked back up at the ceiling. Not too long after, his eyes drifted shut...

• • • •

Tav was now awake in a dream, standing in complete darkness. He looked around to see that every angle was the same: Dark. He took a few steps forward, each step echoing off invisible walls.

"Ah, you're awake," Tav heard a voice say from somewhere in front of him. But, where exactly?

"Come here, let's chat." The voice was calm, but had a twinge of something sinister that Tav could just barely pick out. But, he was dreaming, so whatever, might as well check it out. He walked forward.

"Almost there," the voice reassured Tav. He continued walking forward, and before long he could see a pair of eyes staring back at him, roughly at the height of someone standing. The eyes were black with white pupils, outlined in red to define the edges of the eyelids.

"Good, good," the voice soothed. "Today was interesting, wasn't it? You found out a lot about yourself."

When Tav went to speak, he found that despite opening his mouth, no words came out.

"It's okay, don't worry about talking." Suddenly, the eyes and voice materialized a toothy mouth that twisted into a smirk. "I already know everything."

Tav tried to speak once again, and nothing came out. Tav grabbed his throat and tried to yell. Nothing.

"You're figuring things out, which is great," the voice continued, not reacting to Tav's obvious distress. "But, that means people are going to start noticing. It seems a couple of my old friends came to visit today. What should we do about that?"

Tav instinctively ran forward to throw a punch at the entity, hoping there was a physical body attached to the ethereal eyes and mouth. Mere moments before his fist would have made contact, it disappeared.

"Nice try, good effort." The voice now came from behind Tav. He whipped around to see, and there was nothing. He looked in every direction, and could not find the face he saw moments ago.

"Don't stress yourself out too much, we don't want an *incident* happening again, do we?"

Just like that, Tav was knocked back into the present. He woke
up in real life, sitting up and gasping for air. He looked around the
bedroom. Everything was normal, and there was no sign of the face
that spoke to him moments ago. Exasperated and still tired, Tav
layed back down and tried to forget about it all for the night.

• • • •

CHAPTER 6

"**I**'m telling you, the guy with him, his bodyguard or whatever, had powers too."

Elias looked up at V from his vantage point in the office chair. Now in his human form, he was wearing a grey button-down and khaki pants, typical business-casual. His brown hair was kept neatly short; his good eye was a brilliant blue, and the place where the other one would be was now covered by an eyepatch.

"So what you're telling me," Elias began, "Is that you failed?"

"Well, we don't have him, so..." Rukii trailed off, knowing saying even this much could get him in trouble.

"Cut the shit," Elias retorted sharply. Rukii and V stood nervously at attention before him. Azriel, however, was sitting in an adjacent office chair, behind a desk, watching the encounter go down. The room was large, and had at one point been filled with cubicle dividers. Now, it and the whole building were condemned. It served as the perfect hideout.

"You realize that our job as the Fallen is to neutralize any threat to either realm, and you failed to do so because of a human with artificial powers?"

"To be fair," V raised a finger in careful contradiction. "The boy also has Wrath's powers, and put up a pretty good fight."

Elias sighed.

"Clearly, we need a different plan."

"I've got an idea."

Everyone turned to Azriel, who was currently studying their blade. Without looking up, they continued on. "Isn't he supposed to be on trial for killing his father? If we can find out when and where it's happening, we can just kidnap him during the trial."

The remaining three Fallen looked amongst themselves, then back at Azriel.

"They'll have pretty high security there, it's not like we can just waltz in and take him no problem," V countered once again.

Azriel scoffed.

"You honestly think I'm worried about human security?"

They had a point. With their powers, they could move faster than sound itself, essentially rendering themself invisible to the human eye. This would prove advantageous.

Elias was already on his phone, scrolling a local news article about the trial. "June 10th, at the Supreme Court building," he read. "Must be a public trial."

That was easy, V thought.

"Then it's settled," Azriel said. "I'll go in and make a move, no one will be any the wiser." They looked up at Elias, searching for approval.

Elias nodded.

"I don't see why not. He ideally won't be a problem before the trial, so we can use that time to plan what we do with him once we have him."

Azriel looked back down at the blade. They could perfectly see their own masked face in the polished metal.

"What was the kid's name, again?" Azriel asked.

"Tav," V told them.

Azriel nodded. "Tav..."

• • • •

The next morning, Tav and Rysha were once again at the training facility. The heat had clearly been turned up; Rysha, realizing how well Tav did in an actual moment of battle, decided to get a little more rough. Tav had no problem with it, and was putting up an excellent defense as well as getting his own strike in every once in a while. They were still using practice weapons, however, as Tav had expressed that he truly preferred that until he mastered the techniques. But, Rysha was still curious.

"Hey," Rysha said between clashes of the sticks. "Remember how you were able to create a weapon yesterday?"

Tav nodded and went in for a hit, which Rysha parried.

"Yeah, why?"

"I don't know, it just got me thinking. I wonder if you can do it at will?"

Tav shrugged and blocked Rysha's strike. "Maybe?"

Rysha stopped mid-motion and put down his sword, and this time Tav noticed quickly enough that he stopped himself before going in for another hit.

"I mean, I can do it." Rysha took a few steps back and summoned his sword. Tav watched carefully as it came to fruition in Rysha's hand.

"Hmm," Tav said, "That's really cool."

"Try it, see if you can do it." Rysha took a couple more paces back in preparation.

"Uh, okay." Tav looked down at the mark on his hand, which was surprisingly still there a full 24 hours after Dr. Todd had administered the test.

Concentrate, Tav thought. He put every bit of his thought into creating a sword that he could fully visualize. He even half expected the mysterious voice that had guided him yesterday to pipe up. But, it didn't, and nothing happened.

"Yeah, I don't think I can," Tav said, looking up at Rysha.

"Well, we'll work on that. It takes a lot of practice."

Tav nodded.

"At least you know you *can,* right?" said Rysha. "You did it when we were under attack."

"Right." It was somewhat comforting to know that if he were ever again put in a situation like what happened yesterday, he could do more than just healing himself in the aftermath.

Just then, a voice came from the left of the duo.

"Rysha."

Rysha immediately knew who it was: Allen. He had probably come to talk to him about Tav.

"Stay put," Rysha told Tav. "I'll be right back."

Tav, curious, glanced over at the man without turning his head. He assumed by Rysha's reaction that they knew each other. The man wasn't particularly tall, and not particularly young either. His face was clean shaven, his hair brown with signs of grey peeking through. He was wearing a grey suit and subsequently looked to be some kind of businessman. Tav quickly looked away when their eyes briefly met.

Rysha walked away, and he and Allen wordlessly stepped out onto the upstairs balcony. No one else was there. Once they were situated and the door had fully swung shut, Allen offered his hand for a shake.

"Good to see you again, Rysha," he said as Rysha met his hand for the shake.

"Likewise. How have you been?"

"Busy, as usual," Allen chuckled a little bit. "But, I found the time to come talk to you. Do you have a minute?"

"Sure," Rysha replied, already digging his cigarettes out of his pocket. He noticed that as he lit one up, Allen coughed a little. "Sorry, do you mind?"

"No, no," Allen reassured him, coughing once again. "It's my fault for smoking cigars." Allen chuckled and sent himself into a short coughing fit. He quickly cleared his throat and straightened his tie. "But, regardless, I have something to talk to you about. A proposition."

"Oh?" Rysha asked inquisitively, blowing out a cloud of smoke.

"Yes. It's about the boy. Tav, right?"

Rysha nodded. "What about him?"

"Well, I got to thinking," Allen began. "He's so young, we don't really want to see him go to prison, do we?"

"Well, no, hopefully he will have a good lawyer. Not to mention the fact that I'm going to testify on his behalf as well."

"That's all fine and good, but... What if we took it one step further?"

One of Rysha's eyebrows reflexively dropped.

"What do you mean?"

"I *mean*," Allen lowered his voice to a level much quieter than before. "The organization has slowed down significantly in the past five years, in terms of expenses. We have quite a lot of money sitting around... See what I'm saying?"

Rysha slowly nodded, following along with Allen's implications.

"You're suggesting to me that you want to buy out his trial?"

"Well, not exactly," said Allen, "Consider it more of a trade for services. That's why it's a proposition."

"Okay, shoot. What's the proposition?"

"If we, as the organization of Aim is Up, put money in places that will be advantageous to Tav, then in return, you and Tav will work for us. Something simple, like bodyguard gigs."

Allen paused to let Rysha contemplate. He could tell he was seriously mulling it over, as he had fully turned away from him and was staring off into the city. Allen was right; Rysha *was* giving this proposition serious thought. Tav would more than likely be one of the youngest members of the organization, and may face unique challenges because of it. But, on the other hand, he wouldn't get eaten alive in prison, which seemed at this moment to outweigh the alternative. As for himself, once he returned to work as a detective he would be expected to upkeep his duties both for the NYPD and Aim is Up. He could do it, he thought, but could Tav?

"We'll still have to go through with the trial. It's public knowledge at this point," Allen continued. "But, the outcome is predetermined. It'll be a slam dunk."

Rysha, still not looking directly at Allen, nodded in acknowledgement. Then, after a pause and a sigh, he looked back at him.

"Look, I'll tell you this: I'll run the idea past Tav, and see what he says. I'm not going to make any decisions on his behalf."

Allen smiled.

"That's quite diplomatic of you."

Rysha brushed it off.

"I'll let you know by morning. I'll call."

"Well, that's good enough for me. Just remember that the trial is in two days, so don't forget to bring it up." Allen stepped over to the door and opened it, holding it open for Rysha. "I need time to get the affairs in order before it's too late."

Rysha put out what was left of his cigarette and tossed it into the receptacle. He walked forward to meet Allen at the door.

"I'll let you know by morning," Rysha repeated as he walked in the door. Allen followed close behind.

"Good, I'll talk to you tomorrow?"

"Yup," Rysha replied, looking over to the arena to see where Tav had ended up. Tav was seated on a nearby bench, drinking from a water bottle. *At least he decided to actually sit down this time,* Rysha thought.

Allen squeezed in one more handshake, and then left. Rysha walked over towards Tav. Tav noticed him and gave him a friendly wave.

"What was that about?" Tav asked as Rysha approached.

Rysha waved his hand dismissively. "We'll talk about it later. Wanna go shopping?"

• • • •

CHAPTER 7

Rysha and Tav stepped into the large apparel store. Racks of clothes were organized neatly, women's on the left, men's on the right.

"Let's get you something nice for the trial, yeah?" Rysha had said on the way there.

"Good idea," Tav had replied, very interested in the prospect of wearing something other than the same T-shirt, jeans, and hoodie that he had been wearing and washing for a few days. Now, here they stood, and Tav was sincerely overwhelmed with the choices that lay before him.

"Let's check out the casual stuff first," Rysha said as he pointed over to a section.

"I thought I was getting clothes for the trial? Wouldn't that be like, a suit or something?"

"Well, yes, but," Rysha looked at Tav and smiled. "You need regular clothes too, right?"

"I guess," Tav replied, chuckling nervously. "I don't want you to like, spend a lot of money."

"Please," Rysha smirked. "It's going on the company card, this is *technically* business conducted with the case in mind."

Tav caught on to Rysha's scheme, and returned an equally mischievous expression.

"Well then, I *guess* I don't mind."

Tav and Rysha began to peruse the various types of clothes, and eventually, Tav settled on three t-shirts, a pair of jeans, and a pair of basketball shorts.

"This one is cool," Rysha had pointed out after Tav had already picked out two regular t-shirts. He pulled a shirt off the rack that had "*Brawler 7*" and a few of the game's main characters on it.

Tav laughed, and said "Aren't I too old to wear shirts like that?"

"Well, it *is* in the adult section, isn't it?"

"Good point," Tav replied, taking the shirt out of Rysha's hands to take a better look. It *was* nice, and the material was really soft. He decided to get it.

"Now, the formal stuff," Rysha said as they approached the section. "Have you ever worn a suit before?"

"No," Tav replied, intimidated by the sheer number of options that lay before him.

"Gotcha." Rysha guided Tav over to a section with "Slim Fit" in big letters overhead. "I think one of these will be your best bet. Usually for stuff like this, you'll want grey, brown, or navy blue. Y'know, something you'd wear to Sunday service."

Tav nodded, and looked at the suits with that in mind.

My parents never went to church, Tav thought to himself silently.

"How about this one?" Tav touched the hem of a grey suit jacket with a slightly lighter grey button-up underneath.

"Yeah, I think that would work," Rysha replied, "And these are the matching pants."

Tav looked at both, and nodded.

"Only other thing you'll need is a tie." Rysha flipped through the top sets and picked a specific one out, and did the same with the pants. "Go try these on and tell me what you think."

"Okay." Tav carefully took the three articles and headed over to the changing rooms. Meanwhile, Rysha wandered over to the ties.

"Hmm," he hummed, picking up each tie and carefully inspecting it. Eventually he settled on one that was striped sideways grey and black, with a champagne accent within the stripes. Tav would probably like this.

Shortly after, Tav returned with the suit in hand. He had an astounded look on his face.

"Well?" Rysha asked.

"How did you know *exactly* which size was gonna fit?"

Rysha chuckled, and shrugged. "This isn't my first time shopping for a suit."

"Fair enough," Tav replied. "Well, I like this one."

"Good. Now..." Rysha held up the tie he had picked out. "...This?"

Tav gave the tie a once-over, and touched it to feel the material. It was silky.

"Yeah, I think that'll work," he replied.

"Good!" Rysha smiled. "Let's go check out."

· · · ·

Later that evening, Rysha and Tav were seated on the patio of a fancy restaurant. It was cool outside, and the sun was just starting to go down. Upon Rysha's recommendation, Tav had gotten a strip steak with sides of baked asparagus and mashed potatoes. Rysha had gotten the same, except he substituted the asparagus for sauteed mushrooms.

"I don't like asparagus," he had said.

As the two ate, Rysha was internally searching for the perfect time to bring up Allen's proposition. While he thought it would go well, overall, part of him feared for either choice Tav made. On the one hand, if Tav decided to go through with his trial being bought out, he would now have to face the challenges of being a member of the organization. But, he would have freedom. On the other hand, if for some reason he *didn't* choose to do that, Tav's trial would proceed as normal, and Rysha would be left to silently pray that Tav was appointed a really good lawyer. Regardless, he'd have to explain everything in a way that wasn't overwhelming. Eventually, he decided that now was a better time than ever.

"So," Rysha began after a bite of steak, "That guy I talked to today?"

Tav looked up from his plate.

"Yeah?"

"Well," Rysha said, covering his mouth and clearing his throat, "He runs an organization for people like us that have powers. Y'know, helps them find jobs, helps with life challenges, stuff like that."

"Ah, okay," Tav replied. "Did he just come to check in on you, or?"

"No. He actually wanted to discuss you, as well as the predicament you're currently in."

Tav raised his eyebrows inquisitively.

"Oh?"

"More specifically..." Rysha sighed. "The trial. He..." Rysha found himself still searching for the right words. "... He proposed an idea, and I told him that I was not going to be the one to make the decision, that I'd let you decide."

"Alright," Tav replied, calmly intrigued. "What's the proposition?"

Rysha quietly set down his fork and put his hands together on the table. He dropped his tone to a barely audible level.

"If you so choose, Aim is Up will make sure you win the case, and are given freedom. In exchange, you and I will work for the organization."

Tav stared at Rysha as he spoke.

"The work will be things like being a bodyguard, for example," Rysha continued. "When people in our area need that kind of protection, we'll be the ones to offer it."

Tav felt a pensive expression spread across his face.

"So what you're saying," Tav said quietly, "Is that this organization will give the judge or somebody money, and they'll rule 'not guilty' regardless of what is presented in the trial itself?"

Rysha nodded very slowly.

"Yes."

"And in exchange, you and I will be bodyguards?"

Rysha nodded once again.

"That's right."

"Hm," Tav muttered, leaning back in his chair and putting his hands behind his head. This seemed like a good idea, on the surface, and in exchange for guaranteed freedom, did the details really matter?

"I'll do it," he said after a brief moment.

"Really?" Rysha asked. "And you're sure about it? You-"

"Didn't think about it long?" Tav interjected. "You're right, I didn't. But, I don't think I need to. It seems like a reasonable idea."

Rysha once again picked up his fork.

"Well, in that case, I'll let him know in the morning."

Tav nodded, and smiled. "Sounds good to me."

· · · ·

Later that night, once again, Tav woke up within a dream. This time, he was in a room, albeit dimly lit, and he could make out the outlines of furniture. It looked like a throne room, of sorts, with a massive table in the middle and a throne on the far end. He couldn't tell, however, who was sitting on that throne.

Then, a familiar voice.

"You're back."

Once again, Tav went to speak, and nothing came out.

"Come closer, have a seat."

Tav complied and took a seat at the table facing the throne.

"You probably have a lot of questions, and I'm ready to answer them," the voice began. Tav could hear him adjust forward in his seat, and yet he still couldn't see him.

"For starters, my name is Wrath. That's it, just Wrath. 'Who is that,' you ask? Well, I'm none other than the Son of God."

Tav was now intrigued. *Son of God,* you say?

"The one and only, actually, aside from my sister, *Mercy*." Tav could hear the voice grit its teeth as he spoke his sister's name. He heard the throne shuffle once again as Wrath sat back in his seat.

"We used to all live in the Heavenrealm together, back in the old days. But, that was many, many years ago. Times have changed. Daddy God got mad one day, and now, the Heavenrealm is a long-gone memory to me."

Tav listened attentively. In truth, what choice did he have?

"Well, his anger wasn't entirely without reason. I had thought to myself days, months, *years* prior, 'Isn't there something more to this life? Something better?' So, I challenged him. In fact, I was supposed to have an army behind me when I did, but those ungrateful bastards defected on me. So, I was all alone, facing the almighty God, overseer of the realm, by myself." Wrath shuffled once again. "And... I lost. Pretty badly, in fact. I was cast from the Heavenrealm and sent to a dimension of my own, one barren of life and love and happiness. Those were things I was destined to never feel again.

"Now, I can hear you asking, 'What does this have to do with me?'" Wrath paused for a moment to let out an unnerving laugh. "I'll tell you, with utmost honesty: You are the first human I have witnessed contain such *hatred*, such *power*, in many, many years. I thought to myself, 'I can't let this talent go to waste.' Watching the moment you killed your own father without hesitation gave me hope that I could achieve such a feat myself. To strike down the force that bore me, the same force that later condemned me. So, in that moment, I possessed your body, and bound myself to you with the crest on your hand."

"What do you want from me?"

Tav was surprised to hear himself speak. And he wasn't the only one; Wrath was also taken aback by the fact that his monologue had been rudely interrupted.

"You?" Wrath asked him rhetorically. "*You* are my ticket to success. With not only the artificial powers you inherited from your father, but also the *real* powers I, myself, bring to the table, you're an unstoppable force." Wrath leaned forward, and a beam of light caught his facial features. He wasn't particularly ugly, but not particularly handsome either; His skin bordered on a pale grey, with strong eyebrows and long, dark hair. He had a scar on his right cheek, and several other scars on his neck. He smiled.

"Why don't we take over the Heavenrealm together? Imagine the victory, the luxury, the striking down of a tyrannical overlord. I would separate myself from your body and you would live as my right hand man, bathing in the glory of being the new rulers of the Heavenrealm. What do you say?"

Tav, frozen in fear by the sight of this supposedly powerful entity within him, stammered,

"I don't know."

Was he really being asked to leave his entire life on earth for the promise of hypothetical luxury? He knew in his heart that the answer was a resounding "No", but he greatly feared the consequences if he were to say that right at this moment.

"Tell you what," Wrath began, leaning back on the throne. "I'll give you until this 'trial' of yours is over to decide. Then, perhaps we can strike a deal?"

Tav stayed silent, looking down at the ground.

"Just remember, without me, your powers are weak. Fake. You are the product of man being overzealous, trying to play God for themselves."

With this, Wrath snapped his fingers, and Tav's world faded to black.

• • • •

CHAPTER 8

Today was Wednesday, June 9th. One more day until the trial. Tav woke up incredibly groggy that morning, having spent most of the night thinking about the encounter with Wrath. It was all so strange; Why was Wrath using him, of all people, as a vessel? And what even *is* the Heavenrealm? Tav had never heard of such a thing, so clearly it had no bearing on the happenings of earth. *Did it?*

Tav eventually got out of bed and got dressed. This time, he put on a plain grey t-shirt with dark jeans, with his signature black zip-up hoodie. He still had the same shoes, black canvas sneakers.

I wonder if Rysha wants me to wear different shoes to the trial, Tav thought in a moment of realization. Oh well, he'd worry about that later.

When Tav left his room, he found Rysha fast asleep on the couch. This is where he usually slept, Tav had quickly learned. Right now, his mouth was open and he was drooling a bit, snoring loudly. And, for some reason, he was still in his suit.

"Rysha," Tav said quietly. Tav poked his shoulder a couple times. "Rysha. *Ryyyyyysha.*"

"Huh?" Rysha awoke with a start and shut his mouth, quickly drying the residual drool with his sleeve. He sat up. "Oh, hey buddy. You're up early." He reached over to the side table and put on his glasses.

"Yeah, I guess so," Tav replied. "So, why *do* you sleep on the couch if you have an entire bedroom to yourself?"

"Habit, I guess," Rysha chuckled. He put an arm behind his head and scratched the back of his neck. "My ex-wife always made me sleep out here, 'cuz I'd always get up at odd hours for work."

"Ah, okay," Tav looked away onto the balcony for a moment. "Ex-wife?" Tav asked awkwardly.

"Yeah," Rysha replied with a groan as he stretched. "We got divorced like, six years ago?"

Tav looked back at Rysha, hands in his pockets. "Sorry to hear."

"Well, y'know, sometimes things just don't pan out." Rysha smiled sleepily. "But! Nothing coffee can't fix, right?" Rysha stood up and straightened his clothes, then headed for the kitchen. "Do you want any?" he asked Tav.

"Coffee?"

"Yeah," Rysha was already getting the bag of coffee beans out of the cabinet. "Fresh ground. The good stuff."

"Hmm," Tav thought out loud. "Actually, I've never had coffee."

Rysha's eyes went wide.

"What do you mean, you've 'never had coffee'?"

Tav laughed.

"I just haven't!"

"Well, we're changing that today," Rysha threw some beans into the grinder, shaking his head. "Never had coffee..." Rysha turned to Tav, who had silently migrated into the kitchen and sat at the table. Rysha smirked.

"Don't bully me!" Tav retorted with a laugh.

"I'm not, I swear!" Rysha yelled over the loudness of the grinder. As the beans got ground to a pulp, Rysha readied two mugs. One of them, Rysha's mug, had "LOOK AT YOU, BECOMING A DETECTIVE AND SHIT" printed in large letters across the front. Tav's mug, however, said "I DRINK COFFEE FOR YOUR SURVIVAL".

Tav inspected the mugs that were now set on the counter. "Where did you get such cool mugs?"

"If you drink enough coffee, you begin to just acquire them. Look." Rysha opened the cabinet to reveal what had to be at least 30 mugs, stacked neatly in rows.

Tav raised his eyebrows.

"Wow."

Rysha placed a filter in the top of the coffee maker, and dumped in the grounds. He snapped the filter in place and hit a few buttons. Coffee began to slowly drip into the carafe.

"Tada," he exclaimed, giving Tav a thumbs up.

Tav smiled and gave him two back.

"So," Rysha began, leaning against the counter, "What do you want to do today?"

Tav thought for a moment.

"I thought we were going to do more training?"

"Well, I thought about it, and decided we could give it a break today. But I don't want you to be stuck in the house all day. That would be boring, don't you think?"

The coffee maker beeped. Rysha carefully poured coffee into each of the mugs, his having slightly more in it than Tav's.

"Do you want creamer? It's hazelnut." Rysha asked off-topic.

"Sure? I guess?"

"It makes it less bitter, trust me."

Bitter? Tav thought. *Coffee smells so good, there's no way it tastes bitter.*

Rysha got into the fridge and took out the pint of creamer.

"But yeah," he continued, "I was going to say you could walk around town, check out the sights for yourself without someone breathing down your neck. Y'know?" Rysha handed Tav his coffee, and sat down at the table.

"Yeah, that sounds interesting."

"You still have the phone I gave you, right?"

"Yeah, it's in the room." Frankly, Tav had completely forgotten about it. He wasn't used to carrying a cell phone, so it was hard for him to remember to take it with him.

"Yeah, so I figured that if you need anything, you can just call. There's an art store a couple blocks away. I can send you the walking directions, if you'd like."

"That would be great," Tav replied, gingery taking a sip of his coffee. "Ow." Too hot.

"It helps if you let it cool down first," Rysha remarked smartly, picking up his own mug. "Unless you're old, like me, then you get used to it."

Tav shook his head. "I don't even think you're old."

Rysha scoffed. "Right. Try 38, 39 in November."

"Eh, that's not too old," Tav replied. "My dad is… was… 40."

Rysha nodded, and took a sip of coffee. "Some days I feel old. But, aside from that, you'll want some money for the art store, right?"

"I mean," Tav started in between blowing on his coffee. "I'm fine with just looking around."

"Nonsense," Rysha scoffed as he dug into his pocket to grab his wallet. "You might as well have supplies to do something fun before a really stressful day, right?"

"I guess," Tav replied quietly. "But, you really don't have to."

Rysha handed Tav two $20 bills.

"I know I don't *have* to. I *want* to." Rysha smiled as Tav carefully took the money.

"Thank you, for real," Tav said, stuffing the money into his sweatshirt pocket.

"Not a problem. Now, you promise you'll call if you need anything?"

"For sure. I know the city pretty well, but it's been years. If I get lost, I can always look up a map."

"Atta boy." Rysha took another sip of coffee. He was almost done with his, and Tav was still waiting for his own to cool off.

• • • •

The hot June sun attempted to beat down on the pavement, had it not been for the gigantic skyscrapers that lined the city and cast comfortable shade. Despite that, it was still pretty muggy, and Tav was regretting not wearing shorts. He had set off after eventually finishing his coffee.

"It was really good," he had politely told Rysha. In truth, Tav preferred hot chocolate, but coffee wasn't that awful in comparison. The hazelnut creamer definitely helped.

"In 20 feet, turn right," the GPS on Tav's phone chirped. Tav looked up and saw an intersection. Across the intersection, he saw someone standing amongst a crowd, the only person facing directly towards him. She was wearing sunglasses, so he couldn't tell if she was looking at him. Tav could see that her hair was the exact same shade of blue as the woman that had attacked them yesterday. Tav turned the corner, brushing off the strange encounter and hoping it was a coincidence.

As he walked, Tav felt as though someone was following him. It had to be her. But, he daren't look backwards and give himself away. The art store was about half a mile ahead of him. He could make it. Tav quickened his steps, and the steps behind him quickened as well. In a moment of panic, Tav decided to veer off into an alley to throw off the trail of the person following him.

But, she followed, and soon enough, Tav and V were standing face to face in the alley.

"Hey!"

"Shhhhh," V cautioned while putting a finger to her lips. "I'm here to help, I'm not going to hurt you."

"Why should I believe you?" Tav asked, arms now readied in a defensive position.

V took off her sunglasses, once again revealing her striking amber eyes. "Because, Tav, I'm not like the others. I'm not even technically supposed to be here right now."

Tav didn't let his guard down. "Why?"

"Because, I want to explain some stuff to you. Is that okay?"

Tav, wavering slightly, replied, "Okay, talk. I'm listening."

"Everything sounds really complicated right now, and I'm sure you're scared. But, when I said you're the vessel of someone the other day? I know who it is, and I can tell by the crest on your hand."

Tav looked down at his hand, then back up at V.

"Who is it?" He already knew the answer, but he needed to know what V would say.

"Well, his name is Wrath," V began. "He's God's son. We all used to live together in the Heavenrealm, which is very far away from earth. Wrath wanted us - being me, the guy with me, and two others of us - to help him."

Tav's guard unintentionally lowered as V spoke.

"We quickly realized that if we did that, we'd have to kill all of our friends, and we didn't want to do that. So, we tried to run away. An Archangel caught us, and banished us to our own realm. As for Wrath... We aren't sure what happened to him. That's where you come in."

"Tell her *NOTHING.*" Tav immediately recognized the voice in his head. "Do *not* tell her that I'm here."

"Myself and the rest of the Fallen are certain that Wrath possessed your body," V continued, unaware of what was happening within Tav as she spoke. "So, as opposed to just straight up killing you, we thought it would make more sense to talk to Wrath directly and see what he's up to. See what I'm saying?"

"Y...Yeah..." Tav replied cautiously, eyes looking up and away from her for a moment.

"If you tell her I'm here, I can't promise what will happen next."

But, Tav thought, hoping Wrath could somehow hear him, *She just wants to talk. Nothing is going to happen to you.*

"Bullshit," Wrath replied. "I know what they're up to. They'll kill you to get to me, make no mistake."

"So, do you want to help us out?" V asked carefully.

"I..." Tav was about to tell her the truth, but something happened. Tav could feel his consciousness quickly fading, his vision going dark. He couldn't help but close his eyes.

The body of Tav's eyes opened. They were black with white pupils.

"Hey, V."

• • • •

CHAPTER 9

V readied herself in a battle position. She knew that voice any-where; Wrath had finally completely taken over the body, and he was not about to go down without a fight.

"You bastard," she hissed, swinging her staff in a circle. "'Least you could've done was stay dead."

"I'm not the type." A sword now extended from Wrath's right hand. It was a gorgeous weapon, made of black and red damascus steel with a gunmetal grey hilt. Wrath's crest was on the hilt, as well.

"Why are you still mad?" Wrath asked. "We could've had something great back there, all those years ago. It's not too late, y'know." Within seconds, Wrath's sword was pressed against V's staff.

"I don't want that. I *never* wanted that," V told him through grit-ted teeth.

"Come on, you can't say you *never* wanted to overthrow God." Wrath went in for another aggressive strike, and V parried it. "Re-member all of the shitty things he did to us? Remember how he cursed us to be wretched forever the moment we didn't listen?" An-other strike. "We could have had it all if you had helped me."

"I never wanted to kill my friends, my *family* for it."

And thus, the battle truly began. V's heart raced as Wrath lunged forward with his sword, the blade gleaming ominously in the dim al-ley light. She raised her staff just in time, deflecting the blow with a clash. The impact sent shockwaves through her arms, but she stood her ground.

Wrath's laughter echoed through the alley, his eyes burning with a sinister light.

"You can't hope to stop me, V. It's too late."

Undeterred, V twirled her staff expertly, striking out with calcu-lated precision. She aimed for Wrath's legs, trying to knock him off balance. With a swift swing, she swept his feet from beneath him, but

Wrath levitated slightly with his wings to avoid completely falling over. The clash of their weapons sent sparks flying, each strike a testament to the raw power that coursed through their opposing forces. V's muscles strained as she pushed against Wrath's offense, her determination unwavering. V ducked and weaved, narrowly avoiding the razor-sharp blade. She seized the opportunity to counter, launching a series of rapid strikes with her staff. Each blow was met with Wrath's effortless defense, the clash of their weapons resonating through the alley. V's mind raced, searching for a weakness in Wrath's relentless onslaught.

Then, for a fleeting moment, Wrath's vessel's eyes flashed back to their original grey and white. Now, Tav's own eyes met V's. He was straining, his veins bulging in his arms as he prevented himself from striking her.

"Help... Me..." Tav quietly pleaded in his own voice.

V knew what she had to do. She struck Tav in the head with her staff, rendering him unconscious. As his body dropped to the ground, the sword that was once so formidable slowly dematerialized.

• • • •

It was getting late. Rysha had probably checked his phone six times in the past 15 minutes. Nothing. He hadn't heard a word from Tav. He decided to call him again, just as he had roughly an hour ago. No answer, straight to voicemail.

Damn it, Rysha thought, *This is my fault.* He looked up at the mug on the other end of the table. Tav had forgotten to take it to the sink, which was fine; a missed dish was of least importance right now.

Just then, a knock on the door. Rysha quickly got up to answer it, but by the time he opened it, no one was on the other side. There was, however, a piece of paper, folded in half and blank on the outside. Rysha looked down either side of the hallway and saw no trace of a person having been there. Being inherently precautious, he shut the door and went to the kitchen to grab a pair of gloves. He snapped them on and went back to the door, and picked up the note. Nervously, he opened it, and read the scraggly writing.

"Tav is in good hands. Sorry." It was not signed.

Rysha grunted and shut the door, setting the note on the kitchen table. He read it a few more times, getting angrier with both himself and whoever had left this note with each repetition of "Sorry" in his mind.

Rysha took off the gloves and threw them in the trash, then picked up his phone off the table. He scrolled his contacts for Dr. Angela Todd. He quickly pressed the call button and put it up to his ear. *Brrrrrr. Brrrrrr. Brrrrrr.*

"Hello?"

"Angie. It's Rysha."

Dr. Todd could tell something was wrong by the tone of Rysha's voice.

"Hey. What's going on?"

"It's Tav. I let him explore the city by himself, and..." Rysha took a deep breath to calm himself down so he could talk slower. "... He's still not back yet. It's been hours."

"Okay," Dr. Todd said calmly. "Have you tried calling him?"

"I have, but I think his phone is dead."

"Okay..."

Silence for a moment before Dr. Todd spoke again.

"I know this is crazy and probably not what you want to hear, but if he has a sudden surge in power again it'll show up on my radar I have back at the office."

"But that more than likely means he's in danger," countered Rysha. "Someone left a note at my door, and I have an idea of who left it, but I have no idea where they would be located. It said he's in 'good hands,' but I don't trust that at all."

"Can you call up work and have them send patrol out?"

"They'll know I let him out of my sight, I can't do that."

"Right... Well, it's starting to sound like the radar may be our only option."

Rysha was quiet for a moment. Then, he decided to bare his soul a bit.

"This is all my fault, Angie. I shouldn't have let him go by himself. He was just going to go to the art supply store so he'd have something to keep him occupied until the trial tomorrow."

"Well, now all we can do is deal with the situation at hand," Dr. Todd replied, trying her best to not sound cold or uncaring. "Meet me at the office?"

"Okay. I'll be there in about 20."

"Good. I'll be seeing you."

Rysha took the phone away from his ear, and hung up the call. He sighed heavily.

· · · ·

When Tav awoke, he was in what looked like an abandoned office building. As his eyes blinked fully open, he saw four people standing or sitting in various locations around the room. He also quickly realized that his hands were bound behind the chair he was sitting in, and his ankles were bound as well.

Rukii was the first to notice that he was awake.

"Check it out, guys."

"What?" V quickly got up and went over to Tav, who was battling a gnarly headache and not fully aware yet of what was happening or where he was.

"Hey," V said softly. "You okay?"

Elias walked over and shoved V out of his way.

"Where's Wrath?" he asked Tav sternly.

Tav blinked a few more times, and his eyes got wide with fear.

"I don't know, I-"

"You know exactly what's going on. Now, get out of the way so I can talk to Wrath."

"I can't just... *do* that," Tav said through a shaky breath.

Slap. Elias' palm made square contact with Tav's cheek. Tav returned to his original position and looked up at Elias. Elias grabbed the collar of Tav's shirt, and got very, *very* close to his face.

"Listen here you little shit," Elias spat through gritted teeth. "If you don't switch with Wrath, I'm going to beat him out of you. Understood?"

Tav started breathing heavily, petrified of the man that stood before him.

"Go easy on him!" Both Tav and Elias turned their heads to V, who was being held back by Azriel. "Don't hurt him! He's just a kid!"

Elias let go of Tav's collar.

"He's also the vessel of our sworn enemy, you understand."

V struggled against Azriel, who was not budging. Rukii was watching the whole thing go down from a distance. He didn't know who or how to help, so he stayed silent.

"It isn't his fault," V continued, "He didn't ask for this."

"Do you think it matters?" Elias snarled. "He's one casualty compared to the hundreds there will be if we let Wrath get away."

Tav, at this point, felt tears leaking from his eyes. V noticed this and struggled even harder against Azriel.

"Let it happen," Azriel told her sternly. "It has to."

"No it *DOESN'T!*" V yelled as she pushed Azriel away. She began to run towards Tav.

Tav was incredibly worked up at this point. He was hyperventilating and crying, certain of the horrible things that were about to happen to him. He could feel energy welling up in his chest, like a bomb about to explode.

And then, it did. Tav released a massive explosion of energy, sending each of the Fallen flying across the room.

Tav, barely hanging onto consciousness, realized that he was no longer tied up. He let himself sink back into the chair, and lost his hold on his mind.

• • • •

CHAPTER 10

Rysha sped towards Dr. Todd's office. It was pretty late at night, so hopefully if he *did* get stopped he would be able to talk himself out of a speeding ticket. But, so far it didn't seem like there were many officers out and about, so he should be fine. He turned onto the road and put the pedal to the floor. Not much farther to go now, just pass a couple buildings and her office was right there.

When Rysha pulled into the parking lot, he saw a car already parked with its headlights on.

Good, he thought, *She's already here.* Rysha whipped the car into the adjacent spot and threw it in park, quickly shutting off the lights.

Dr. Todd saw Rysha and got out of her own car.

"Glad you made it in one piece," she said jokingly as Rysha shut his car door.

"Yeah," Rysha replied with a huff. The two silently walked up to the door, and Dr. Todd got out her keys to unlock it. As she did and they stepped in, an alarm began to beep. Dr. Todd walked over to the panel and punched in her code, disabling the alarm.

"This way," she motioned, and she and Rysha walked down the dark hallway.

"Thank you for doing this," Rysha said after a moment.

"Yeah, don't worry about it," Dr. Todd replied. "He seems like a good kid, it's the least I can do."

They walked in silence for a few seconds more. Then, Dr. Todd asked,

"Who do you think left the note?"

"Well, Tav and I were ambushed in my apartment complex the other day, I think it was one of those two. More than likely the woman, the other man didn't seem like the type."

"Any idea what they wanted?"

"The woman said something about Tav being the 'vessel of some-one important' or something, so I have my speculations."

"I see..."

The two arrived at the end of the hallway, where the double doors of a large lab stood. Dr. Todd once again brought out her keys, and quickly flipped through them until she found the right one. She unlocked the door and held it open for Rysha, who carefully stepped inside. Dr. Todd flipped on the lights, revealing various stations with various pieces of equipment.

"This over here should do the trick," said Dr. Todd as she wheeled over a large machine. "Y'know, half of my lab techs have no idea what this is," she remarked with a chuckle. "I actually have the patent on this." She patted the top of the machine as if it were a car, or maybe a boat.

"Wow, that's interesting," Rysha replied with a weak smile. He wished he could truly gush about how cool he found that fact to be, but he was simply too stressed out. Dr. Todd sensed this and didn't press the issue. She booted up the machine and it made a few beeps and whirs, then a radar popped up on the screen.

"Now, we wait." Dr. Todd went over and grabbed a couple chairs, then set them in front of the machine. She sat down and patted the other seat for Rysha to sit as well. He did.

The two stared at the screen for a moment in complete silence. As much as he didn't want to, Rysha waited with baited breath for a blip to appear. The situation wasn't ideal, but it was better than the alternative of breaking and entering every possible location in New York where they could be hiding. That's not even taking into consideration the possibility that they left the city with him. Or the state. Or the country. Hell, if they really *were* some type of celestial beings, they could have whisked him off to an entirely different dimension by now.

"So, how has work been?" Dr. Todd's voice broke Rysha from his internal spiral.

"It's been work," Rysha replied, running a hand over his hair to smooth the flyaways. "This case is like none other that I've ever encountered."

"Yeah, I don't think you've ever been entrusted with the care of a 16-year-old dad-killer, have you?"

Rysha couldn't help but titter at the phrasing.

"No, I haven't."

"Well, it's good practice for having a teenager around. You're still married, aren't you?"

Rysha swore that he physically tensed up at the question.

"No, no I'm not," he responded as dryly as he could manage.

"Oh..." Dr. Todd realized she struck a nerve. "Sorry."

"No, no, it's fine," Rysha reassured her. "It was doomed from the start. We thought we could work it out, but she couldn't handle being married to a detective that works all hours of the night."

"Yeah, I imagine that's not for everyone," Dr. Todd replied. "My husband ended up leaving me for a younger, prettier doctor." She laughed a little bit. "He must have had a type."

"That's the worst," Rysha said, laughing a little bit along with her. He understood that she was trying to relate to the situation, but a strange little part of his brain couldn't help but wonder...

"Look." Dr. Todd pointed urgently at the screen. Rysha hadn't even noticed the quick succession of *beeps* that had started to emit from the machine.

"Bingo," exclaimed Dr. Todd, "That's it. Quick, you got a notebook?"

"Yeah, for sure." Rysha quickly dug in his jacket pocket for his notepad.

"Write down those coordinates," Dr. Todd ordered. This was it. This *had* to be Tav.

. . . .

Wrath laughed as he once again took control of the body. He opened his arms wide and released a sort of cry of victory.

"Finally, we meet again, you *scoundrels*," said Wrath, now donning his own eyes and wings.

"I just want to talk," Elias told him, standing up from his position across the room where he had landed after the blast.

"Oh, now that you actually *see* me, you're taking a different approach." Wrath laughed some more. "You were ready to torture a teenager just a second ago." Wrath materialized his sword. "What is up with that?"

All of the Fallen stood and readied themselves. Elias now held a scythe in both hands. The blade was dark and ethereal, as if a piece of the sky was condensed within it. Azriel had twin blade daggers with a shining blue streak through one, and a red streak through the other. Rukii had his bow and the potential for a clone with a sword, and V had her staff. They were ready.

Azriel decided to make the first move. Before Wrath could even blink, they were up close and personal, and got in a strike with the dagger right across his neck. They quickly blitzed backwards to avoid Wrath's imminent strike. Instead, Wrath paused and lowered his weapon. He felt the blood on his neck with his hand, and an off-putting smile spread across his face.

"Man, it's been so *long*," Wrath said, lust weaved through every word. "Do it again, I dare you."

Elias went for the next hit. He charged and swung his scythe, hoping to catch Wrath's blade and disarm him. But Wrath was simply too quick. He countered the scythe blade and redirected the force in the opposite direction. Elias almost completely lost grip, but caught the handle right before it escaped his hands. With insane strength, Elias gripped his palm around the tip of the handle and swung it right for Wrath's neck.

At this same moment, Rukii fired a regular arrow. It flew towards Wrath with incredible speed, but before it could make contact, Wrath dodged out of the way of both the scythe strike and the arrow. As he did so, he was met with an onslaught of quick strikes from Azriel's daggers. Wrath dodged each of them with ease, as if he was floating in the wind. His footwork was incredible, every step was so carefully realized that it looked effortless. His swordsmanship was beyond perfect, with an accurate prediction of every move that came at him, even from four different sources. The Fallen truly couldn't touch him.

V was up now, it was her time to shine. She swung the staff with incredible skill, but it was no match for the blade of the Son of God. Wrath easily knocked her backwards, completely throwing off her balance.

BAM. Everyone, including Wrath, turned to see that the large metal door had been slammed open. In it stood Rysha, gun ablaze.

"Wait, wait, wait, stop," said Wrath, lowering his weapon as if there was no immediate threat. "How the hell did *you* get here?"

Rysha quickly realized that the Tav that stood before him was not the same Tav that had been captured. The voice that came from his mouth was eerie, even transcendental. Tav's grey eyes had been replaced with black orbs with white pupils. This must be what they meant when they said Tav was a vessel.

Azriel, not aware of who this intruder was, went after Rysha and drove the dagger into his midsection. Rysha gasped at the pain, and upon realizing that not even a gun was not going to be fast enough, dropped it and materialized his blade of flames. He swung at Azriel and barely missed them, Azriel having removed the dagger and moved out of the way just in time. Blood began to drip from Rysha onto the floor.

"Tav! What happened to you?" Rysha said breathlessly before Azriel could get another strike in.

"Oh, he's not here right now," Wrath said effortlessly through Tav's body's mouth. "You'll have to go through me."

"What..." Rysha stammered before Azriel went in for another attack. Rysha frustratedly yet successfully blocked the strike from the dagger, wincing as he moved.

Elias looked between Wrath and Rysha. This must have been the man that Rukii and V had talked about. Azriel clearly saw him as a threat, but they should really be focusing on the task at hand, being Wrath.

"Stay with the objective!" He called out.

Azriel paused and looked at him.

"What if he's going to help him?"

"And what if he doesn't?"

Azriel begrudgingly agreed with their leader, and shifted their attention back to Wrath. Wrath was still just standing there, not wasting even an ounce of energy where it wasn't worth it.

"You can attack me all you want," Wrath chided. "Nothing will change my mind, and I'm going to hold this body captive until he agrees to help me out. Besides, I'm having entirely too much fun to kill any of you off yet."

Then, once again, a barrage of hits from the Fallen. Each used their respective powers to push the offensive, Wrath effortlessly parrying every strike and arrow.

Rysha, meanwhile, was left bleeding out and quite confused. Should he protect Tav, even though his body has been taken over, or should he help neutralize what could be considered an imminent threat? No amount of training could have prepared him for this strangely unique dilemma. He was truly dealing with otherworldly forces.

After a while, it was evident that Wrath was finally starting to get bored. He decided to end this, and quickly. With one swift motion,

Wrath swung his sword and sent a wave of energy crashing through his opponents. Everyone was sent flying backwards.

"Now, who to take out first," Wrath thought out loud. "Perhaps the dearly appointed leader? Or perhaps one of the annoying henchmen?"

Suddenly, Wrath felt his consciousness fading. *There's no way,* he thought. His eyes began to droop, and he dropped his head down.

When it came back up, Tav's eyes had replaced Wrath's. He quickly scanned the room and saw the Fallen scattered across the other side. Even further beyond them, at the entrance, Rysha was on his knees. Tav saw the blood dripping from Rysha's shirt and onto the floor.

"Rysha..." He whispered barely audibly.

Tav ran forward, with no goal in mind other than helping his mentor. Unfortunately for him, he was stopped in his tracks. Wrath took over once again. Now, he spoke to Tav out loud.

"Can't you see I'm busy? You pest, know your place. If it weren't for you I'd be in the Heavenrealm already."

Tav pushed his voice through his own body, overtaking Wrath's control for a fleeting moment.

"If it weren't for me, you wouldn't have a body to control!"

Tav quickly took the blade in his right hand and switched it to his left. Without any forethought and with great force, he brought the sword down and sliced off his right hand at the wrist. He watched his hand drop to the ground, not yet aware of the pain that awaited him in the aftermath of the adrenaline. He watched as his entire hand dissipated into nothingness. He looked up. Every single one of the Fallen, as well as Rysha, had watched this event transpire.

V's mouth was wide open in surprise.

"T...Tav..." She stammered.

Tav looked down once again at where his hand once was. It was bleeding profusely. He screamed. Elias quickly realized what this meant; The boy was no longer possessed by Wrath, and the threat was now gone. He looked around at his battered comrades.

Shit, he thought. Elias carefully stood up, and using his scythe, made a cutting motion in the air. Where the slash had cut the air, a portal appeared. Within it, there were hundreds of thousands of stars amongst the vast void of space.

"Quick," Elias motioned. The Fallen realized that now was their chance for escape, and one by one disappeared into the portal.

All that remained in the silent, abandoned office were Tav and Rysha, both who were on the verge of bleeding out.

• • • •

"What the hell!" Dr. Todd stormed through the metal door, bag of medical supplies at the ready. She saw that Rysha was propped up against the wall, hand over his stomach, and Tav was crouched in front of him.

"Quick, over here!" Tav yelled. Dr. Todd ran over to the duo and assessed the situation. Rysha was losing blood fast, and Tav... *Tav?*

"Tav, what... What happened to your hand?"

Tav looked down at the stump that had already begun to scab over.

"Don't worry about it," he told Dr. Todd. "Work on him first."

Dr. Todd nodded and attended to Rysha.

"Just in time," Rysha remarked with a weak smile.

"Yeah, yeah," Dr. Todd replied with soft sarcasm. "What did you get yourself into?"

Rysha winced as Dr. Todd put disinfectant on the wound in his side. "It would take me longer to explain than I probably have left."

"Oh come on, don't say that," Dr. Todd applied pressure and cleaned up around the wound. "You're pretty damn lucky, whoever did this narrowly missed anything important."

"Well that's good, at least."

"So he's gonna be okay?" Tav asked.

"I certainly believe so," Dr Todd reassured him. "Nothing taking it easy for a while won't fix. Now, as for you," Dr. Todd turned to Tav and motioned for him to show her what was left of his wrist. Tav carefully brought it up for her to see. It was weird to look at, like something was *supposed* to be there and wasn't. Surprisingly enough, it didn't hurt much now, not nearly as much as the moment after he cut it off.

"Walk me through what happened," coached Dr. Todd.

"Well, I got kidnapped by one of the people that attacked us the other day, so I ended up here. Then..." Tav paused, thinking of the easiest way to explain the strange and complex lore that had befallen him. "There's an entity, Wrath, that possessed me. That's who these people were after. I freaked out and lost consciousness for a bit, but internally I could feel myself fighting for it. And eventually, I won. And to remove the possession of Wrath, I cut off his seal." Tav looked down. "My hand just so happened to go with it."

"Wrath?" Dr. Todd asked incredulously.

"Yeah, he was these people's enemy and the Son of God, or something," Tav began, "And he was gonna use me to take over the Heavenrealm, which I guess is a thing?" The more he spoke, the more he questioned his own sanity.

As for Dr. Todd, hearing these things come out of Tav's mouth confused her even more. She looked over to Rysha, who was already looking a bit better. He just nodded.

"He's right, y'know. That's pretty much what happened."

Dr. Todd looked at the ground for a moment, then back up at Tav.

"Man, you really haven't had a great week, have you?"

Tav shook his head. "No, not really."

• • • •

"Damn it, damn it, *damn it!*" Wrath screamed into the void that now surrounded him once again. He was right back where he started, back in his old nether dimension. He stood on dark grey dirt, and looked up into the starless black sky. He plopped himself down onto the ground.

"What am I supposed to do now..." He thought to himself out loud. He had been enjoying his time on Earth; For the first time in as long as he could remember, he was part of an actual *fight*. It's different when your dad is the one who wants you dead, but when it's ex-comrades that were supposed to help you take over a realm? It adds a whole new dynamic.

As Wrath delved deep into his thoughts, a shimmer appeared mere feet from where he sat. He looked up, and a shadowy figure slowly materialized.

"Wrath, Son of God, Fallen from Grace," the figure boomed. It had been a minute since Wrath had heard his full, formal title.

"I have come to offer aid in your endeavours."

• • • •

CHAPTER 11

Finally, the day of the trial had arrived. After the "excitement" of last night, Tav wanted nothing more than to lay in bed for as long as he could. He sleepily looked over at the clock, which read 5:45 AM. He had a little bit more time, as he didn't have to be up until 7:00 and ready by 8:00. He rolled over and closed his eyes once again.

Rysha, for once, had decided to sleep in his own bed. He had truly forgotten how soft it was. The relief offered was immeasurable, even though Dr. Todd had instructed him to only sleep on his back until he was fully healed. Rysha blinked his eyes open and looked at the ceiling. It was still dark, so he had some more time to sleep before his alarm would go off. His thoughts slowly drifted…

• • • •

"I feel like I'm living with a stranger," Emily had said.

Rysha looked up from his paperwork. He had been so engrossed in the technicalities of the case that he hadn't heard what she had said previously. But this, *this* stood out.

"What do you mean?"

"You know exactly what I mean. You're never home, and when you *are* home you're so invested in your work that it's impossible to talk to you."

Rysha looked back down. This was not the discussion he wanted to be having right now. He tried to stop himself from heaving a heavy sigh, but it was too late.

"You know I don't do this job for fun, Emily. I have a duty to uphold. And besides, how else are we supposed to pay bills?"

Emily took that personally. "Oh, so you think just because I don't work that you can throw yourself into working and expect me to be okay with it?"

"That's not what I'm saying," Rysha said calmly. "I'm saying that I'm doing this to keep us afloat."

"You could literally do anything else; work at a factory, or as a business manager, anything."

"It's not that simple."

Emily was standing now in front of the table where Rysha was sitting.

"What do you mean 'It's not that simple'? I could probably find a hundred people in this city that actually want to be with their wife!"

Rysha looked up once again. Their eyes met. The gaze that had once been so soft, so caring, now stared back at him with burning hatred. Rysha wasn't sure how his own face looked right now, but he certainly knew how he was feeling: Tired. Worn out. Ragged.

"Go, then. Find one of those 100 people." Part of Rysha was surprised that he actually said it out loud. Emily just gasped.

"I can't believe you. You know what? I think I will." She walked over to the couch and picked up her purse. She headed for the door, and as she opened it, she turned to get one last word in.

"I'll be back for my stuff."

With that, the door slammed, and Rysha was alone in the apartment.

· · · ·

BEEP, BEEP, BEEP. There it is, the alarm clock. Time to get up. Rysha carefully rolled over and pressed the button on the clock, and the beeping stopped. He winced a little as he sat up, remembering the pain of yesterday as if it was happening right in that moment. Nothing coffee and a couple ibuprofen can't fix, though.

"Hey, bud, time to get up," Rysha called as he cracked Tav's door open. Tav was already awake, though. He had already gotten dressed; well, as dressed as he *could* get. His dress shirt was untucked, his pants had no belt, and his suit jacket was crumpled up in a pile on the bed.

Rysha peeked his head in and saw the state of things, then looked back at Tav.

"Oh, you're up already."

Tav just nodded.

"Well," Rysha remarked as he stepped fully into the room, "Do you need help? Do you need a belt? And socks that aren't white and dingy?"

Tav looked down at his socks. They were on crooked, and the bottoms of them were brown.

"Hmm, probably," Tav replied.

"Okay, give me just a sec." Rysha left the room, and came back with a pair of black socks with a gold band across the top. He also had a black leather belt that he hoped would be small enough for Tav.

"Here you go. And... Tuck in your shirt." Rysha handed the items to Tav, who quickly exchanged his socks for the nice ones. Rysha picked the jacket up off the bed and smacked it a few times to knock the wrinkles out.

"You usually try to keep these flat, so they don't get this wrinkled," Rysha kindly corrected.

"I know, I was going to," Tav insisted casually.

Rysha laid the jacket flat across the bed.

"Where's your tie?" He asked.

"Oh, over here." Tav went over to the dresser and picked up the tie, which was also crumpled in a pile. "I, uh... Don't know how to tie this. And I don't think that even if I *did,* I *could.*"

"That's okay, I'll help you." Rysha took the tie from Tav and began to instruct him. "Just so you know how, first you make kind of a loop, like this." Rysha folded the large end of the tie over the smaller one. "Then, you bring this around, and put it up through the loop."

Tav watched attentively, unsure if he would ever be able to replicate this himself.

"Last, you tuck this part down through the knot, and there you go." Rysha now held a fully tied tie with perfect proportions. "If you want, you can just put this over your head and tighten it so you don't have to do all that. Here." Rysha handed the tie to Tav, and Tav held it in his hand like it was some kind of holy grail.

"Don't worry, it shouldn't come undone until you take it off."

Tav nodded and put it over his head. He decided to wear it like a headband for a moment.

"Imagine if I showed up like this," Tav said with a chuckle.

Rysha laughed. "Yeah, I don't think that'd help your case much."

Tav finished putting on the tie correctly. Then he grabbed the suit jacket. He put half of it on, and struggled with the other half.

Rysha noticed this and asked, "Need help?"

Tav looked up from his struggles, and nodded. Rysha walked over and held up the right half of the jacket, and Tav slipped his arm through. Tav sighed.

"This is going to take some getting used to."

"Yeah, I imagine..." Rysha patted Tav on the shoulder. "Don't worry. After today, we'll get things sorted out and get you in with people that can help."

Tav smiled weakly.

"I sure hope so."

Rysha stepped back.

"Now, shoes..." Rysha trailed off at the realization that he and Tav had never bought dress shoes. Tav walked over and picked up a sneaker with his remaining hand.

"I have these?" He held the shoe up like he was holding a dust bunny he had caught.

Rysha smiled awkwardly.

"Ehh," he said, making a gesture with his hands. "Hang on, I think I might have a pair you can borrow." Rysha disappeared once again and came back with black dress shoes.

"Those are too big," Tav said. "I can tell by looking at them."

"Well, try 'em on anyways," Rysha told him as he set the shoes down. Tav slipped into one, and poked at the toe. There were a good couple inches between his toes and the end of the shoe.

"I mean, it *should* work," remarked Tav. He took a couple steps with one shoe on, and then backwards to return to his original position. "I might crease them, though."

"Don't worry about it, I've got plenty." Rysha smiled warmly. "Not to mention, you don't have to tie these, which is nice."

"For sure," replied Tav.

"I'll let you finish getting situated. Just come out when you're ready, okay? We'll leave at about 8:00."

Tav nodded, and Rysha left the room, shutting the door behind him. He sighed and looked at the clock: 7:40 AM. He sat back down on the bed and began to think. Had arrangements really been made for this trial to be an easy win? Was anyone going to notice his hand was missing?

Holy shit, he thought, *my hand is missing.* Tav poked the stump up through the sleeve and looked at it. It was fully healed, as if a surgeon with peak precision had performed the amputation instead of a probably-crazy teenager with an otherworldly sword, and as though it had been done months or even years prior to this moment and not yesterday. It was weird, but considering all things, it was significantly better than the alternative.

Back to the trial. This Allen guy, he was supposed to take care of things. Was this really fair? Regardless, it did happen in self-defense, and in any other situation, Tav would not have survived the bullet wounds. It was complicated, more complicated than Tav was certain he could stand up for himself for. They would call him to the stand, and he'd have to tell them exactly what happened. Which was fine, as he had no intention of lying. He just hoped that the judge was at least vaguely familiar with the concept of humans having powers.

Tav looked at the clock again; 7:50. He walked over to the bedroom door and carefully opened it. When he walked out, he noticed that Rysha was out on the balcony, smoking. He had changed into a different suit and fixed his hair, still in a ponytail, but now with less unruly strands, and a red hairband to match his tie. His face was freshly shaved, except for the goatee, and he looked ready to go.

Damn, he gets ready fast, Tav thought to himself.

Rysha noticed Tav and gave him a wave, then put out his cigarette. He stepped inside.

"You ready?" he asked.

"I think so," replied Tav.

· · · ·

"Court is now in session."

Tav sat nervously between Rysha and his attorney, all of which were seated behind a bench desk. Papers were neatly spread across it, with words on them that Tav could not even begin to comprehend. Tav had hardly even spoken to his attorney, spare for a brief handshake encounter before entering the courtroom. Apparently, he hadn't needed to, as he had been told that she had "all of the information she needed". Whatever that meant.

Tav couldn't believe this was all finally happening. Everything felt like it had taken place so long ago. His entire life had been turned upside down in a matter of days, and it still didn't feel real. To Tav, it felt like he *had* actually died when he was shot, and this was all just a messed-up afterlife. But no, it wasn't, as Tav had felt true pain since then, which proved to him that he was actually alive. He looked down at his right sleeve, and kept it concealed beneath the bench.

"The Prosecution calls Tav Segol to the stand."

Here we go. Tav stood up and walked over to the witness stand, feeling the eyes of every member of the courtroom upon him. He sat down and pushed the hair out of his eyes with his left hand, opposite of his usual reflexive use of his right.

"Mr. Segol," the Prosecutor began, "Can you recount the events of the night of June 7th, 2018?"

Tav gulped. "Yes, sir." Tav was silent for a moment, gathering his thoughts. He hadn't mentally practiced that much, as he thought it would be as simple as telling the truth. But now, as he felt the stares of strangers, it was proving to be much more complex than that. "My father and I were having dinner," Tav began. "I asked him about a news article I had seen talking about the 'Anomaly Project.' He got angry at the mention of it, and left the kitchen. He went into the living room and got into the drawer, and got out his gun. He then said, 'You were never supposed to know about this,' and shot me."

"Mmhm," said the Prosecutor. "Okay. Mr. Segol, is it true that you survived those injuries due to having 'Self-Healing Powers', as described by the Unified Code of Abilities and Powers as being Class C?"

"Yes, sir," replied Tav.

"Do you recall the events in which you killed your father?"

"Objection. Leading."

"Objection sustained."

Tav wasn't entirely sure what this meant, but he had a theory that it was because the question was inappropriate in some way.

"Mr. Segol," the Prosecutor began once again, "After your father shot you, did you defend yourself against any further attacks?"

This was still a tricky question. Technically, Tav did not remember what happened after he was shot. Should he say that outright, or should he put himself at risk by saying he remembered even though he didn't? Tav glanced over to his attorney, then at Rysha, then back at the prosecutor.

"Something came over me and I have no recollection of the events after I had been shot."

"No further questions." The Prosecutor collected his papers, and sat back down. Tav looked over at the judge, unsure of if he was allowed to move yet.

"You may be seated," the judge quietly told him. Tav got up and returned to his seat.

"Your Honour, the Defense calls Detective Rysha Barlett to the stand."

Rysha's steps were calculated as he walked up to the witness stand. Despite his injury, he had a strong presence; Tav swore he looked taller than usual. His naturally playful demeanor was now fully masked behind a refined air of diplomacy. Rysha sat down at the witness stand.

The Defense attorney was now standing at the podium. He organized a few papers, then began. "Mr. Barlett, can you describe the scene that you witnessed as you arrived at the location of the incident?"

"Yes, sir," Rysha's voice was now incredibly serious. "When I arrived on scene, I found Tav and Joseph Segol in the kitchen of the home. Joseph Segol was soon pronounced deceased, and Tav Segol was in a trance state. Tav was crouched and bleeding from three gunshot wounds to the chest."

"Did you observe any signs of a struggle?"

"Yes, sir. The body of the father indicated signs of a struggle, and Tav had sustained three bullet wounds."

"Did Tav say anything to you?"

"No, sir, he was in a state of shock and unable to speak before he inevitably collapsed."

"No further questions, Your Honor."

The Defense attorney returned to his seat, and Rysha stayed put on the witness stand.

"You may proceed with cross-examination," said the judge.

"Thank you, Your Honor," said the Prosecutor as he returned to the podium. "Mr. Barlett, is it true that you are a member of an organization that specializes in the assistance and rehabilitation of individuals with powers, as defined by the Unified Code of Abilities and Powers?"

"Yes, sir," said Rysha.

"And Mr. Tav Segol, having powers described as Class C under that Unified Code, would fall under this jurisdiction?"

"Yes, sir."

"So therefore, you are connected to an organization that would advocate on behalf of someone such as Mr. Segol, is that correct?"

"Yes, sir."

"Do you feel that this in any way, shape, or form, influences your observation of the crime scene?"

Rysha didn't flinch.

"My testimony is based on the unbiased evidence that was gathered at the crime scene."

The Prosecutor smirked ever so slightly. "Of course. No further questions, Your Honor."

Underneath Rysha's cool demeanor, he was mentally sweating a bit. Even though the outcome of this trial was already decided, and everything leading up to its conclusion was essentially superficial, this Prosecutor was playing a convincing part. If the jury was swayed in a direction that was incongruent to the decided outcome, things were going to look quite suspicious. Rysha quietly returned to his seat.

"The Defense calls Tav Segol to the stand."

Oh boy, his turn again. Tav got up and walked over to the witness stand, sitting down. He could feel himself shaking slightly, hopefully not obviously enough that it was evident to anyone else.

"Tav, can you confirm the events that led to your father's death?"

"Yes, sir. We were sitting at dinner, I mentioned an article I had seen about the 'Anomaly Project', he became agitated and left the kitchen and went into the living room. He then grabbed his gun and shot me, and I blacked out."

"Did you possess the intent to harm or kill your father?"

"No, sir, I acted in self-defense."

"Did you have any history of violence with your father?"

"No, sir," Tav replied. "We had our disagreements that were typical of a father and son, but nothing to the severity of what happened that night."

"Thank you. No further questions."

With that, the Defense attorney left the podium, and Tav got the hint that he was allowed to return to his seat. There was palpable silence in the courtroom for a moment. Then, the judge spoke once again:

"Ladies and gentlemen of the jury, you have heard the testimonies of the witnesses and the arguments presented by the Prosecution and the Defense. It is now time for us to deliberate on the matter at hand. The defendant is presumed innocent until proven guilty beyond a reasonable doubt."

The judge cracked his gavel then rose from his bench, and Tav could hear the jury filing out of the courtroom behind him. Tav glanced over to Rysha, who glanced back and gave a small nod. Tav found this reassuring; Hopefully everything had truly been sorted out, and this case was about to be a thing of the past.

Within an hour, the jurors returned to their station in the courtroom. Tav glanced backwards at the sound of them, but Rysha quickly tapped Tav's leg to turn back around, so he did. Tav's heart was now pounding, not only from having committed a small yet possibly relevant *faux pas,* but that the fate of his future hung in the hands of the jury.

"Ladies and gentlemen of the jury, have we reached a verdict?" asked the judge.

The foreperson of the jury stepped forward, and said simply,

"We have, Your Honor." Such a brief statement, yet it held so much power. Tav maintained his sight on the wall across the room from him, as did Rysha and the attorney.

"In the case of The State of New York vs. Tav Segol, the jury finds the defendant Tav Segol not guilty of involuntary manslaughter."

Tav could feel himself drop in relief. He lowered his head a moment before quickly bringing it back up and turning to Rysha. Rysha smiled and nodded, not very well hiding his own true sense of relief.

"Thank you," said the judge. "The court recognizes the jury's verdict of not guilty. Mr. Tav Segol, you are free to go."

• • • •

For the first time in three days, Tav took his first steps out of the courtroom as a free man. He took a deep breath, then sighed. His eyes felt like they had truly opened for the first time since the incident. But, he couldn't help but think, *now what?* The life he had lived before was now entirely behind him. His *own father* was now a memory of the past, and not a pressing reality.

Tav's thoughts were quickly interrupted. Rysha nudged Tav and he looked up to see the same man that had come to visit them at the training facility: Allen. Tav prepared himself for whatever was about to happen next.

"All's well that ends well," Allen started with a grin on his face. He stuck his hand out to Tav for a handshake, and Tav, realizing he could not feasibly shake a hand right now, just nodded in return. Allen then turned to Rysha.

"Can I take Tav off your hands for a minute?"

It was weird for Tav to hear his name being said by someone he hadn't actually met before.

"You okay with that?" Rysha asked Tav.

Unsure as to whether or not he should say yes, Tav ultimately decided to say,

"Sure."

"Great. Come with me, this way." Allen motioned for Tav to follow him. He took him over to an empty conference room, knocking politely on the already open door before entering. No one replied, so Allen fully walked into the room. He motioned for Tav to step in, and he did. Allen softly shut the door behind them.

"Have a seat, Tav," instructed Allen. Tav truly couldn't tell if he was about to be confronted or congratulated, as Allen's tone was thoroughly ambiguous. Tav went to the other end of the conference table and sat down, and Allen sat perpendicular to him.

"Congratulations on the successful trial," Allen began.

Tav stared at him nervously.

"You can relax, my man, nothing is going to hurt you here." Allen offered a smile, and Tav did not take it. He was still talking to a stranger, even if this stranger arranged for him to win his trial.

Allen recognized the push-back and took on a tone of business.

"I came to talk to you about something, I'm sure Rysha mentioned it already. If you don't know, I'm Allen Wilson, and I'm the CEO of Aim is Up. That's the organization that helps people with powers, like you." Allen could tell Tav was listening, so he continued. "I'm the one who came up with the idea for you to work for us, in exchange for a smooth trial. Remember that?"

Tav nodded.

"Good. So, I assume you have come to a consensus about it?"

"Yeah," said Tav, speaking for the first time in several minutes.

"And what might that be?"

"I'll do it," Tav replied.

"Well," Allen said with a twinge of surprise in his voice at such a confident and concise answer, "That's great! You'll be assigned various missions, like being a bodyguard or helping old people cross the street. Stuff like that."

With the exception of the "old people" part, that was pretty much what Rysha had already told Tav.

"Now, onto a different matter..." Allen held up his right hand. "Let me see."

"What?" asked Tav.

"Let me see," Allen repeated. Tav finally got it. He was asking to see what had happened to his hand. Tav carefully held up his arm, bent at the elbow, and pulled down the sleeve to reveal the stump.

"Hmm," said Allen as he gave it a once-over. "It wasn't like that the other day, now was it?"

"No," replied Tav calmly.

"Do you mind telling me what happened?"

Tav hesitated. He honestly wasn't sure what he should and should not tell him. Rysha hadn't prepared him for a meeting like this. Then again, telling by Rysha's reaction to Allen approaching the two after the trial, it was possible Rysha didn't even know this meeting was going to happen in the first place.

"An accident," Tav said flatly.

"An accident, huh?" Allen questioned him. "Amputated limbs don't usually heal that fast after an accident, do they?"

Tav didn't waver. He put his arm back down under the table.

"You know you can trust me, this isn't my first rodeo," Allen reassured him. "I've seen my fair share of crazy situations in my day. You're not the first person to have healing powers."

Allen *sounded* genuine, but was he? Tav thought about it, and realized that considering the circumstances, he was pretty much obligated to tell him at this point in time. So, he did. Tav calmly explained everything; The fact that he was possessed by the spirit of the Son of God, then confronted by that spirit's ex-underlings, then the battle, and then his ultimate decision to remove the possession by removing the seal. And, now, here he was.

Allen leaned way back in the chair and put his hands behind his head. "Interesting," he breathed through a sigh. "That is certainly interesting."

Tav waited in silence to see what kind of a response his seemingly outlandish story would elicit. Yet, as the seconds ticked on, Allen didn't look particularly shaken by it. After a moment, Allen finally conjured up a response.

"Well, I can tell you this much: As a member of Aim is Up, you won't have to worry about such, er, *otherworldly* threats," he began. "We offer protection against such things as much as we are able to. And, I imagine with Rysha as your legal guardian, you won't have anything to worry about."

Tav realized that he hadn't mentioned that Rysha was there when it all happened. Not to discredit Rysha's own toughness or anything, anyone of any strength would be caught off guard by a celestial being disguised as a human plunging a dagger into your side.

"So," Allen continued, "You are going to be well taken care of with us. Trust me."

This time, when Allen smiled, Tav returned it, be it weakly.

"So, you're in for real?" Allen asked.

Tav nodded.

"For real."

"Sounds good to me," Allen said as he stood up. Tav stood up as well. "Well, we'd better tell Rysha, don't you think?"

Meanwhile, Rysha had stepped outside for a cigarette. His hands were shaking slightly as he lit it, due to a combination of a huge release of nervousness and having skipped breakfast *and* coffee that morning. Not too far into his smoke, Dr. Todd walked up beside him.

"Oh shit, I didn't realize you were here," Rysha said, quickly taking the cigarette out of his mouth.

Dr. Todd just laughed.

"You're a grown man, I don't care if you smoke."

Rysha shook his head.

"I meant at the trial in general," he clarified.

"Ah, well, I couldn't miss the verdict on the kid, y'know?"

Rysha nodded as he put the cigarette back in his mouth.

"I think it went well."

"I agree," replied Dr. Todd. "I was hoping for the best for him, truly. He's a good kid."

"Yeah, he is," said Rysha.

"You've really done a good job with him."

Rysha's eyes met hers for the first time since she had walked up to him.

"You really think so?"

"I do," she replied genuinely, softening her own gaze. "It sounds like his bio-dad wasn't great to begin with. At such an impressionable age, he needs good influence, and I think you're able to provide that."

Rysha smiled.

"Well, that's nice to hear. Thank you."

Just then, Allen and Tav walked out of the courthouse. Allen pointed at Rysha and sauntered over to him with Tav in tow.

"Mr. Barlett, Dr. Todd," Allen began formally while nodding at each of them, "I'd like to introduce the newest member of Aim is Up." Allen grabbed Tav's left hand, and brought it up as though to celebrate a victory.

"Mr. Tav Segol!"

• • • •

PART II

U<small>NRAVELING</small>

CHAPTER 12

"So, what's this thing like?" Tav had asked Rysha.

"It's a big convention that happens twice a year where all of the members of Aim is Up talk about important stuff," replied Rysha. "I haven't been to one in a few years, due to work."

"Right, right."

"They'll probably run through a list of new members, including you," Rysha elaborated. "Probably handshakes all around or some kind of a 'Woop.'"

Tav chuckled.

"Sounds like entirely too much attention." He looked down at his right hand, which was now fitted with a high-tech prosthetic. A month went by between the incident and when Tav had gotten in with a doctor, then a prosthetist, then a physical therapist. Tav was a fighter, though, and he *wasn't* scared of needles. So, he got through it, and emerged fully able to use his new hand.

Handshakes, however, were still a formidable foe. He was always afraid that he'd squeeze too hard and crush the hand on the receiving end.

"OW!" He could already hear the other person exclaim.

"It usually is," Rysha replied, breaking Tav of his nervous thought process. "These guys like to party, that's for sure."

Rysha threw on his turn signal and pulled into the convention center parking lot. It was packed; People from all over the U.S. travelled for this meeting, as the Anomaly Project had occurred nationwide. This was definitely a bigger crowd than last time he had attended, Rysha observed.

"Hmm." Rysha turned the music down so he could see better. He pushed his glasses down his nose and looked around, scanning for a parking spot. After a couple rounds of up-this-way, down-that-way, he found one. He pulled in and shut the car off.

"Ready?" Rysha asked.

"Ready," replied Tav.

The two got out of the car, and Rysha clicked the fob a couple times to lock the doors. As they approached the giant convention center, Tav noticed rather quickly that the building and the surrounding area were decked out with huge signs. "AIM IS UP SUMMIT," "THIS WAY," and similar.

"Wow," remarked Tav. "This thing is a pretty big deal, isn't it?"

"Yeah, it kind of is," Rysha replied, scanning the building up and down. He was internally wondering what kinds of people he'd run into. He knew some of them from the New York chapter, but more as a formality than actually knowing who they were.

When they stepped inside, they were met with the sight of hundreds of people standing at various booths, if not talking amongst themselves. It was truly a bazaar.

"We've got time before the big meeting starts, wanna look around?"

"Sure."

Rysha and Tav wandered around a bit, glancing over at the vast array of booths. Some of them had people in fun costumes, selling healing remedies or other products. Some offered things more along the lines of services, like lawyers or counseling centers. The arrangement of it all led Tav to believe that being a part of the Anomaly Project was more common than he had originally thought.

Rysha nudged Tav on the shoulder.

"Check that out." He pointed to a booth where someone was selling art prints of varying sizes, from small picture frame sized all the way up to posters.

"Ooo," said Tav, "Let's go look there."

The booth wasn't very busy, so Tav could probably talk with the person a bit about their art work.

"Hi!" they said as Tav and Rysha approached. "Welcome to my art booth, let me know if you have any questions!"

"Thanks!" Tav gave them a thumbs up. They looked like an interesting person, and their eccentricity was truly reflected in their artwork. As Tav browsed, he noticed a common theme of what appeared to be self-reflection. There were various abstract depictions of a person in the center, with swirling imagery around the subject. Tav was particularly struck by a small piece that had a person painted in gold in the middle, with silvery wings sprouting from their back.

"This one is really nice," said Tav, "Can I look at it?"

"Of course!" they replied cheerfully. Tav picked up the picture and closely inspected it. It was done with acrylics, he suspected, and the attention to detail was immaculate.

"How much is this one?"

"$30," they said as they pointed at the sign. Small prints were $30, with prices ranging all the way up to $200 for the large prints. Considering the quality of craftsmanship, both Tav and Rysha found this reasonable.

"I'll take this one, for sure."

"Great!" The person reached under the table and brought up a card reader. Tav noticed just then that they were in a wheelchair.

"Whenever you're ready."

Tav dug in his pocket and got out his wallet, and took out his card. Rysha had helped him set up a bank account not too long ago, and had given him some money to start off with. Tav inserted the card.

"Acrylics, right?" Tav asked as he waited for his card to process.

"Yep yep! You're observant." They smiled.

Tav smiled back.

"I do art, too. Mostly pencil and notebook paper though."

"Hey, any medium is a good medium," the person affirmed. "I started off doing doodles in a digital workspace, but I found that physical mediums made more sense, if that makes sense?"

"For sure." The kiosk beeped and Tav took out his card. "I feel the same way."

The person hit a few buttons on the kiosk, then looked up at Tav.

"Thank you so much! Oh, here," they reached over to a stack of business cards and handed one to Tav. "Here's my card, it's got all my info and stuff. Hit me up if you ever want to talk about art!"

Tav gave the card a once-over. It had a great design, and a little self-portrait of the artist themself.

"Thanks a bunch!" said Tav.

"Yes, thank you," concurred Rysha with a smile.

"Of course! Enjoy!"

With that, Tav and Rysha wandered off. Tav shuffled his backpack to where he could get into it, and carefully stuck the canvas down into it. As they walked, he took another look at the card. "Rowan Berry, They/Them." What followed was a little paragraph about their story, and the type of art they make.

Cool, Tav thought. He stuck the card in his pocket.

Rysha, meanwhile, was looking around for a familiar face. He was still awestruck at the sheer *amount* of people. Something must have changed. But, most of them looked to be around Rysha's age, if not a little older. Some people had even brought their kids. Maybe that was it. Or, maybe the concept of powers was a little more widely accepted, so more people felt safe attending a convention around the concept. Regardless, it was getting close to time for the big meeting, and people were slowly starting to shuffle into the conference hall part of the complex.

"Let's head that way," Rysha directed.

"Okay," replied Tav. He was still curious what this big meeting could be about, aside from introducing new members. Clearly it wasn't just that, there was no way. The more Tav thought about it, the more he theorized that Rysha didn't have any idea, either.

The conference hall was huge. It was honestly more like an auditorium, with the large amount of seats as well as the stage at the front. It looked like a place where important people would give special talks. Rysha scanned the room.

"Over there?" Rysha pointed.

Tav nodded.

"That way if you have to get up when they introduce you, everyone will see you." Rysha winked, and Tav chuckled.

"Right," Tav agreed, shuffling some sarcasm into his tone.

They made their way over to the seats and sat down. It looked like they had gotten there just in time, as the other seats were slowly starting to fill up. Tav took a look around. These people really did just look like normal people. No one really looked out of place. Tav still, however, felt like he stuck out, even though he truly knew that he didn't. It was a strange feeling.

Not much later, the lights flickered a few times to indicate that it was almost time to start. Rysha got out his phone and put it on silent, then stuck it back in his pocket. Tav's phone was already on silent, so he didn't have to worry about it.

Then, it started. The lights went down and the spotlights centered on the stage. After a moment and with no introduction, Allen walked out on stage.

"*Gooooood* afternoon, lovely people! How are we doing today?"

The crowd whooped and hollered, but Rysha stayed silent. Rysha and Tav looked at each other, and Rysha playfully rolled his eyes. In a moment of mutual understanding, they both returned their attention forward.

"Sounds good to me," Allen continued through the microphone. "There are a lot of you this year, that's fantastic. You know, I think that's one of the most important things about this organization, and that's a sense of community."

Here he goes, Rysha thought to himself.

"Without you guys, there would be no Aim is Up. With that being said, I'd like to start off today by introducing our new members. Go ahead and stand and stay standing when your name is called, if you could. " Allen shuffled through a stack of papers until he found the list.

"At least he's getting it over with early," Rysha whispered to Tav with a nudge. Tav looked over to him and nodded.

As Allen rattled off names, people began to pop up all over the hall. It sounded like he was going down the list alphabetically, so Tav had a minute to prepare himself. He took note of the people that were standing; Most, if not all of them looked to be about Rysha's age. Was he about to be the youngest new member?

"Tav Segol."

Here it is. Tav carefully shuffled out of his seat and stood up, feeling as though there were a million eyes upon him. Then, Allen moved onto the next name, and Tav could feel the eyes shifting their attention. This was all so foreign to him; he had never been recognized like this. Even at home school stuff, he was always just a kid in a class, never a part of anything special. But this? *This* was special.

"Let's give it up for the newest members of Aim is Up!"

The crowd clapped and cheered, and it further reinforced Tav's feelings of specialness. As the applause dwindled, everyone sat back down, and Tav did the same.

"Now, onto internal affairs," said Allen. He clicked a few buttons on a remote, and a large screen that Tav hadn't even noticed before lit up. On it, a statistics chart nearly blinded the audience with how bright the colours were.

"Since 2013, two years ago, the outreach of the company has increased by over 150%," he stated. This was numbers stuff. Tav found it hard to keep his attention focused as Allen broke down various points of interest. Rysha, however, had scooted his glasses down to the end of his nose, and was carefully studying each slide of the presentation.

Nerd, Tav thought. But, not really, as Rysha hadn't been heavily involved in the organization in a while, so he had reason to be interested in what had happened since he was gone.

"So, what does that mean for us?" Tav zoned back in just in time to hear Allen ask this question. "Well, it means you have all been doing a great job, and should be proud of yourselves. Let's keep this trend going and shoot for even better next year. Thanks, everyone."

With that, the crowd applauded once again, and Allen walked off stage. The lights went up. People began to shuffle themselves out of the hall.

"Now that wasn't too bad, now was it?" Rysha asked.

"Nah," replied Tav. "The numbers were kinda boring, but other than that it was fine."

"I'm sure you're not the only one who thought that. Allen is a numbers guy, through and through."

"I guess so," agreed Tav.

When Rysha and Tav got out of the conference hall, it didn't take long before Dr. Todd came running up to them. If it wasn't for her glasses, Tav wouldn't have recognized her without a doctor's coat.

"Tav! They called your name!"

Tav awkwardly scratched the back of his neck.

"Yay," he replied with playful unenthusiasm.

"Ah c'mon, it was cool." Dr. Todd put an arm around Tav, and turned to Rysha. "You must be pretty proud of your boy here."

"Yeah, yeah, I guess." Rysha smiled, hoping his sarcasm landed. Dr. Todd removed herself from Tav's side, and stood rather formally in front of the two. It was strange for Tav to see her outside of a medical context, and even stranger that she was so... Outgoing.

"We're going out for drinks tonight, you guys wanna come?"

Rysha and Tav looked at each other.

"You want to?" Rysha asked Tav.

"Can I even go into a bar?" Tav asked.

"It's a restaurant, so you'll be fine, you'll just have to get lemonade or something," countered Dr. Todd.

Rysha looked back at her and shrugged pleasantly.

"Sure, why not?"

"Great! Meet us at The Mystic Bear in about half an hour, we'll have a table ready."

Rysha nodded. "Sounds good to me."

· · · ·

Roaring laughter filled the crowded restaurant. Rysha and Tav were situated across from each other at a huge table with about 20 other people, most of which were doctors and other higher-ups from the organization.

"And so I said, 'So what? The worst that'll happen is that you'll piss laser beams.'"

More laughter. One of the doctors was recounting a story with one of his early patients, back when the Anomaly Project had first started.

"We didn't know much, back then," he continued. "Nowadays they hopefully have a pill for that."

Tav looked over at Rysha. He was quietly enjoying a cup of coffee.

"I don't drink," he had said earlier when offered. Something told Tav that there was more to that statement, but he didn't ask.

"Rysha," said Dr. Todd.

Rysha looked up.

"Hmm?"

"Why don't you introduce him to everybody?" Dr. Todd once again put an arm around Tav. This time, she seemed a little less than sober.

"Of course," Rysha cleared his throat. "Friends, this is Tav."

Tav awkwardly waved at everyone at the table. A few people waved back, some said, "Hi, Tav!"

"Why don't you guys introduce yourselves, too?" asked Dr. Todd. Everyone went around in a less-than orderly fashion and told Tav who they were. Some of them made it a point to add "MD," "PhD," or "NA" after their name. The others just muttered their name and left it at that, one even stating,

"I'm just so-and-so's husband."

"Y'know, it's crazy that someone so young is a part of the org now," one of them said. "The people that we worked with have kids and such now."

"It opens up a whole new area of study," said another doctor. "If only we could get the funding like we had the first time."

"Right," the first person replied. "Fat chance of that."

As the night went on, more drinks were served, more food was had, more laughter was shared. It was refreshing for Rysha to see such comradery. He hadn't been out like this in a while, as work usually prevented it. The hours ticked on, and the group slowly disbanded. Eventually, it was down to Rysha, Tav, Dr. Todd, and another man.

"I'm gonna get a taxi," the man responded when Dr. Todd had asked how he was going to get home. She then looked over to Rysha, who was finishing up the last of his coffee.

"Would you, maybe, be able to swing me home?" she asked as coherently as she could muster.

"Yeah, of course," Rysha replied. "Do you mind, Tav?"

"No, that's cool," Tav looked over at Dr. Todd, who looked like she was starting to get sleepy.

"Yay," said Dr. Todd quietly. "Let me pay my tab and we'll head out." She looked down at the receipt in front of her. She shoved her glasses to the end of her nose, made a face, then dug some money out of her purse and set it on top of the receipt. Rysha did the same, with the exception of the face, and the group made their way out of the restaurant. As they stepped out, Rysha lit up a cigarette, and they all headed for the parking lot.

"I still can't believe you smoke," Dr. Todd admitted candidly. "Last I knew you were a fresh 18-year-old headed right for the Academy."

Rysha just chuckled. "Well, unfortunately, we get older and pick up bad habits."

"Ain't that the truth." Dr. Todd turned to Tav and pointed a finger at him as they walked. "Don't do anything dumb, like smoking or drinking or stuff like that. Be a good boy." She took her finger and bonked Tav on the nose.

Tav shook his head in response.

"I'm good," he said simply, suppressing a laugh.

They made it to the car, and Rysha opened the passenger door for Dr. Todd. She bowed dramatically and stumbled into the car. Tav climbed into the backseat.

"You're really an angel for this," Dr. Todd told Rysha as they drove.

"It's not a problem, I promise."

Then, silence for a moment. Rysha hit the button to turn on the radio, and classical music quietly filled the car.

"I know this," remarked Dr. Todd after the music played for a few seconds. "Chopin's Waltz in A Minor." She gestured in the air as though she was conducting an invisible orchestra.

"I believe you're right," replied Rysha, concealing his true pride in her knowledge. Music had always been important to him, and he was happy to know he wasn't the only one who knew a thing or two.

The music played on, and Dr. Todd nodded her head along with it. Tav noticed that Rysha would occasionally steal a quick glance over to her before returning his gaze to the road.

Tav was certain he knew what was happening here.

• • • •

CHAPTER 13

"So, how would you feel about going back to school?"

Tav looked up from his drawing. He was sitting at the kitchen table, taking advantage of the natural light from the afternoon August sun. Rysha was on the couch, looking at his phone.

"Hmm," Tav thought out loud. "I hadn't really thought about it, I guess."

"Well..." Rysha got up off the couch and walked over to Tav. "This one looks cool. They seem to heavily emphasize the arts. Here, take a look." Rysha handed Tav his phone, and Tav began to scroll. He picked out key phrases, like "Independently Funded", "Nationally Accredited," "Success Rate". He supposed those were all good things.

"Looks interesting," Tav noted before handing Rysha his phone.

"Yeah." Rysha smiled and pushed up his glasses. "I don't know, worth a thought, right?"

"For sure..." Tav looked down at his drawing, then back up at Rysha, who was now back on the couch. "Why did you ask?"

Rysha looked up from his phone.

"Hm?"

"I mean, why did you ask if I want to go back to school?" Tav was certain there was something that prompted this, and that it wasn't just out of the blue.

He was right.

"Oh, I talked to Allen briefly earlier today, he asked if you were in school. He also offered for the organization to pay for it, if you did want to go back."

"Right, right," replied Tav. He once again looked down at his drawing. It was the beginning sketches of a sword, specifically the one Wrath had conjured during that unfortunate meeting with the Fallen. He remembered it in immaculate detail, right down to how the material of the hilt felt in his hand. It all seemed like it had just happened yesterday.

But... School might actually be a good idea, Tav thought. He could sharpen his skills, finish his education, and, most terrifyingly, make friends.

"If you *were* to go back to school," Rysha began, "Do you think you could handle the responsibility of school as well as working for Aim is Up?"

Tav thought about it for a moment. It would be a balancing act, but he felt that he could manage it decently well.

"Yeah, I think I could," Tav ultimately responded. Rysha looked over to him, glasses perched on the end of his nose.

"Do you want to go back to school?"

Tav looked around, then nodded.

"Yeah. I do."

• • • •

"I have come to offer aid in your endeavours."

Wrath studied the figure that now stood before him. He was cloaked in dark shadow, hiding his true form. He did, however, have wings, and those wings looked like those that would belong to an Archangel.

"How, pray tell, do you suppose you'll do that?" Wrath asked casually, bringing himself up off the ground.

The Archangel did not waver. "My offer will yield what you and I commonly desire."

Wrath raised an eyebrow.

"I share your discontent," the Archangel continued. "The Heavenrealm has become a stagnant den of corruption, of clinging to power with no regard for its effects."

"Sounds about right," remarked Wrath.

"I believe you possess necessary assets. Combined with my knowledge of the current climate of the Heavenrealm, and your formidable skills, we will be an unstoppable force."

Silence hung between them for a moment before Wrath spoke again.

"There is one problem, though. I'm now bound to the body of a specific human in any realm that isn't this one, and that human is probably living out a normal life on Earth by now."

"Not a problem," reassured the Archangel. "I know of this human and his situation. An opportunity will soon arise for us."

Wrath was still skeptical, but it was worth a shot, right?

"Fine, then, I'll accept your help. But, how do I know this isn't some elaborate trap?"

"Trust is to be earned, I understand," said the Archangel. "However, in these desperate times, I feel it is necessary for us to work towards the common goal."

Cryptic, but also true, thought Wrath.

"What was your name?" Wrath asked, a twinge of distrust still tainting his voice.

"Michael," replied the Archangel simply.

• • • •

CHAPTER 14

It didn't take long for Tav to get enrolled at Dalton High. A simple online application, a meeting with the principal, and it was done.

"You're just in time, actually. Enrollment closes tomorrow," the principal had said. So, he was given a uniform, and sent on his way with a pleasant, "See you in a week!"

Now, the day had come: The first day of school. Tav would be in his sophomore year, despite having dropped out around the middle of his freshman year. He was, surprisingly enough, ahead in credits at the time, and roughly at the level that new sophomores at this school would be.

Tav rolled out of bed and stood up. He carefully picked up his prosthetic and the silicone sleeve that went with it. He slipped the sleeve onto his wrist, then the prosthetic hand over top of it, flexing the fingers a few times to be sure he had put it on right. He looked over to his uniform that was hung neatly on the door handle of the closet. It was basically a suit, at least to Tav. It was navy blue with a white button-up and a red tie. Luckily, it was one of those ties that you just slipped over your head and didn't actually have to tie.

Tav took the uniform off the hanger. It was such a strange concept, to go to a building that requires you to wear specific clothes, and be surrounded by hundreds of people your age who have to do the same thing. He put on the uniform and looked at himself in the mirror. He looked awkward. He tugged at the collar of the shirt and adjusted his tie. His pants were quite a bit too short, to the point of exposing his ankles.

No way I can wear these, Tav thought. He quickly exchanged the pants for the pants he had worn the day of the trial. If he recalled correctly, he could wear whatever pants he wanted as long as they were

111

slacks or dress pants, as well as being grey, navy, or black. So, these grey ones would work, despite not matching the jacket.

"Better," he whispered to himself, turning around a couple times in the mirror. He was ready. He stepped out of his room to see Rysha already up and ready, drinking coffee at the kitchen table.

"Hey, bud!" Rysha greeted Tav cheerfully. "Ready for your first day?"

"I hope so," replied Tav. "This is so weird."

"What's weird? The uniform?" Rysha asked.

"Well, yes, but also... All of it."

"Sit down, talk to me about it. We've got a minute before we have to leave."

Tav complied and sat at the opposite end of the table. He figured now was a better time than any to spill his guts.

"The fact that not two months ago, I was battling otherworldly beings and being the vessel to some great evil. And before that, the whole incident back home. Now I'm living some version of a normal life, and..." Tav looked up from his ramble and directly at Rysha, not sure how to finish his thoughts.

"Well," Rysha eventually began, "You're right. Things have moved rather quickly for you, and you have every right to feel a little disoriented. I think that being in school will bring some regiment into your life that will be advantageous."

"Yeah, you're right," Tav replied.

Rysha looked down at his phone, and turned it on to check the time.

"Time to head out," he said. "Got your backpack?"

"Crap! I almost forgot!" Tav darted to his room and came back with his backpack, chock full of, hopefully, everything he would need.

"You're welcome," Rysha smirked.

The school was about a 20 minute drive from the apartment. In this traffic, Rysha allowed for 45 minutes, to ensure Tav would get there on time.

"You nervous?" he asked Tav in the car.

"A little," Tav replied candidly.

"You'll have a great time. You'll learn all sorts of new things, make new friends, have all of these great experiences."

"How do you make friends?"

Boy, was *that* a loaded question.

"Just talk about stuff you like, about cool experiences you've had. I wouldn't talk about the 'powers' thing, though, that might raise some eyebrows."

Tav wholeheartedly agreed. He wanted to come off as "normal" as possible. Rysha pulled into the parking lot and noticed there was a huge line of parents dropping off their kids, as well as buses pulling into the other half of the parking lot. It was a mess.

"*Hrrm*," Rysha grumbled as he brought the car up into the line. He hadn't accounted for this.

"I can just get out here," Tav remarked, noticing Rysha's mild frustration. "The door isn't too far."

"You sure?" Rysha asked.

"Yeah! I walk really fast."

Rysha laughed.

"Okay, if you say so." He unlocked the doors, and Tav stepped out onto the school grounds.

"Have a good day!" Rysha told Tav with a thumbs up.

"I will," replied Tav with a wave. And with that, he was off to his first day as a normal high school student.

• • • •

So many people, Tav thought to himself as he walked into the main building. There were pods of students gathered in various spots outside the building, and inside students busily made their way to their classes. There were three buildings on the campus: This one, which housed core classes like Math and English; The Arts building, which had mixed media and the music classes; and the Sports building, which had the gym and the pool and things of that nature. Tav didn't plan to spend much time in the Sports building, as he hadn't enrolled in any of those courses. But, he may eventually take up fencing, as he had heard from the principal that they had a great fencing program.

But, for now, he needed directions to his first class. The principal had taken them on a walk-around of the campus, but Tav had already completely forgotten how the room numbers worked. He held his schedule tightly in his hands, and walked up to the front desk.

"Excuse me," Tav began quietly, "Can you tell me where Room 107B is?"

"Sure, hun!" replied the receptionist. "You'll go down that hall-way on the left, take a right, and it'll be on the left a little ways down." She made pointing gestures in each direction as she spoke.

"Left, right, left," Tav muttered to himself. "Thanks!" he told the receptionist.

"Not a problem, hun," she replied as Tav walked off.

Hallway on the left, that's this one, Tav thought to himself as he made his way down. He was walking pretty fast, his long legs carry-ing him past people that were walking at a more leisurely pace. His walking speed definitely earned him a few weird glances.

Take a right. Tav swiveled on his heel and turned into the new hallway. This one was a lot more densely crowded. Tav mentally de-bated if he wanted to wait for the crowd to move, or push his way through. He *really* didn't want to be late on his first day. So, Tav de-cided to strategically push his way through, carefully weaving in and out of the crowd as he scanned the tops of doors for the number.

104B, 104B, he mentally repeated to himself. *There it is.*

The door was blocked by a group of boys, chatting it up about their lobby on *Bulletspace* the night previous.

"Dude, I no-scoped that kid so hard."

Tav attempted to interject.

"Excuse me."

"Yeah no literally, we owned those guys."

"... Excuse me."

"Bunch of noobs."

"Hey," Tav finally asserted more loudly than before. The boys stopped talking and turned to him. Tav was a good six inches taller than these boys, and they all had to crane their necks to look at him. Tav smiled.

"Can I get through?"

One of the boys turned to his friends, then back to Tav. He dramatically stepped away, leaving a clearing to the classroom door.

"My good sir," the boy said with a twinge of sarcasm.

"Thanks!"

Tav, ever-oblivious, walked through the group and on into class. He could just barely hear the boys snickering behind him.

· · · ·

Tav's day flew. Math, then English, then Science, then History. He made it through his core classes like a breeze; This was all easy stuff, so far, mostly just the handing out of syllabi and the teachers introducing themselves. The English teacher was insistent on the students themselves doing a little introduction. When it came around to Tav, he had to think about his response.

"Tell us your name, pronouns, and a fun fact about yourself."

"I'm Tav. I use, uh, boy pronouns, and I like to draw."

The teacher had smiled, doing her best not to laugh at the usage of "boy pronouns," and moved on to the next student.

Now, Tav was at lunch. The second half of his day would be spent in the Arts building, so he had that to look forward to. He wondered what an art class would be like. He had only ever watched tutorial videos on the internet, and never received instruction from an actual *teacher*. But, regardless of the intimidating nature of the situation, he was optimistic.

He chose to sit by himself at a smaller table in the lunchroom. The view was pretty expansive, as he could see most of the other tables from where he was at. Occasionally he'd look up from his actually-quite-good turkey sandwich and green beans and take a look at the other students. There was so much variety, he was certain he had never seen this many people his age in one place. It filled him with a dual sense of curiosity and fear.

After lunch, Tav made his way to the Arts building, more specifically the studio where his classes would be held. And, yes, they did refer to it as a *studio*.

He looked up at the massive set of doors to the studio. "ART" was in fancy lettering above them, and it looked as though students had done murals down the sides of the walls surrounding the door. Tav stepped in and took in the sights before him; on one side, there was what looked like the outline of a regular classroom, with desks in neat rows and a teacher's desk at the front. The other half, separated by a very clear invisible line, was the actual *studio* part of the studio. There were easels, drying racks, and cupboards that were more than likely full of every kind of tool and supply imaginable. It smelled great in there, too, like dried paint and something floral that Tav couldn't quite pick out.

Tav walked a little further in and over to the classroom half. Some students had already picked out a desk. Just as he had done in the rest of his classes, he chose a desk right in the middle. It seemed neutral enough; he had already gathered that the teacher's pets sat in the front rows, and the rowdy or weird and quiet kids sat in the back.

So, Tav found it appropriate that he would be right smack in the center of those two conflicting ideas.

The bell rang, and the last of the students filtered in and took their seats. As everyone settled, the teacher walked in as well. She really did look exactly how Tav had anticipated an art teacher to look; tall, crazy hair, big round glasses, and a multicolour boho dress.

"Good morning, class," she began as the chattering came to a screeching halt at her appearance. "How's everyone doing today?"

"*Goooooood,*" the class chanted seemingly in unison.

"Great to hear. For those of you who don't know, and I see a few new faces here today, I'm Mrs. Edwards. You can call me Mrs. Edwards, Mrs. Ed, or Ed-Boss."

A few students giggled at that last one. Mrs. Edwards smiled at the thought of her joke landing accordingly.

"I'll be your Arts teacher this semester, and hopefully next semester too."

At this time, she walked over to her desk and grabbed a stack of papers. She handed it to the first student in the first row.

"Go ahead and take a syllabus and pass it around, then once everyone has one, we'll go over it."

Tav was still intrigued by the concept of a paper syllabus. Back when he was homeschooled, there was a digital list of the stuff that a class would cover, but a paper one? That seemed entirely better.

Tav felt a paper smack his shoulder. The boy sitting next to him had caught Tav in thought and off-guard, so he quickly took the stack and grabbed a paper before passing it to his right. He briefly made eye contact with the girl on his right: She was pretty, and had big round glasses just like the art teacher. She smiled at him, flashing her teeth as well as her pink-and-green braces, and took the stack of papers before continuing to pass them.

Tav began to look the syllabus over. The list of things they were going to cover included, but was not limited to: Pencil Drawing,

Acrylic Painting, Sculpting, and an Intro to Digital Arts. Everything else was various types of art history, or something of the like. It all looked interesting, and it all excited Tav.

Mrs. Edwards then went over the syllabus, stopping at each point and briefly explaining it. When she was through, she exclaimed,

"Phew! That sounds like a lot, right? Don't worry, we'll spend just the right amount of time on each topic. I teach according to what my students are interested in. For example, if I find that this class has an overall knack for Acrylics, we'll work on that a little longer. If I find that you guys really don't enjoy sculpting, we'll keep it short and move onto the next topic. Sound good?"

A couple students gave her a "Yeah," and the rest, including Tav, nodded more to themselves than to the teacher.

"Awesome. Today, I'm going to ask you to do something simple. Get out a notebook, any notebook."

Tav dug through his backpack and found his sketchbook that he had bought specifically for this class. He figured that he would need it, despite preferring to draw on regular lined notebook paper.

"It doesn't have to be a dedicated sketchbook, even paper is fine."

Crap, Tav thought. *People are going to think I'm a nerd.* But, he had already gotten it out, so he might as well stick with it.

"Now, turn to a new page, and here's what I'd like for you to do..." Mrs. Edwards sat down at her desk and put her elbows on it, holding her chin in her hands. "Draw me how you're feeling today."

A few students exchanged confused glances amongst themselves before looking back to the teacher for guidance.

"Draw me how you feel," Mrs. Edwards repeated. "Happy, sad, nervous, bored. Whatever it is, draw me a picture of it. You've got 5 minutes starting..." She picked up a stopwatch and hit a button. "... Now."

Tav turned his attention to the blank page. How *was* he feeling? His initial thought was "excited for art class," but he wasn't sure how he'd draw that. Honestly, he wasn't sure how he was going to draw anything that wasn't a sword or weird geometry. But, that's the point of art class, to learn how to do different things than just one specific area of expertise.

Tav clicked his mechanical pencil a few times and got to work. He carefully drew lines and edges, shading and crosshatching.

"Time's up, show me what you've got."

Tav looked over the drawing. It was a quick sketch of a bunny, sitting in a patch of grass. To him, it represented a new beginning; a fresh start.

"Show of hands, who wants to talk about their drawing?"

Hands shot up all over the classroom. Tav looked around, and slowly brought his left hand into the air.

"Let's start with you. Tell us your name, what you drew, and why you drew it."

Phew. It wasn't him. The nervousness really set in the moment he put up his hand. But, luckily, she had picked someone else.

"My name is Ashley, and I drew a smiley face because I'm happy today," the girl said simply.

"Good! Now, show it around so everyone can see."

Emily proudly swung her notebook around, a little too quick for Tav to get more than a brief glance at it. But, it was a smiley face alright. Simple enough.

"Great! Who wants to go next?"

Hands shot up again, and Tav gave it a second shot. Again, she picked someone else. This boy decided to stand up.

"My name is Jack, and I drew me and my friends because I'm happy to see them again."

"Very good. Let everyone see."

Jack carefully displayed his drawing to the class. It was three stick figures labeled "Isaiah, Me, Cole," in that order. The only difference between the figures is that the boy in the middle was wearing a hat, just as he was in real life. He quickly sat back down.

"One more, let's see it."

Tav put his hand up once again, certain that she wouldn't pick him. If she hadn't by now, she wasn't going to.

"You in the middle, what did you draw?"

Bam. Like a gunshot, she pointed directly at Tav and pulled the trigger. He shuffled his hand back down and picked up the notebook.

"I'm Tav, and, uh…"

Tav looked down at his drawing. Was it too emotional? Was it *lame*?

"And… I drew a bunny, because this year is a new beginning for me."

"Very nice, very nice. Let everyone see."

Tav turned the notebook around and let everyone get a look. He could feel their stares analyzing every line, every blade of grass, every hair on the bunny. He returned the notebook to a flat position on his desk.

"Sounds like you guys are going to do great this year. I'm really looking forward to teaching all of you."

· · · ·

Tav walked in the front door and carefully shut it behind him. He had taken the bus home, and after carefully learning the route the day before, got back to the apartment in one piece. Rysha had asked if he wanted a ride home, and Tav had replied that he'd "better learn the bus route sooner rather than later." Rysha insisted that he at least drop him off on his first day, and Tav, finding the gesture endearing, said that would be all right.

Tav walked into his room and shut the door. He stripped himself of his uniform and threw on a t-shirt and basketball shorts. Being in a stuffy uniform all day was terrible, he had quickly concluded. He was happy to be home.

Tav stepped out of his room and looked around for Rysha. Eventually, he spotted him on the balcony, smoking, and Tav decided that before he secluded himself, he should probably tell Rysha about his day.

"Heyo," chirped Tav as he slid the glass door open.

"Hey bud," Rysha returned. "How was your day? Sit down, tell me all about it."

Tav could sense a certain tiredness in Rysha's voice. Nonetheless, he ran through the course of his day, and how great everything was.

Rysha smiled wide.

"That's fantastic to hear."

"How was your day?" Tav asked.

"Oh, me?" Rysha took a long drag off his cigarette before blowing out a cloud of smoke. "My day was interesting. I'll be going back to work this week, now that you're all settled in."

"Really?" Tav had been internally curious as to when Rysha would return to his duties, but hadn't thought to ask.

"Yup yup," replied Rysha. "Wednesday night, I'm back on the team."

"Well, that's a good thing, right?"

"Oh yeah, yeah," Rysha reassured him. "I'll be honest, I was enjoying the break, but it'll be good for me to get back into the swing of things." He took another drag. "Remember how I was talking about having a schedule, a regiment, of sorts?"

Tav nodded.

"Well, that's how it is for me, too. There's a perfect balance of what is expected of me and what is entirely up to chance."

"Right," Tav replied. "So, what exactly do you do at your job?"

"I'm a homicide detective," Rysha told Tav matter-of-factly. "I can't talk about the details of work, but I go to crime scenes and investigate the situation."

Makes sense, Tav thought. That explains why Rysha was assigned to *his* case all those months ago.

"Do you work nights?"

"Usually, yes," replied Rysha. "It really depends on what they need at any given time. My sleep schedule will go back to being nonexistent." Rysha chuckled and finished off his smoke before tossing it into the ashtray. He sighed. "It's one of those things that, as difficult as it is, is necessary. I help the families of the victims get the closure that they wouldn't otherwise have."

Tav nodded once again. He looked off the balcony into the expansive cityscape.

"But, now," Rysha continued as he leaned forward in his seat, "I'll have the duties of the organization to attend to as well."

"Right," said Tav.

"So, my plan is to drink a lot of coffee and hope for the best." Rysha gave Tav a half-hearted thumbs up. Tav laughed.

"That usually works, right?"

"I've done it for 20-some odd years now, so I think it does."

The two laughed a little before Tav piped up.

"Well, we'll be going on missions together, so I'll pick up the slack if you're tired that day."

"Sounds good to me," Rysha replied with an obviously joking sense of relief. "But really, it'll be fine, I'm not at all worried about it."

"Good."

The two sat on the balcony a moment before Rysha stood up.

"So, dinner?"

"Definitely," Tav told him, relieved that the hunger in the pit of his stomach would soon find relief.

• • • •

The landscape within Tav's dream was nothing short of otherworldly. Large willow trees lined the streets that were illuminated by old-fashioned street lights. There were several houses, four to be exact, and a building that somewhat resembled a town hall. Beyond where Tav was standing, he could see that the road dropped off into a pier. He could not, for the life of him, figure out where he was.

So, he started walking. Something, or someone, would reveal themselves soon enough.

"Tav!"

Tav turned around to see an entity sprinting at him full speed. He attempted to conjure a weapon to no avail. He put his arms up in a defensive position.

"No, Tav! It's me!"

Tav recognized that voice from somewhere, but *where* exactly?

"It's me! V!"

That's who it was. Tav took a good look at the figure that now stood before him. V didn't look like herself; She now had four eyes instead of two, her hair was in odd strands all over her head, and she looked more like a bog creature than anything even remotely human.

"...V?" Tav eventually stammered out.

"Yeah... Sorry," she apologized. "This is probably pretty scary for you."

"No, just... Surprising is all." Tav mustered a smile in an attempt to comfort V in her self consciousness.

"Well, I didn't bring you here for no reason," V began. "We, being the Fallen, talked about your situation. And in all truth, you may still be in danger."

While Tav was listening, he took note of the three moons that hung in the sky before looking back to V.

"There's a chance Wrath can possess you again," said V. "You really have to be careful with what you do and who you trust."

"I mean, yeah," replied Tav. "I always am."

V smiled, relieved. "That's good to hear. I wanted to warn you because I was worried about you."

"That's thoughtful of you. Thank you."

"Of course."

The two stood in the silence of the street.

"Are any of the others here?" Tav asked.

"No, they aren't here. Since I pulled you into this realm while you were sleeping, you and I are the only ones here. It's like a private server for a video game."

Tav chuckled. "I'm surprised you'd make that kind of an analogy."

V rolled her eyes, all four of them.

"What? Do you think I don't know what video games are?"

"I don't know, maybe..." Tav trailed off. After thinking about it for a moment, he said, "I always assumed celestial beings to be hundreds of years old or something."

"While that's technically true, most of us are aware of the happenings of Earth. Me, moreso, because I was a Watcher."

Tav raised an eyebrow. "Watcher?"

"Yeah, it was my job to observe humanity and make sure nothing crazy happened. And, if it did, to tell someone."

"Hmm," pondered Tav. "Did you ever actually see anything crazy?"

"Not really," V replied. "A few murders here and there, but unfortunately those seem to be relatively common amongst humanity."

"Right, right..."

"Well, I should probably send you back..." V said, breaking herself from the conversation. "... Now that you've reassured me. You have school tomorrow, right?"

"Yeah, I do," Tav replied.

"I hope you have a good day."

Tav smiled. "Thank you." He felt a wave of black wash over his consciousness as he drifted back to silent sleep.

• • • •

It was the next morning. Tav was up bright and early once again, and this time he would have to catch the bus. He threw on his uniform. Beyond the bedroom door, Tav thought he could hear Rysha talking in the living room. He walked over to the door and pressed his ear to it.

"Yeah, we can stop by this morning, not a problem. Okay, alright, see you then, bye."

Tav removed his ear from the door and stepped back. He was very much curious who Rysha had been talking to, but he figured he would find out soon enough.

"Morning, bud," Rysha greeted Tav as he walked out of his bedroom door.

"Morning," Tav returned. He really wanted to be all like, "Who were you talking to? Does it pertain to me?" But, he decided to just let it play out.

"I just got off the phone with Allen," Rysha told Tav as he turned to him from the couch. "He wants us to meet with him this morning."

Tav was entirely right in his prediction.

"But, what about school?"

"I'm going to call you off. Remember, we told them at the first meeting that you would have to miss certain days for 'extracurricular activities.'"

Tav did remember that. He also remembered how Rysha didn't straight up tell the school what he would be doing, but had carefully crafted a situation that the administration couldn't say no to.

"Well, do I have to wear my uniform?" Tav asked.

"No. Honestly, I'd say you can wear whatever you want."

"*Phew.*" Tav quickly stepped back into his room and swapped his uniform for a pullover hoodie and basketball shorts.

"Much better," Tav said as he reentered the living room.

"Good. We should probably get going, then."

Rysha opened the front door for Tav, who stepped out first, and shut it behind him. Things were about to be interesting.

• • • •

CHAPTER 15

"Hello, we're here to see Allen."

The receptionist looked up from his computer and smiled.

"Okay, can I get your names?"

"Rysha Barlett," Rysha motioned to Tav, "Tav Segol."

"Gotcha." The receptionist typed away on his computer for a second. "Alright, I'll let him know you two are here."

"Thank you."

Rysha and Tav went over to the lobby section and sat down. The office space was huge, even despite being part of a bigger building that housed several other businesses. Tav assumed from the setup of things that Aim is Up occupied two floors, this one for the lobby, and the upstairs for the offices. Not to mention, the art in this lobby was fantastic. There were sculptures on tables, and paintings that looked like they were done by real human beings on the walls.

Allen must really enjoy art, Tav thought.

"There's my boys!"

Boys? Rysha thought. He turned to the sound of Allen's voice and saw him essentially gallivanting into the lobby. Tav's attention was also caught.

"Come on up, I'll show you my office," Allen beckoned with a big swoop of his arm. Rysha and Tav made brief eye contact before slowly getting up to follow him.

He's in a strangely peppy mood, Rysha thought as the group walked down the hallway and into the elevator. Allen pushed the "2" button, and the elevator doors shut.

"So, Tav, I heard you're in school now?"

Tav nodded.

"Today was going to be my second day." He hoped that statement didn't come across as annoyed, but there was a small part of him that hoped Allen would still get the message.

"Oh yes, sorry to pull you out of school for this," Allen apologized. "I just wanted to meet with you two as soon as possible. To discuss technicalities."

The elevator dinged and the doors slowly pulled apart. Allen stepped out first, Tav and Rysha followed. After a short walk they arrived at Allen's office, evident by the golden nameplate on the left side of the door.

"Come on in, have a seat," Allen politely directed. Rysha and Tav took the two seats in front of the desk, and Allen sat down in his somewhat comically oversized desk chair. "Now, the first order of business is a matter of personal curiosity." Allen turned to Tav. "Let me see your new hand," he directed bluntly.

"Oh, this?" Tav replied casually as he brought up his right arm. He was so used to it by now that it didn't seem strange anymore. He flexed his muscles a few times to activate the hand, and it slowly opened and closed.

"Wow," Allen remarked. "Technology truly is amazing, isn't it?"

"For sure," said Tav. He put his arm back down to rest on the chair.

"Well, I'm happy that all of that worked out. You just let us know if you need anything, okay?"

Tav nodded.

"Now, Rysha," Allen adjusted himself to where he was facing only Rysha now. "You will be resuming work as a detective tomorrow, correct?"

Rysha silently nodded. He was highly suspicious of the circumstance he was currently in. Why would he request to see both Tav and himself on such short notice? And why had it seemed like an entirely superficial meeting thus far? He kept his guard up.

"And your schedule will be, for the most part, occupied?"

"Depending on when they need me, yes. I am essentially on-call."

"I see..." Allen shuffled in his seat. "See, the thing about that is, you will essentially be on-call for us as well. Do you feel you will be able to manage both means of employment?"

Odd question, thought Rysha silently, his steady eyes never indicating anything untoward. "I don't believe it will be a problem," he stated.

"See, *believing* in something is much different than *knowing for certain.* See what I'm saying?"

"It won't be a problem." Rysha's tone now had a twinge of coldness to it. Allen smiled in response.

"Well, if that's the case, then I'll have you sign this contract." Allen slid a paper contract forward to Rysha's half of the desk.

Rysha had seen this coming a mile away, though. Despite having been a member of the organization, he was never technically employed with them. He adjusted his glasses down to the end of his nose and began to read the contract *very* carefully.

"I have one for you as well," Allen said as he pushed a paper towards Tav. "You're 16, right? Don't need a work permit?"

"Yeah, I'm 16," Tav said as he took the paper in his hands. Without even looking, Rysha put a hand over the paper before Tav even had the chance to start reading it.

"He doesn't sign anything until I review it."

Tav, understanding now what was happening, guided the paper into Rysha's hand.

"Thank you," Rysha told Tav as he took his contract and put it on top of his own. He began reading it; From his understanding, Tav's contract was a simple contract of employment, valid for a year. The rate of pay is dependent on the contracted work that is given. It included the terms of employment, details of benefits and vacation time, and a confidentiality agreement. Everything seemed in order, nothing out of the ordinary. Rysha handed the sheet back to Tav.

"Read it before you sign it," Rysha sternly cautioned Tav.

"I will," Tav reassured him, and he began to look it over.

Meanwhile, Rysha now had his own contract to worry about. So far, it looked exactly the same as Tav's. But then, he arrived at a clause close to the bottom of the page.

"VIII: THE EMPLOYEE MAY REFUSE ANY CON-TRACT WORK ASSIGNED TO THEM, UNDER THE STIP-ULATION THAT THEIR EMPLOYMENT MAY BE TERMI-NATED UPON REFUSAL."

They'll drop you if you refuse a job, Rysha confirmed to himself. For some reason, Tav's paper didn't say that. He decided to bring it up.

"Clause Eight on my contract," Rysha began, "About the refusal of contract work."

"Yes?" inquired Allen.

"Am I correct in my noticing that this clause is not present on Tav's contract?"

"Well, I made some modifications. With him being a minor and all."

"I see."

Rysha and Tav finished filling out their sheets at roughly the same time, leaving Rysha under the impression that Tav had actually taken the time to read his. They pushed their sheets forward, and Allen collected them up.

"Very good," he said as he took a quick glance at Tav's contract, then Rysha's. "Casey? That's cool," Allen remarked after seeing Rysha's contract. That was, indeed, his middle name. Tav wondered why he didn't say anything about *his* middle name. "Dylan" was pretty cool; At least, *he* thought so.

"That settles it then. Gentlemen," Allen set down the papers, and everyone stood for handshakes; Rysha first, then Tav. "Welcome to the team. You'll begin work in September, after the tournament takes place."

"Tournament?" Tav asked as he released Allen's hand back to him.

"Oh, yes, did Rysha not mention it?"

Both Allen and Tav looked at Rysha. Rysha just shook his head.

"I hadn't mentioned it."

"Well if that's the case," Allen sat back down in his chair. "We should see if it interests him, shouldn't we?"

Rysha silently looked over to Tav, who was fully anticipating Allen's next words.

"The organization of Aim is Up hosts a tournament every couple of years, all across the United States. This year, it's happening in New York City, and I would like to be the first to invite you to participate."

Tav's eyebrows raised. "What's it like?"

Allen smiled at Tav's earnestness. "People with powers, such as yourself, compete against each other for a grand prize, of monetary value."

Tav nodded.

"Hmm."

"Yes. So, it's worth thinking about. You can talk to Rysha about it, he should know a thing or two." Allen winked, and Rysha stood steadfast. Allen stood back up and made his way to the door. "I will be seeing you both soon, I imagine?"

"Yep," Tav told him, slightly out of turn, but not wanting Rysha's silence to cause a problem. With that, Rysha and Tav were now on the other side of Allen's office door.

• • • •

"So, what kind of work are we going to be assigned? Is it really being a bodyguard and walking old people across the street?"

"Is that really what he told you?"

"Yeah."

Rysha glanced over at Tav, then into the rearview mirror, before returning his eyes to the road.

"It depends. I'm surprised he didn't go over it more extensively. Seemed like he cared more about the tournament."

Tav looked over at Rysha. He had a certain *look* on his face. Like, he was mad, but more mad at a situation than a specific person.

"You okay?"

"Yeah, for sure," Rysha replied, now with a forced pep in his tone. He didn't want Tav to know how he was truly feeling about the whole situation, but apparently his face was more revealing than he thought. So, he gave Tav a big cheesy smile.

Tav laughed a little.

"Whatever you say."

"I will say, though," Rysha began, "That the tournament may be a good opportunity for you."

"Yeah?"

"Mmhm. It's nothing super serious, but it will give you a chance to see what other people's powers are like."

"Right." Tav's interest was definitely piqued by the situation. Now that he was living a relatively normal life, he would need something to keep himself occupied, outside of school and work, of course. Something fun, something physical to get his energy out. This sounded *way* more interesting than the school fencing club.

"So I should do it then, right?" Tav asked.

"Sure, if you want to. Not telling you to or even recommending it, with everything else you have going on, but if you decide you'd like to do it, I'll help you train."

"Really?"

"Sure," replied Rysha. "I've already helped you with the basics. Polish that up and you'll be more than ready."

Tav was definitely invested now. "For sure. I'll do it."

Rysha nodded to himself. "Want to run some sets at the gym? We've got the rest of the day to kill."

"Definitely." Tav felt like everything in his new life was starting to come together.

• • • •

Allen was packing up his things for the end of his day when a shadow was suddenly cast across his desk. He looked up, and there stood a tall, muscular man in a formal suit. His hair was dark and curled atop his head, and his golden eyes seemed to pierce the dwindling light of the evening.

"We're closed, why did the receptionist send you up?" Allen asked, frustrated that his day was now not yet over.

The man silently put out a hand, and within an instant, Allen was encapsulated in an energy field. The man brought his hand up and Allen slowly rose to the ceiling, seemingly frozen in time and space.

The man spoke.

"I formally request to be a part of your organization."

Allen, still frozen, could not respond. The man gently put Allen back in his seat. When the energy field dissipated, Allen looked even more annoyed than he originally had.

"Nice try, but it's going to take more than a simple levitation trick to convince me."

The man realized he would have to change his tactics, as pure, raw strength clearly wasn't going to cut it.

"Fair enough," said the man. He put his hands together, and just like a magic trick, a large stack of cash materialized in between his hands. The man set the stack on the desk and stood back.

"Hmm," Allen remarked. He picked up the stack and ran through it. It was legit. "Now we're talking. Tell you what, we've got a tournament coming up next month. Show up for that and we'll see what we can do."

The man nodded. His golden eyes seemed to glow a bit now.

"Thank you." The man turned on his heel to walk out the door.

"Hey, man, you never told me your name."

The man turned his head only partially to Allen.

"Michael."

• • • •

CHAPTER 16

The sound of Kendo sticks clashing filled the arena as Tav and Rysha sparred. Rysha was pushing the offensive, and Tav was skillfully countering him. This was the first time they had sparred in the past few months, and the first time Tav had held a weapon with his new hand. It was easier than he had anticipated, as he had initially struggled in occupational therapy with holding a pencil. But, to him it made more sense now that was holding a larger object that didn't require as much in terms of fine motor skills.

Tav decided to switch things up a bit. He started pushing the offensive now, Rysha slowly moving backwards towards the corner. The fluidity of the motions was near perfect, and despite Tav being without Wrath's battle sense, he still had a deep understanding of the art of the fight.

Rysha suddenly stopped. His phone was going off. Tav stepped backwards and put the kendo stick at his side, and Rysha dug his phone out of his pocket.

"Just a second," he told Tav as he looked at the caller ID on the screen. "It's work."

"Got it."

"Detective Barlett," Rysha formally answered the phone.

Tav took this as a good time to grab a drink. He walked over to the bench and propped the stick upwards against it, and grabbed his water bottle. He took a few large swigs, mentally blocking out the conversation Rysha was having on the other side of the arena. If it was work, it was probably important, even though Tav remembered that Rysha wasn't technically back on duty until tomorrow, Wednesday.

Maybe they're just debriefing him on something, Tav concluded to himself. He looked over to Rysha and saw that he was quickly walking towards him.

"We gotta go," he briefly told Tav as he picked up Tav's kendo stick.

"Wait, what happened?" By the time Tav asked, Rysha had already returned the practice weapons to the rack, and was headed back over to the bench to grab his stuff.

"They need me for a case, immediately," Rysha hastily told Tav.

"Oh? Are you dropping me off first?"

Rysha quickly and frustratedly shook his head as he picked up his bag.

"Unfortunately, there isn't time. You'll have to go with me."

Tav could feel his eyes going wide. A crime scene? Weren't civilians not supposed to see that stuff?

"You will stay in the car, and you will put your sweatshirt up over your window so you can't see anything." Rysha looked behind himself to Tav as he turned in the direction of the escalator. "Got it?"

Tav audibly gulped, and nodded. This side of Rysha was similar to the version of him he had witnessed in the courtroom; Brief, to-the-point, and serious.

"Let's get going," Rysha told Tav as he strode towards the escalator. Tav quickly followed behind.

• • • •

It was evening now, and a light rain pattered on the windshield of the car. Tav was in the passenger seat, holding his sweatshirt up over the window to cover the scene that lay mere feet away from the car.

Tav carefully tracked Rysha through the windshield as he approached the home, and once he was behind what the sweatshirt covered, had no idea where he was. Tav's arms were starting to get a bit tired from being stuck in this position, but he knew that he had to do what he had to do. Nevertheless, he was still curious. He had never seen a real-life crime scene, despite having been involved in one. Everything he knew about this was what he had seen in crime shows on TV, which was usually dramatized anyways, he assumed. He decided to get brave and take a peek.

What he saw was nothing short of extraordinary. There were several cop cars surrounding the home, an ambulance towards the front, and another vehicle that Tav did not recognize.

Maybe it's a van? He asked himself. Regardless, there was a lot happening. Officers were scattered throughout the scene; People in white coats and latex gloves were placing down markers in the yard and on the street; And, Tav assumed, there were several detectives actually within the building, including Rysha.

Moments after moving the sweatshirt so he could see, Tav saw an object on wheels being rolled out of the house by two people. When they turned, Tav realized what it was: A gurney, covered by a blue sheet, with what he presumed to be a dead body underneath. Tav had to stop himself from gagging, and he quickly put the sweatshirt back up. He was truly disgusted. Someone died here, and seeing this in real life really sealed the feelings Tav suddenly felt racing through his mind. His breaths quickened, and he could feel tears welling up in his eyes. This was all too familiar. This was probably what happened with his father. This was a crime scene.

The more he thought, the more the panic set in, and Tav's vision began to double. He was breathing so fast now that each breath he took in felt shorter than the last, and he felt as though he was barely exhaling. His arms slowly dropped from the window, and Tav hugged the sweatshirt close to his body, shivering.

Rysha, meanwhile, stepped out of the building. He said a few parting words to the CSI that was taking photos, and stuck his notebook back in his pocket.

The CSI looked over to Rysha's car, and saw a head of dark red hair bobbing back and forth, as though crying.

"Hey, did you bring your kid with you?" the CSI asked.

"What?" Rysha turned his head to his car and saw Tav had dropped the sweatshirt down, and was now visible in the car. "Um, yeah," Rysha replied, "Didn't have time to drop him off. I told him it'd be quick."

"I get it," the CSI told Rysha. "Sucks that a kid has to see this, though."

"He wasn't supposed to..." Rysha muttered more to himself than the CSI. "Excuse me." Rysha took his leave and rushed back to the car. When he opened his door, Tav's head snapped up in response. His face was red, his eyes like saucers, and snot ran down his nose and over his lip. He was a mess.

"Tav," Rysha started calmly as he sat down in the car and quietly shut the door. "Are you okay?"

Tav quickly shook his head. His breathing was still way too fast. Rysha had to do something.

"Hey, take some deep breaths for me." His tone was calming, just as it had been all those months ago in the hospital. Tav drew in a deep breath, and shakily let it out.

"Can you tell me what's going on?" Rysha asked.

"It's... It's..." Tav quietly sobbed. "It's like it's happening all over again."

"Okay," Rysha replied quietly. "I realize that I should have taken you home first, and that I put you in a compromising position. It won't happen again."

Tav's big eyes once again looked up at Rysha. Rysha's face was sincere with concern.

"Can you talk to me about how you're feeling?"

Tav brought the sweatshirt up and wiped his nose, then gave Rysha a slight nod.

"It made me remember what happened with my dad," Tav told Rysha through tears that came slower now. "Seeing a body that you know is dead is... Scary."

Rysha nodded. "I understand. You shouldn't have seen that, and I am sincerely sorry that you did."

"It's just crazy," Tav said, now rushing his words. "I killed my dad because he tried to kill me. I didn't even mean to kill him, I just meant to defend myself. He wasn't a great person, I'll admit that, and he did me wrong more than right. But, did he actually deserve to *die*? And my mom, she didn't deserve to die, either, and I wasn't even there when that happened. I never actually got to see her in the hospital."

Rysha watched as Tav laid it all out in front of him. He was relieved that Tav considered him a safe person to express his feelings to.

"Sometimes," Rysha said to Tav, "Things happen that are beyond our control. The only thing you can do is process your emotions accordingly, which is exactly what you're doing right now. I'm proud of you, very proud."

Tav sniffled.

"Really?"

"Yes, really," Rysha replied. "You're so young for so many things to have happened to you already. There are people my age who would really be struggling with the reality that you live every day. But here you are, going to school, making friends, *living your life*."

Tav had stopped crying by now. He wiped the residual tears from his eyes and looked over to Rysha.

"I couldn't have done it without you."

Rysha's expression softened, and he smiled at Tav.

"I'm honoured that you feel that way. I intend to help you however I can, and..." Rysha paused, choosing his next words carefully. "... I want to be a fatherly figure in your life, because it seems to me that that is something you need."

Tav looked down for a moment, then back up at Rysha.

"Well, you are."

Just like that, Tav flung himself into Rysha for a hug. Rysha chuckled a little bit and carefully wrapped his arms around Tav.

"Tell me how you really feel," Rysha joked.

Tav pulled away and chuckled quietly.

"I think that just about sums it up."

• • • •

CHAPTER 17

The weekend had finally arrived. Tav finished out his week at school, and had busted out all of his homework Friday night. That's how he had always done it; finish the assignments Friday night so he'd have the whole weekend to relax. He was a good student, and so far doing great in all of his classes, *especially* Art. In Art, they were covering all of the basics that Tav had a pretty good grasp on, so he truly felt a little bit ahead of some of his peers who seemed to struggle with those basic concepts. Maybe this would eventually lead to a tutoring gig, later in the year.

Tav was already up early, drawing at the desk in his room. The morning light filtering through the tall room window, combined with the warm glow of the desk light, was nothing short of perfect. Tav was working on something different this time; in Art, the teacher had introduced the concept of perspective, and Tav was trying out the "1-Point" technique. This meant that everything in the drawing was drawn with one point of perspective in mind, usually either in the center or close to it. For this specific drawing, Tav had chosen his point in the middle, and was drawing skyscrapers from the view of someone at street level looking straight up. Every once in a while, he would look out the window to the real skyscrapers within his view, and envision what it would be like to be at the bottom. Lines came naturally to him; everything was composed of either lines, squares, or...

Something else, he thought.

Knock, knock, knock.

"Come in," Tav told Rysha, not moving from his seat at the desk.

"Hey, bud," Rysha spoke in a cheerful tone. "Ready for an adventure?"

Tav looked up for the first time since Rysha had entered his room, and was met with quite the surprise: Rysha was dressed in cargo shorts and a tank top, with a backpack slung over one shoulder. He was wearing a large hat that resembled something you'd wear on a safari, as well as hiking boots. This was the first time Tav had ever seen Rysha in something other than a suit.

"What..." Tav trailed off as he gestured in Rysha's direction.

Rysha beamed.

"We're going on an adventure."

Tav furrowed his brow.

"Where?"

"You'll see," Rysha replied with a teasing tone. "Wear something for being outside, I'll meet you at the car."

"O-okay," Tav stammered. With that, Rysha left the room and quietly shut the door. Tav was still in his pajamas, which he figured would be less than suitable for being outside. *Outside?* Tav asked himself. *What is Rysha up to?*

Tav got up and slipped off his shirt, trading it for a clean yet similar one. It was August, so it was still relatively warm, but not as bad as the months that had preceded it. He then filed through his drawer for a pair of cargo shorts; Green camo, of course, what other colour can cargo shorts be?

Once he was dressed, he stepped out into the living room. Rysha was at the car by now. By the smell wafting from the kitchen, he had already made a coffee to bring with him, so Tav figured they would be gone for at least a little while. Tav slipped on his tennis shoes and stepped out the door, carefully locking it behind him.

• • • •

As Rysha pulled into the gravel parking lot, Tav quickly realized that they were arriving at a nature preserve of some sort. It was beautiful, with trees as far as the eye could see; all kinds of them, too, not just the stuff that was planted in planter boxes in the city. Tav and Rysha stepped out, and Rysha drew in a deep breath.

"Nice to finally breathe air that isn't stuffy, right?" Rysha remarked.

Tav followed suit and took in his own deep breath. It was such a complex smell that he couldn't distinguish anything specific about it. It just smelled like *nature.*

"Ready to hit the trail?" Rysha asked.

"Of course."

Rysha hit the keyfob a few times to lock the car, and the two started for the marked trail nearby.

As they walked, Tav eventually broke the silence.

"Y'know, I think my mom brought me here once when I was little."

"Oh, really?" Rysha asked inquisitively as the brush and rocks of the trail crunched beneath their feet.

"Yeah. It seems really familiar."

"Well, I picked a good spot, then," Rysha remarked. "Do you remember the lake?"

"The lake?" Tav repeated. Just then, the trail tapered off into a cliff, and their steps stopped feet from the edge. Below them, a huge, crystal blue lake, that continued farther than the eye could see.

"Oh, the *lake,*" said Tav.

"Mmhm."

They stood there a moment, taking it all in. It truly was beautiful, invoking feelings that were beyond definition. The sun shone bright in the clear blue sky, casting shadows from the trees behind them. The lake itself seemed to shimmer slightly as the gentle wind cascaded across its surface.

Tav closed his eyes. As he listened carefully, he could hear birds from the direction of the woods. He heard the breeze blowing past his ears, and felt it in his hair.

Rysha looked over to Tav, who seemed at this point to be in a state of complete zen.

Good, he thought, *he seems to be enjoying it.*

Just then, Tav opened his eyes. He looked over to Rysha and smiled.

"Did you remember to pack lunch?"

"Sure did," Rysha replied. He swung the backpack around to this front, and after carefully unzipping the main compartment, pulled out two equally sized brown paper bags. "I always come prepared."

Tav clapped his hands together.

"Perfect!"

• • • •

"So," Tav started between bites of his ham and cheese sandwich, "You know so much about me already. Why don't you tell me about you?"

Rysha looked over to Tav from the other end of the picnic table. He finished his bite and covered his mouth as he swallowed.

"Sure," he told him. "What do you want to know?"

Tav shrugged.

"I don't know. Just tell me stuff."

Rysha chuckled.

"Okay. Well," Rysha tapped his chin as he thought of interesting things to say. "I graduated from the Academy when I was 24, with a major in Criminal Justice and a minor in Psychology. I got married when I was 30 and divorced when I was 36. I work in homicide, but you already knew that. I-"

"What's your favourite colour?" Tav asked before Rysha could continue.

"Hmm..." Rysha thought about it. "Blue."

"Good answer," Tav told him. "Mine is red."

"That makes sense," Rysha replied with a chuckle. "What's your favourite animal?"

"I really like rabbits," Tav told Rysha. "What about you?"

"Definitely Friesian horses. I know, oddly specific, but they're so *cool*," Rysha told Tav with a childlike sense of wonder.

"That's a good one," Tav replied. Then, he got to thinking, "Hey, you never mentioned the Anomaly Project."

"I was about to," Rysha remarked with a chuckle. "That happened right before I went to college."

"What was it like?" Tav asked.

"It was fairly straightforward, surprisingly." Rysha took a bite of his sandwich, then covered his mouth again as he spoke. "You basically walked in and signed up on a list. In a few days, they'd call you back with your appointment date. Mine was a few days after I signed up. If I remember correctly, I was one of the first people on the list."

"Right," said Tav, listening intently.

"Then, I went in for my appointment. That's where I met Dr. Todd. She was a young medical student back then, about to graduate from college." Rysha's tone softened ever so slightly at the mention of her. "She's the one who administered the actual shot. And yeah, it was a shot, I can't explain exactly how it works, as I'm not a scientist like her. But, within a few weeks, I started testing the waters; Jumping up to see if I could fly, concentrating really hard in front of a mirror to see if I could turn invisible. See, that was the interesting thing, is that it was a complete gamble as to what kind of powers you'd get.

"Eventually, I figured out that I could cast flames. More as a joke, I was with some friends, and made a motion like I was doing a *Kamehameha.* Y'know, like from *Dragon Ball*?"

Tav raised his eyebrows at Rysha's mention of an anime. Wasn't he too old to know what *Dragon Ball* was? Now that he thought of it, though, the series was released in the United States in the 90's, so Rysha would be the right age to have seen it and the subsequent series, *Dragon Ball Z,* as a young adult.

"Yeah, I'm familiar," Tav commented after his quick internal calculations.

"And when I did," Rysha continued, "Flames came shooting out. Luckily no one was standing in the way, but it was *very* strange."

"Oh I imagine," Tav replied. "I still feel strange creating weapons and healing so fast."

"Right," said Rysha, "It takes some getting used to, doesn't it?" He sighed. "That was many years ago. The world has changed since then."

Tav watched as Rysha looked off into the distance reflectively. After a moment, Rysha pushed up his glasses and returned his attention to Tav.

"Ready for the hike back?"

"Absolutely," Tav replied as he gathered up his trash.

· · · ·

Wrath patiently waited for Michael to return to him. It had been several days since their last meeting, where Michael had mentioned something about an "opportunity arising." Wrath still wondered what exactly he had meant by that, and now would be his chance to ask.

Just then, as if on cue, Michael's form slowly materialized before Wrath. Since he was in a realm other than Earth, he once again took on the appearance of an Archangel.

"Well?" Wrath asked with eager anticipation.

"I have accomplished the first step," Michael began. "I have infiltrated the organization that the boy and his protector are members of."

"Good, good," Wrath rubbed his hands together. "Now what?"

"As I said, the perfect opportunity for our strike will soon arise."

Wrath decided to just come right out and ask.

"What do you mean by that?"

"There will be a tournament next month amongst the members of the organization. The boy is surely going to participate."

"*Ohhhh...*" Wrath drawled. "So what you're saying is that you're going to enter this tournament and kick his ass?"

"Hm..." Michael hummed, furrowing his brow. "That's not exactly how I would portray it, but regardless, I will take the necessary steps to ensure that he and I are matched against each other. He's strong, so there is no doubt that he will succeed within the brackets. As will I; the humans' artificial powers pale in comparison to my own."

"Got that right," Wrath concurred. "So, you'll go up against him, and then...?"

"That is where you come in," Michael finished Wrath's thought for him. "After his defeat, he will be in a weakened state, and prime for repossessing."

A creepy smirk crawled across Wrath's face.

"Excellent. Next month, you say?"

"Yes," Michael replied.

"So, what are you going to do in the meantime?"

"You must trust the process," Michael told him.

Wrath just shrugged.

"Whatever you say."

• • • •

CHAPTER 18

Sunday went fast, then Monday came. Tav was sitting alone at lunch, just as he had done the previous week. He preferred it that way; it gave him the chance to observe everyone from a comfortable distance, like a photographer observing wildlife. Chatter filled the lunchroom like a cacophony of crickets, but Tav could still pick out bits and pieces of conversations.

However, Tav wasn't alone for long.

"What's happening, handsome?" one of the boys asked as he set down his tray. Tav looked over to him, an eyebrow raised. This was one of the guys that was standing in the doorway the other day, bragging about his "pro gamer strats."

Tav stayed silent, hoping that the group would collectively get the hint that he wasn't interested in conversation.

"We figured you looked lonely," another of the boys chimed in. "Maybe we could be of some assistance with that."

"Cool," replied Tav flatly.

Snickers erupted amongst them before they returned their attention to Tav.

"So, a bunny in art class, huh? Are bunnies your favourite animal?" the presumed leader of the boys chided.

"Yeah, actually," Tav replied with a small smile. Internally, though, he wondered how they had found out about that. He didn't recognize any of them from the class. Maybe one of them had sat behind him, in the back rows, so he hadn't noticed them.

"We've got a real tough guy on our hands, boys."

More snickers, some of which couldn't help but evolve into full-blown laughter.

"What's up with the robot arm, anyways? You a cyborg or some shit?" One of the boys reached across the table to touch Tav's arm, but before he had the chance Tav withdrew it.

"Don't touch me," Tav warned, his patience quickly wearing thin.

"Ah c'mon, I'm just curious," the boy insisted.

"Don't bother," the leader of the group told his friend. "He's too good for us, you realize."

"Don't you guys have something better to do?" Tav asked, attempting to balance his annoyance and what was left of his patience.

"Better than bothering the new guy? Of course not," the leader replied.

Tav assessed his current options: He could sit here and entertain these individuals, or go somewhere else and hope that they didn't follow. Regardless, he couldn't... really...

... *Do anything about it. They'll look desperate for attention if they follow me,* Tav thought to himself.

In one swift motion, he picked up his tray and stood.

"*Oh no,*" one of the other boys drawled. "He must be getting pissed off."

As Tav turned to walk away, the leader quickly stood up and took hold of Tav's tray.

"Where do you think *you're* going?"

"Away," Tav replied coolly, tugging slightly on his tray, hoping to free it from the boy's grasp.

"Not yet, you aren't," the leader told Tav, his tone fiending sincerity.

Tav, frustrated, set his tray down on the table. He was still standing, and quite a bit taller than the square boy that now faced him. Their eyes were locked in.

"You have my undivided attention," Tav told him.

"Smartass." The boy hurled a fist at Tav's face, landing squarely on his nose. The lunchroom quieted at the noise the contact of the hit had made.

Tav took a few steps back and put his hand up to his face. Yep, his nose was bleeding. He put his sleeve under his nose and looked over to the boy, fire dancing in his eyes.

"Hey!"

A teacher that had watched the entire confrontation go down stormed over to the boy and caught his fist right before it went in for another hit. The rest of the boys had backed up by now, not wanting to catch any of the fate that now awaited their leader. The teacher restrained the boy on the ground, and called on his radio for backup.

Unbeknownst to Tav, someone else had watched the encounter go down. Tav looked over to see the same girl from art class rushing over to him, her curls bouncing with every hurried step.

"Are you okay?" she asked as she approached Tav.

"I'm fine," he told her through his sleeve. The two of them watched the boy get carted away by who they presumed to be the school security guards. The original teacher that had restrained the boy now approached Tav.

"What happened?" he asked.

Tav wiped his nose, which had by now stopped bleeding, thankfully.

"They sat down around me, and I got up to leave. I guess they didn't like that."

"I see," replied the teacher, looking down at the plethora of trays that now remained unclaimed at the table. He looked back up at Tav. "Do you want to press charges?"

Tav quickly shook his head.

"Okay. Well, regardless, I'm going to have you fill out an incident report. Let's go to my office." The teacher started for his office, and Tav followed behind him. Before they got very far away, he turned to the girl that had come to check on him.

"Thank you," he quietly told her.

• • • •

Finally, Tav remarked to himself as he stepped into the art studio. His nose was still a little sore, but so far there didn't seem to be any bruises. *Guess there's more advantages to healing powers than surviving bullet wounds,* he told himself.

Class was now in full swing, and Mrs. Edwards was going over a brief history lesson about ancient art. As Tav listened, he felt a slight tap on his shoulder. He looked over, and the girl from earlier was in the process of slipping a piece of paper onto his desk. Tav, now very curious, unfolded the note.

"Your name is Tav, right? I remember from the other day."

Tav snuck a glance over to her, only to see that she was looking straight forward. Tav looked back at the paper. He carefully grabbed his pencil and clicked it a few times.

"Yes. What's your name?" He finished dotting his question mark and folded the paper back up, then very sneakily placed the note back on her desk. He returned his attention to the teacher. After a moment, out of the corner of his eye, he watched the note return to his desk. Again, he opened it, this time with eager anticipation.

"Carlina :)". The "i" was dotted with a small heart.

That's cute, Tav found himself thinking. Then again, *Carlina* was cute. And for some reason, she was talking to him? And came to check on him? This was all very strange. He hesitated with his pencil a moment, then ultimately wrote,

"That's nice, I like it!"

He passed the note to her once again. As he did, they made brief eye contact. Her eyes were emerald green, and her mouth was curled in a lopsided smile.

"Okay, class, can anyone tell me where the first cave paintings were discovered?"

Tav and Carlina quickly broke eye contact and returned their attention to the teacher. It would definitely suck if they got caught passing notes, especially in the one class they both cared so much about.

"Yes, Carlina?"

Tav hadn't even noticed that she had raised her hand.

"Spain?"

"Yep! You got it!"

Tav stole one more glance at her; Carlina was quietly beaming with pride.

She must be good at the history stuff, he thought. *Maybe she can help me study.*

After the lesson, the bell rang for class to be over. Tav collected his papers into his backpack, and headed out the door.

"Hey," he heard behind him. He turned around to see Carlina standing there, papers clutched between her arms. Tav raised his eyebrows, anticipating a response.

"Um, I was wondering," Carlina began, "if you wanted to come over after school and play video games with us? Me and my friends, I mean."

Tav could feel a smile spreading across his face. His cheeks began to heat up.

"Definitely," he told her, hoping that his excitement wasn't *too* obvious. He still wanted to play it cool as much as he possibly could.

"Awesome!" Carlina smiled wide. Her smile seemed to make time slow down around them; everything else was irrelevant. "I should probably send you my address, right?"

Tav chuckled.

"That would probably help."

Carlina reached into her pocket and took out her phone.

"What's your number? I'll text it to you."

"*Uhhhhh...*" Tav scrambled into his own pocket for his phone. He didn't have his number memorized yet. "*Gooooood queeeeestion,*" he elongated as he quickly pressed buttons on his screen. "I think I found it? Maybe?"

"Cool! What is it?"

Tav read off the number, occasionally looking up to Carlina to see if she was following along. She was.

"Perfect. I just texted you, see if you got it."

At that exact moment, Tav watched "Hi!" pop up at the top of his screen.

"I did," Tav told her with a smile as he returned his phone to his pocket.

"Yeah, we did it!"

Tav's smile grew wider. She's so *spunky*.

"Well," Carlina put her hand out to Tav for a fist bump, "I'll see you later, then?"

Tav, realizing that she was waiting for him, flexed his right hand into a fist and returned the fist bump.

"For sure, I-I'll see you then," He stammered, nervous that she would be taken aback by getting fist bumped by a probably-cold hunk of metal. But, she didn't even flinch. With that, she turned the other direction and walked down the hallway.

Tav couldn't help but watch her leave. Even the way she *walked* was perfect. Perfectly elegant, like an ice skater gliding across the rink. He swore he could feel hearts appearing in the gleam of his eyes.

• • • •

"Oh shit!" Tav's opponent exclaimed as Tav charged his character in for a hit. He got the combo off perfectly, and finished him off in a series of swift motions. After delivering the finishing blow, Tav turned to the boy that sat next to him on the couch.

"Gotcha," Tav told him with a twinge of pride.

The boy set down the controller and stuck out his hand for a shake.

"*GG, GG,*" he told Tav. Tav returned the shake firmly, and the boy shuffled off the couch.

"Who's up next against our reigning champion, here?" the boy asked. He was right; Tav *had* won every game since he had arrived.

"Ooh! Me, me, me!"

Carlina got up from her spot on the floor and took the previous player's place on the couch. The whole couch shook as she plopped down, sending Tav upwards like the other end of a seesaw. Well, maybe not quite, but it made Tav giggle regardless.

"Get ready for the taste of defeat, boy," Carlina told Tav, cheekily smiling in his direction.

"That's what you think," Tav replied with a smirk. He wasn't yet sure what level of banter she was comfortable with, so he was testing the waters a bit. Tav was proud of himself, though; this was the first time he had played *Brawler 7* since the incident. Tav had opted to not go back and get his stuff, and later told the police that processed the crime scene to "donate it all to someone who needed it." Unfortunately, though, that left him without a console at Rysha's house. Regardless, he was doing really well, and had no problems using his new hand with the controller.

"Bring it," Carlina told him as she perused the character screen. "*Hmm,*" she muttered. "I'm gonna go Neema."

"Good choice, good choice," Tav encouraged her. "She's a good Damien counter." His character, "Damien the Great", was the character he had used the most, and subsequently felt he was decent with by now.

"Exactly," Carlina concurred as they loaded into the arena.

"THREE, TWO, ONE, FIGHT!" the TV boomed. With that, they were off to the races. Carlina was already coming off strong, landing hits left and right as Tav struggled to counter.

Oh man, she's good, Tav quickly concluded. He was going to have to push a bit.

"Come on, Carlina!"

"You got this!"

"Go Tav!"

The small group of high schoolers cheered as the on-screen battle raged on. The rapid clicking of controller buttons barely broke through the sound coming from the TV, which was turned up *loud*. Tav felt the controller shake with every hit he landed, which was not happening very often. Carlina was truly kicking his ass. He briefly looked up to his health bar and saw that it was glowing red. He was done for.

"*Grrrr,*" Carlina playfully growled as she combo'ed into the final hit. Tav watched "Damien the Great", the once formidable sword-wielding vampire, crumple to the ground on-screen.

"Hell yeah!" one of Carlina's friends yelled as she went in to hug Carlina's shoulders.

"Yeah, baby!" Carlina exclaimed as she watched Neema do a victory stance over Damien. "First loss of the night, how does it feel?" she laughed to Tav.

Tav laughed back.

"Terrible. It feels terrible."

"Aww." Carlina leaned over to Tav and slugged him on the shoulder. "There's always next time, don't you worry."

Tav waved his hand in the air dismissively.

"You picked a good counter, what can I say?"

The night didn't end there. One by one, everyone got a turn against each other. Tav chalked up a few more wins, as well as a few more losses.

"Well," Tav eventually said, looking down at his phone screen. "We've got class tomorrow, so I'm going to get going."

"Okay!" Carlina told him from the kitchen. She walked back into the living room with a bag of chips and a two-litre of pop, and set them down on the coffee table. She ran over to Tav and trapped him in a big hug.

"Thanks for coming," she muttered into his chest before pulling away. Tav hadn't even had time to react, it was so quick. He could feel the heat rising in his cheeks again.

"Th-thanks for having me," he stammered with an awkward grin on his face.

"Good to meet you, Tav!" one of Carlina's friends shouted to him with a wave.

"Same!" Tav told her. He walked closer to the door and cracked it open. "See you guys later."

"Bye," the group told him in a varied chorus. Tav carefully shut the door behind him, and took a deep breath.

Is this how you make friends?

• • • •

About an hour after he left Carlina's place, Tav arrived home. He was getting pretty good at navigating the bus system, knowing which bus to take to get to where he needed to go. He set his backpack down next to his bedroom door, and wandered into the kitchen for a drink. He noticed that Rysha wasn't around, and around the same time, he saw a notebook turned open to a page on the kitchen table. He picked it up and read it.

"Working a case, see you in the morning!"

Tav nodded to himself in understanding. He was going to have to get used to having the house to himself at night. It was a little scary, but nothing he couldn't realistically handle. Tav walked back over to the front door and locked it, then headed for his room.

"Phew, finally," he breathed to himself as he shed his uniform. He noticed that there was still a little blood on the sleeve from his nose. *Crap,* he thought. Maybe Rysha knew how to get blood out of clothes? He only had the one uniform jacket, so he'd have to take care of it tonight before school tomorrow. Tav took out his phone and shot Rysha a text, hoping he'd respond soon. Tav set the phone on the nightstand and finished getting into his pajamas.

Shortly after, Tav's phone began to vibrate. Rysha was *calling*.

"Hello?" Tav answered, still awkward about how to answer a phone call on his very own cell phone.

"Hey, bud," Rysha began on the other end of the line. "How did you get blood on your uniform?"

"Well," Tav began, "Some punk punched me in the nose today."

"Yeah, I knew that already," Rysha told him. "They called me from the school right after it happened. I was hoping I'd get to talk to you about it before work today, but I didn't get to."

"Yeah."

"Last thing I'll say about it: I'm proud of you for not kicking his teeth in."

Tav chuckled.

"Thanks."

"Now, you know where the laundry room is, right?"

"Yeah, off the kitchen?"

"Yes. Take your jacket and go in there."

"Got it." Tav walked out of his room, through the kitchen, and into the laundry room. "Now what?"

"Okay, so you see the shelf with all the cleaning stuff on it?"

"Yeah."

"Good. Get the stuff called 'Squeaky Klean'. It's in a spray bottle."

Tav set the jacket down on top of the washer and got the bottle. "Okay. Now what?"

"Spray the spot, let it sit for like an hour, and then throw it in the washer with cold water on a small load."

"Cold water... Small..." He cranked the dials on the washer in advance so he would remember when he actually had to start it. "... Got it. That's it?"

"Yup, that's it," Rysha told him. "If that doesn't work, we'll try it again tomorrow after school. Just don't forget to throw it in the dryer for a bit before school in the morning, okay?"

"Right," Tav affirmed. Wash it tonight, dry it in the morning. Easy enough. "Thanks, *Dad*."

Tav held his breath at the sudden realization of what he had just said. He meant for it to be more of a "*Thaaaanks, Daaaad,*" some kind of joke on the fact that Rysha was teaching him how to get blood out of clothes, which is a relatively fatherly thing to be asking for advice on. However, it accidentally ended up sounding more genuine than anything else.

There was a brief pause on the line.

"... *Dad?*" Rysha eventually asked, his tone unreadable to Tav.

"Um, uh," Tav stammered. "Okay bye." Tav quickly hung up. *Oh boy.* He might be in some kind of trouble for this one. But, after Tav stared at his screen for a moment, Rysha did not call back to yell at him, or more likely, considering Rysha's personality, to ask a million questions. So, he turned his attention to the matter at hand: Getting this stupid blood stain out.

Tav sprayed the spot a couple times with the spray, then set the cleaning solution back on the shelf.

Great, I'll have to stay up a while before I throw it in the wash, he remarked to himself silently. Surely, there was something good on TV at this hour.

• • • •

The next morning, Tav got up early to give his jacket time to dry. He carefully cracked his bedroom door, and stepped out. Rysha was sound asleep, once again, on the couch.

He must've gotten back early this morning, Tav concluded to himself. He carefully walked through the kitchen and into the laundry room, and got his jacket out of the washer. Looked to him like the spot was gone. *Hell yeah, thanks, Rysha.* Tav was suddenly reminded of the "Dad" incident from last night. That was awkward. Did Rysha actually mind him calling him that? Tav shook his head to clear his thoughts, and threw the jacket into the dryer. He hit a few buttons, and the dryer happily chirped as it started its cycle. Tav hoped the beeping wouldn't wake Rysha. But, as he walked past the couch back to his room, Tav saw that Rysha was asleep in the exact same position that he had originally been in: Glasses still on, mouth wide open, snoring, with an arm hanging off the side of the couch. Tav smiled at the sight of such a man in such a strange state of sleep, and went back into his room.

• • • •

Later in the day, Tav was back in his usual spot at lunch. Hopefully, the threat of events like that of yesterday transpiring were neutralized. Tav picked away at his mac and cheese, and, once, again, green beans.

This school must like green beans, Tav thought. It's not like green beans were bad, but there were so many other vegetables. Like baked asparagus. Tav thought fondly back to the fancy steak dinner he and Rysha had partaken in all those months ago. *Yum.*

"Tav!"

The sound of his name pulled him from his thoughts, and he looked up to see Carlina walking towards him.

"Oh, hey," he greeted her with a smile.

"Can I sit with you?" Carlina asked, already hovering her tray across the table.

"Of course," Tav told her.

"Awesome." Carlina set down her tray and clapped her hands together. "I have exciting news."

"Oh?" Tav asked inquisitively.

"As of last night, I am happy to invite you to the newly-formed Dalton High Video Games Club. Whaddya say?"

"Video Games Club?" Tav repeated.

Carlina beamed. "Yep! Me and the crew talked last night, and we decided that we already get together often enough to play games, why don't we make a club out of it?"

Tav took a bite of mac and cheese as she spoke. He swallowed, then gave her an enthusiastic nod. "Sounds like a great idea, to me."

"I know, right?" Carlina's face glowed with pride. "So, you in?"

Tav took another bite, and nodded once again.

"Sweet!" Carlina shuffled her backpack to her side, and pulled out a clipboard. She slid it across the table. "Go ahead and sign this. It's the list of all of the members we've recruited."

Tav took the clipboard up in his hands and looked it over. Names took up one line a piece on the notebook paper, with "Video Games Club" written neatly in Carlina's handwriting at the top. Tav recognized a few of the names as people that he had met last night. He scratched his name on a new line, and handed the clipboard back to Carlina.

"How often are we going to meet?" Tav asked. He wondered how much this was going to conflict with his duties at Aim is Up.

"Probably once a week," Carlina replied. "Why? Is a specific day better for you?"

"No, no," Tav was carefully contemplating what exactly he should tell her. "I'm training a couple times a week for a..." he hesitated. What was a not-crazy way to tell her that he was training for a...

"Martial Arts tournament," he ultimately settled on.

Carlina's eyes went wide with wonder.

"Martial Arts? I had no idea you did that stuff."

Tav laughed nervously.

"Yep, sure do."

"That's really cool, seriously," Carlina told him. "Can I come to the tournament?"

Tav felt the colour drain from his face. He wasn't off the hook just yet.

"Well, um," he stalled as he searched for words. "I'm not sure if it's a public event, but I'll let you know, okay?"

"Okay!" Carlina gave Tav a thumbs up and a huge smile. "Hey, no wonder you're so good at fighter games. You know how all that stuff works already."

Tav chuckled.

"I mean, it *does* help, that's for sure."

"Still kicked your ass, though," Carlina remarked through a laugh.

Tav nodded solemnly, trying his best to hide his smile. "A worthy opponent, you are."

Carlina laughed once again.

"You're funny, y'know?"

Tav reflexively brushed the hair out of his eyes, before looking over to Carlina.

"Thanks."

• • • •

CHAPTER 19

The week came and went just as fast as it has started. Tav's work was starting to pick up in his core classes, and his Art class was delving deeper into individual lessons. Now, it was Saturday. All of his homework was done, and he had the day to himself. Not to mention, there was exactly one week until the Aim is Up tournament. Tav swore the month had flown right past him, and was surprised how rapidly the date was approaching.

I'd better start getting serious, he told himself. He rolled over to the side of his bed and unplugged his prosthetic, slipping it on with the usual ease. He got up and stood in the center of the room; Maybe he should use today to train? Maybe Rysha wouldn't mind taking him over to the training facility? Regardless, he should start doing some workout stuff at home. He walked over to the dresser and picked up his phone. He navigated to the search bar, and looked up "beginner workout", and before long, page after page of suggestions began to pop up.

"Hmm," Tav mumbled to himself as he scrolled. He tapped on one that looked promising, and scanned it for key details: 30 Jumping Jacks, 20 Squats, 10 Sit-Ups, 10 Push-Ups, and 30 Arm Crosses, if he wanted to focus on upper body flexibility. Seemed easy enough.

Tav set his phone back on the dresser and returned to the center of the room. He wasn't sure if he was light enough to not shake the whole apartment by doing jumping jacks, so he decided to skip that.

20 squats. Easy. One, two, three,... He continued counting to himself as he performed each squat. *... 19, 20.* That was done, and it wasn't even that hard.

Next, sit-ups. He situated himself on the floor, and did 10 sit-ups. Easy.

Now, push-ups.

Can my wrist even bend like that? Tav asked himself. He turned over to his knees and left hand, hovering his right hand above the ground. He very carefully brought the hand down, and he heard a mechanical *whirr* as the wrist bent to a 90 degree angle. He wasn't sure if he should be supporting his own bodyweight with the prosthetic, but as he carefully brought his knees up off the ground, it didn't budge. *Should be fine,* he thought. He bent his elbows and dropped his chest to the ground, before coming up again. Nothing bad happened, so he could do the rest. *Two, three, four... nine, 10.* He swung himself up to half-sitting on his knees, and heaved a deep breath. *That* had proved to be a little more challenging than what he had already done. He stood up, feeling his leg muscles twitch just a little bit as he did. All that was left were the arm crosses. Those were easy enough.

... 29, 30. He brought his arms down to his sides. All done. Now, hopefully, he was warmed up enough to put up a good fight against Rysha in the arena.

Tav walked out of his room and shut the door behind him, and upon walking into the living room, heard faint snoring coming from the couch. *That* put a hitch in the plans, for sure. Tav stood there and contemplated for a moment; he could just go to the training facility by himself, couldn't he? He knew where it was, and figured it wouldn't be hard to figure out which bus to take to get there. Tav looked over to the kitchen and saw that the notepad was still sitting on the table. *Perfect.*

"Went to the gym, took the bus, I'll be back." Tav thought for a moment if he should say anything else, and decided that that should cover it. He set the pencil down and walked over to the front door. He cracked it, and looked over to Rysha to see if he had heard the door and woken up. Nope. Sound asleep. Tav stepped out of the apartment and shut the door behind him.

• • • •

It was weird training by himself. Tav had only ever trained with Rysha, who guided every exercise in a way that made sense. Now, he was alone. When he got to the second floor, he realized that there wasn't anyone else around. *Strange.* Oh well, he knew where everything was, and now he didn't have to worry about being in anyone's way. He decided it was in his best interest to train with a practice weapon, considering he was without the guidance of Rysha, as well as to not raise any eyebrows if someone *were* to show up. Even now, he still wasn't sure where powers and traditional weaponry stood in the public eye.

Tav walked over to the rack and picked up a kendo stick.

You know what? He thought. *Maybe I should practice dual wielding.* He picked up another kendo stick and stepped back from the rack, then swung them each in a circle a few times. It already felt good, so it was worth a shot. He walked over to the practice dummies and stationed himself squarely in front of one that was around his height. The dummy's uncoloured eyes stared off into the distance; Its expression was steadfast, unfeeling, unchanging. Tav almost felt bad for beating on something that couldn't defend itself. He very carefully brought his right stick up, and gently struck the side of the dummy. It didn't budge, nor did it yelp out in pain. Tav went for another hit, this time with the left stick. Much of the same. He very slowly cycled hits with each weapon, right then left. Eventually, he was in a groove. The rhythmic *smacks* of the sticks against the dummy were almost musical, and Tav slowly increased the tempo.

He was so in the zone that he didn't hear the footsteps approaching him.

"Hey."

Tav, startled, swung around and actively stopped himself from smacking the voice with the same motions he had just been using on the dummy. Before him stood a tall man with short, dark brown hair, and unnaturally golden eyes. He had to be at least 6'5", even taller than Rysha.

Tav made an inquisitive face.

"Can I help you?"

"Looks like you're training for something," The man reported in a quiet yet somehow booming voice.

"I mean, yeah," Tav answered. He found it strange that not only was this man remarking on his training, but had seemingly appeared out of *nowhere*.

"You're doing well, keep up the good work."

"Thanks...?" Tav was still more confused than anything.

The man stuck out his hand for a shake.

"I'm Michael. And you are?"

Tav propped up the stick against his leg and shook Michael's hand.

"Tav," he told him.

"Tav? As in Tav Segol, from Aim is Up?"

Now, Tav was *very* confused, and increasingly cautious.

"How did you know that?"

Michael reached within his jacket and pulled out an ID badge. On it was a photo of him as well as various credentials. "Aim is Up" was printed in large letters across the top of the badge.

"I'm from the Indiana chapter," Michael explained, sticking the badge back into his pocket. "I'm actually here for the tournament next Saturday. Allen told me about you."

"Oh," Tav remarked, feeling slight internal relief. "Really?"

"Mmhm," Michael uttered. "He told me you were the new up-and-coming face of the New York chapter."

"Huh," remarked Tav. Did Allen really feel that way? "Well, that's cool I guess."

"I was told this is the best training facility in the city," Michael continued, "So I thought I'd come check it out."

"Yeah," Tav replied. Now, he was just curious without the caution. "So, you have powers too?"

Michael nodded. "Nothing crazy, just levitation. I believe I'll be competing in the beginner's bracket."

"Beginner's bracket?" Tav asked.

"Oh, did no one tell you?" Michael asked in return. "The tournament will be separated into two brackets: The beginner's bracket, and the expert's bracket."

"Ah, okay," Tav nodded along with the new information. He wondered if Rysha knew about the brackets, and if he had anything to say about it.

"Yeah. So, since you don't have a practice partner, would you like to run a couple rounds?" Michael asked.

Tav looked back at the dummy, then to Michael. He might as well, I mean... He said he's a beginner, as long as he plays nice, nothing bad should happen. Besides, Tav knew that he was more than capable of taking someone down, even without Wrath's powers.

"Sure," he eventually replied.

"Cool, cool," said Michael. "We'll use that big arena over there, meet me in it when you're ready."

"Got it."

Michael walked towards the arena, shedding his jacket as he walked. He was wearing a long sleeve button-up underneath, as well as dress pants and dress shoes; Not exactly an ideal outfit for maximum flexibility, but Tav wasn't about to judge. He himself usually wore his zip-up hoodie and jeans to train.

Tav made his way over to the arena, where Michael was doing some light stretches. Tav slipped under the ring and stood opposite of him, halfway between the corner and the center of the ring.

"I need more practice with dual wielding anyways," Tav remarked to Michael.

"Right, right. It can be tricky, takes a lot of practice," replied Michael.

Tav noticed that Michael had settled on a staff, which would make for an interesting counter to his own setup. He limbered himself up a bit, swung his sticks, and planted his feet.

"Ready?" Michael asked Tav.

"Ready," he confirmed.

Michael and Tav walked from their respective corners to the center of the arena, as though they were duelling sheriffs at high noon.

"Want to count us off?" Michael asked.

Tav nodded. "Three... Two... One... GO!"

Michael was the first to strike, going in for an overhead hit. He was quick, but not to the point where Tav couldn't block it. Tav felt that he now had twice as many tactics for blocking, having two weapons. Michael went in for another strike, with Tav blocking it yet again.

This guy is like a robot, Tav thought to himself after a couple strikes. *Maybe I should initiate.* Tav took a gratuitous step forward and planted a hit with the left stick right at Michael's midsection. Michael huffed, and Tav took a step backwards. Had he hurt him?

"Nice," Michael breathed quietly.

Tav just nodded, assessing the state of his opponent.

"Don't be shy," Michael said, straightening up and rolling his neck. "Come at me."

That was enough of an invitation, but was Michael actually going to put up a fight? Tav decided to go all-in and see what happened.

His enthusiasm seemed to pay off. Michael met each of Tav's strikes with a perfect block, swinging the staff in perfect harmony with the barrage of attacks coming from Tav's two sticks. Tav realized he was quickly pushing Michael back into his corner, and before long, he had nowhere to go.

"I'd call that good for this round," Michael said between heaving breaths. "You win."

Tav backed up and lowered his weapons. He hadn't even broken a sweat; if this guy was going to compete in the tournament, he'd probably been one of the first ones out, if this is what got him to surrender.

"That was great. Who taught you all of this?" Michael asked.

Tav wasn't sure how much information he should reveal, so he decided to keep it simple.

"Someone else in the organization."

"Well, regardless, you've got moves, kid."

Tav nodded.

"Thank you."

• • • •

Rysha blinked his eyes open. Daylight streamed through the balcony doors. *What time is it?* He asked himself. He pulled out his phone.

"12:30?" Rysha asked aloud. He tossed his phone down onto the floor and groaned. He *really* overslept today. He sat up and ran a hand through his hair, then put on his glasses.

Wait a minute. *Where's Tav?* He should have been up by now. Maybe he was still in his room? Rysha got up and walked towards Tav's bedroom. Before he opened the door, he caught a glance of the notebook on the kitchen table. It was flipped to a new page, and Tav's handwriting was scrawled across it.

"Went to the gym, took the bus, I'll be back," Rysha read to himself. Interesting. *Tav must've not wanted to wake me,* he thought as he contemplated the note. He set down the paper and walked back over to the couch to pick up his phone.

"Hey, I'm up, are you doing okay?" He texted Tav. He sat down on the couch and sighed. Now, to wait.

• • • •

Tav felt his phone vibrate in his pocket. "Wait a second," he told Michael amidst their sparring session. He dropped his left kendo stick and dug his phone out.

"Oh crap," Tav muttered to himself after a moment.

"Everything okay?" Michael asked, lowering his guard.

"Yeah, just give me a second," Tav told him. He began quickly typing: "Yeah, still at the gym," he replied to Rysha. He stuck his phone back in his pocket. "I should probably get going anyways."

"No problem," Michael told him. "Here, I'll put those up for you if you're in a rush."

"Oh, okay, sure," Tav put the two sticks together and handed them to Michael. Michael's hands were big enough that he could grasp both sticks in one hand.

"Good sparring with you today," Michael told Tav as he walked over to the rack.

"Yeah, same," Tav replied to Michael's back. He gathered up his water bottle and turned to Michael, who was walking back towards him.

"I imagine we'll meet again at the tournament?"

"More than likely." Tav took out his phone once again. He saw a message preview, from Rysha: "Okay, let me know if..." That's all he could see.

Michael smiled. "See you then."

"See ya." With that, Tav turned and headed for the escalator. Overall, the encounter was strange, but harmless. Strange in the fact that this Michael guy knew who he was, and harmless in that he had average, maybe even below average, skills. Did he *really* have powers? He had an ID from Aim is Up, so he must be some variation of legit.

Tav walked outside into the September sun. It was cooler today; A slight breeze blew Tav's hair into his eyes. He brushed it away, and turned his phone back on to reply to Rysha.

"Let me know if you need a ride," the text from Rysha said in full.

"Sure, that'd be fine," Tav texted him.

. . . .

"So, how was it?" Rysha asked Tav during the drive home.

"It was fine. I actually sparred with a guy from the organization."

"Oh?" Rysha asked. Tav could see an eyebrow of Rysha's shoot up through the rearview mirror.

"Yeah. His name was Michael."

"Michael, Michael..." Rysha parsed through his mental catalogue of names, but *Michael* didn't ring a bell. "Was he from the New York chapter?"

"No, Indiana," Tav answered. "He had a fancy ID badge he showed me."

Now, Rysha's interest was particularly piqued. Last he knew, Aim is Up didn't give out ID badges. At least, *he* never had one.

"And, he knew who I was?" Tav continued. "He said Allen had told him about me, said I'm the 'up-and-coming face of the New York chapter', or something."

Very interesting.

"What did he look like?" Rysha asked.

Tav mentally thought back to the man that had initially approached him.

"Tall, like really tall. Taller than you. Brown hair, kinda gold-ish eyes."

"What was he like in the ring?"

"He was... Kinda boring, if I'm honest."

"Really?"

"Yeah, he didn't put up much of a fight. I won, mostly. And he said he's going to be in the beginner's bracket, whatever that means."

Rysha's eyes darted over to Tav, then back to the road.

"Was anyone else up there?"

"No," Tav told him simply.

Red flag after red flag, this encounter was. Rysha's tone got serious.

"If you see him again before the tournament, don't spar with him."

Tav looked over to Rysha.

"Why not?"

"Because I said so."

That was *not* a typical answer from Rysha, the man who generally explained everything.

"Why do you say so?" Tav quickly worked up the courage to challenge Rysha just a little bit.

Rysha contemplated his answer carefully. Should he just be straight up and tell him that he doesn't trust this guy? He didn't want to sound overbearing, but he also wanted Tav to err on the side of caution. He sighed.

"All things considered," Rysha began, "I don't think it's wise to spar with someone with whom you aren't fully certain of their capabilities. He could have lied about his strength and seriously hurt you."

Tav thought about Rysha's response. He was right, fundamentally.

"Nothing bad happened, though," said Tav.

"Who's to say it wouldn't next time?"

Tav stayed silent. He didn't want to push his luck any further.

Rysha looked over to Tav, and saw that he had propped himself up against the window, facing the other way.

"I'm sorry if it sounded like I don't trust you."

Tav turned to Rysha.

"It's not that I don't," Rysha continued, "I just want you to be careful. You never know about people. Not everyone who took part in the Anomaly Project was a 'good guy.'"

It was then that Tav remembered the advice that V had given him in the dream the other night. She pulled him *into her realm* to tell him to be careful. Had he completely forgotten her caution?

"I understand," Tav told Rysha, not revealing the heed of warning that his sort-of-ally, sort-of-enemy had told him. "I'll be more careful next time."

"Good," said Rysha. "Don't be afraid to wake me up, okay? We can go to the gym any time after school this week."

"Okay," said Tav.

Rysha could sense apprehension in his voice.

"Really, I mean it. It isn't a problem."

"I know," Tav replied. But honestly, he didn't want to bother Rysha if he was working nights. Then again, on any normal day, he would probably be up by the time Tav got out of school. So, ideally, Rysha was right in that it wouldn't be a problem.

· · · ·

Every day, after school, Rysha took Tav to the training facility. They trained hard, and subsequently rested hard. Tav spent most of his evenings laying in bed, utterly wiped out from the intensity of the training. Rysha, however, went to work every night, and always returned in the wee hours of the morning. Now, it was Friday. Tav had gotten all of his homework done on the bus ride home, so he wouldn't be stuck doing it Sunday after the tournament.

Right, tomorrow is the tournament, he thought to himself as Rysha pulled into the training facility's parking lot.

"I think we should practice with actual weapons today," Rysha told Tav as he locked up the car.

"Really?" Tav asked. "Aren't people going to notice if we use our powers?"

"Surprisingly enough, people tend to mind their business here," Rysha replied confidently. "Besides, we aren't the only ones here practicing with powers, I imagine, especially if you ran into someone who explicitly told you they were from the organization."

Rysha and Tav walked into the building and made their way upstairs. Today, Rysha wore a t-shirt and sweatpants, which was unusual. Tav had swapped his school uniform for a t-shirt and basketball shorts, as well as his signature hoodie.

"They'll give you a uniform at the tournament," Rysha had told Tav the previous day. "I think it's like a karate uniform. A *gi.*"

The gym was busy today, as it had been all week. More and more people seemed to have learned of the training facility's existence, specifically those training for the tournament.

Lots of new faces, both Rysha and Tav had silently observed to themselves.

Currently, both arenas were being used, so Tav made a suggestion.

"I dual wielded the other day, wanna see?"

"Of course," Rysha replied. They had spent the rest of the week on single wield, refining techniques and introducing a few new concepts. Now, Tav was excited to show off his new tech. He walked over to the rack and picked up two kendo sticks.

"Better to use these on the dummy, right?"

Rysha chuckled.

"Don't want to have to pay for slicing it up, I see?"

"For sure," laughed Tav. They headed over to an unoccupied dummy, which just so happened to be the same one that Tav had used the previous Saturday. Rysha stood a good distance away, but close enough that he could see. Tav stanced himself, and began to strike. It didn't seem to flow as well as it did that Saturday. Maybe he was nervous now that someone was watching him.

"When you're going in on the left side," Rysha walked over to Tav and stood beside him, copying his stance, "Swing like this." Rysha swung an invisible stick at an angle that Tav had not previously considered. "That way, they'll be less likely to parry."

"*Ohhh.*" Tav adjusted the strike angle on the left, then hit from the right. "That makes so much more sense," he told Rysha.

Rysha just smiled.

"Keep going."

Tav began to strike the dummy once again, and before long, was in a perfect rhythm just as he had been in the other day.

"Good," Rysha remarked. "If you were to duel wield actual weapons, what do you think you'd choose?"

Tav stopped striking and looked at the dummy.

"Well, what are my options?"

"Anything, really," Rysha replied. "If you can make a sword, you can make two swords, or two axes, or two daggers, like that one Fallen had."

Tav remembered back to the encounter with the Fallen. The shorter blonde that had stabbed Rysha had two daggers. He was honestly surprised that Rysha had mentioned that.

"The list goes on," Rysha continued. "If you're strong enough, any weapon that you can use with one hand, you can have two of. Not to mention, you have the advantage of only one wrist getting tired, assuming you remember to charge your hand."

Tav smiled awkwardly and scratched the back of his head with the kendo stick. He *had* forgotten to charge his hand the night before Wednesday, and had to explain to his teachers at school that he couldn't write because... *No hand.*

"See?" Tav would hold up his stump to each teacher. Some didn't flinch, others had stifled a grimace. Tav had derived some joy out of their mixed reactions, not to mention he was off the hook for schoolwork. Unfortunately, though, he inevitably had to do the work later, but it was assigned the next day instead.

"I'm pretty good about not doing that," Tav told Rysha, returning the stick to his side. "I guess I was so tired Tuesday night that I totally forgot about it."

Rysha smiled.

"Well, ideally you'll remember tonight, so you'll be ready for tomorrow."

"Crazy that it's happening tomorrow," Tav remarked, turning himself once again to face the dummy.

"Yeah, this month flew by." Rysha looked over to the arenas, and saw that the bigger of the two had opened up. "Let's head over there," he told Tav, motioning with his head in that direction.

Tav held up the two sticks, silently questioning if he was going to need them. Rysha shook his head.

"We'll try for real this time."

Tav nodded, and walked the sticks back over to the rack. He and Rysha met in the larger arena, standing on opposite sides, as they always did.

"During the tournament, one of you will come out first, and the other will follow," Rysha told Tav. "You'll make a little bit of a dramatic entrance. Practice waving or something."

Tav awkwardly walked forward. *Waving?* He stuck his right hand in the air and moved it back and forth rigidly.

"No, pretend you're a famous wrestler. They just called your name, the crowd is going wild. What would you do?"

Tav smiled wide, internally amused at the thought of professional wrestlers. He flexed his arms and made an angry face.

"*Grrrr,*" he growled, trying his best not to laugh.

"There you go!" Rysha told him, also stifling laughter. "That's the spirit. Now..." Rysha put out his hand, and summoned his sword. This time, there were no flames, yet the blade seemed to be glowing white hot.

"Try making a weapon."

Tav hadn't conjured a weapon since he had removed Wrath's possession. In truth, he wasn't even sure if he would be able to, especially now that one of his hands was artificial.

"How?" Tav asked.

"Hmm," Rysha quietly hummed. "Imagine it's in your hand and you're looking at it. If you're summoning two, try putting your hands out in front of you, like this," Rysha put his fists out in front of him, sword still in hand. "So you can see both."

"Right, okay..." Tav stuck his hands out in front of him. He closed his eyes, and imagined the sight of two short swords appearing in his grasp.

"Channel the energy from your core," Rysha guided.

Tav focused his attention on his sternum. He swore he could feel heat there, as if the energy was charging up. His fists didn't waver in front of him. Suddenly, Tav felt the energy shoot from his chest out through his arms. He opened his eyes, and two gleaming damascus steel swords were now in his hands.

"Yes!" Tav exclaimed, laughing triumphantly. "I did it!"

"Nice!" Rysha could feel Tav's pride radiating from him.

Tav took the swords and swung them around himself. It felt so *perfect* to dual wield. It almost felt more symmetrical than using just one weapon.

"Ready?" Rysha asked from across the arena.

Tav nodded, and without saying a word, charged for Rysha. In one swift series of events, Tav went in for a right-sided strike, Rysha parried it, then disarmed Tav's left sword. Tav watched as the sword that now lay on the ground dematerialized into thin air.

"What..." Tav was shocked. How had Rysha done that so easily? He looked up to Rysha, who had a huge smirk on his face.

"See? Dual wielding isn't as easy as you think."

Tav stepped back and looked at his now-empty left hand.

"Now what?" he asked Rysha.

"Just make it again. You can make a certain amount before you run out of energy."

Tav closed his eyes, and concentrated once again. He felt this energy shoot out to his hand, except this time, upon opening his eyes, he was met with the sight of a dagger similar in style to the sword he already had. He looked up at Rysha.

"Why did it do that?"

"My guess is that you're still working on harnessing your energy. Sometimes that produces unpredictable results."

Well *that* was annoying.

"Why haven't you taught me more about controlling the energy?"

"I didn't think you needed it," Rysha replied simply.

Didn't need it? Tav thought. "Isn't that like, the whole point?"

"Ultimately, the person you're fighting is going to be concentrating more on their own set of powers, not what weapon they're approached with. You have to learn to adapt."

Right. Adapting to the situation. Rysha had talked about that before. So, with a dagger in one hand and a short sword in the other, Tav rushed Rysha.

I can go in for a strike with the sword, and catch him off guard with the dagger, Tav plotted to himself as he ran forward.

At this moment, Rysha glanced to the other half of the arena, beside Tav. There stood a tall man, in a suit, with unnaturally golden eyes.

"Rysha!"

Rysha's attention was quickly returned to Tav, who was about to strike. In the last possible moment, Rysha blocked the sword. Tav's dagger, however, was headed straight for Rysha's midsection. Rysha hurled himself to the side, and landed in a crouched position.

Tav, brow furrowed, lowered his weapons.

"What happened there?"

Rysha once again looked at the man standing on Tav's side of the arena. Their eyes met, and the tall man smiled with an ever-so-slightly detectable hint of malice.

"... Nothing," Rysha eventually muttered.

• • • •

The drive home was silent. They had gone a few more rounds after Tav's near-miss, but Rysha seemed entirely preoccupied. Tav never once looked behind himself to see the man standing there, but had he, would have immediately recognized who it was.

"So, are you ready for tomorrow?" Rysha asked, breaking the silence and taking a hit off his cigarette.

"I think so," Tav replied. "I feel like I kind of hit a ceiling, though."

"How so?" Rysha asked.

"I don't know," Tav admitted. "Maybe just because I've already gotten pretty good at everything you've taught me. I don't know what I'm missing."

"It's normal to feel that way," said Rysha. "But, as you already know, the heat of battle can teach you things that you didn't even know were possible."

Tav thought about it. That was certainly true; the battle between himself and Rysha versus V and Rukii had taught him a lot, and that was only one specific instance. He had no idea what kind of people, nor powers, he would be up against at the tournament.

"You're right," Tav said after a moment. "Do you think I'll have an energy explosion like I have in the past?"

"Ideally, no," Rysha replied frankly. "If you feel it coming, take a few steps back and take a deep breath. If you need to tap out, tap out."

Tav didn't like the idea of tapping out, but it was better than the potentially deadly alternative.

"I don't think it'll happen, personally," Rysha continued. "You've learned a lot of self-discipline since you first started training."

"Thanks," Tav replied. He felt his phone vibrate in his pocket, and pulled it out. It was Carlina.

"Hey! When's that tournament thing you were talking about? :)"

Crap. Tav had completely forgotten that he had told Carlina about it.

"Oh, hey," Tav began aloud. "Is this thing a public event?"

"Yes, you just have to buy tickets. Why?"

"Well..." Tav trailed off as he began typing a response to Carlina. "Tomorrow," he told her. "I invited a friend, on the off chance it was a public event," he told Rysha.

Rysha looked over to see Tav shove his phone back into his pocket, then look up to him. He looked like he was hiding something in a mischievous, teenager-type way.

"A friend, you say?"

"Yeah. From Art class."

"That's cool. Did they just ask about it?"

"Yeah," Tav admitted.

"Well, tell them that it will be at the Marks Arena, in town," Rysha explained. "And that they have to order tickets before Midnight tonight."

"Gotcha, I'm telling her now," said Tav as he began relaying the information in a text to Carlina. He really hoped that she could make it tomorrow.

"So she knows about you?" Rysha asked Tav, glancing at him through the rearview mirror.

"Well, not exactly," Tav replied. "I told her it was a martial arts tournament."

"Ah, I see," Rysha remarked. "She's going to find out regardless. You should have been honest."

Tav's phone vibrated in his hands, and he read the message.

"Okay great! I'll ask my parents. :) Hopefully I'll see you tomorrow!" Carlina texted.

Tav put his phone away again. "You told me to not talk about the 'powers' thing."

Rysha remembered that he had, indeed, told him that.

"Good point, I apologize."

"No worries," Tav told him. "You're right, though, she's going to find out. She seems really nice, though, I don't think she'd use it against me."

Rysha could feel Tav's tone brighten as he mentioned the mystery girl he was currently texting.

"What's her name?" he asked him.

"Carlina," Tav responded, trying his best to keep his tone level even at the mere mention of her.

"Nice. Carlina," Rysha repeated more to himself than Tav. "Well, maybe you guys can sit together before it's your turn, right?"

Tav could feel a blush spreading across his face.

"Right..."

He hoped Rysha didn't see it. But, he did.

• • • •

"It's tomorrow, isn't it? The tournament?" Wrath asked Michael, who was standing facing the voided sky within Wrath's dimension.

"Yes, it is," Michael responded simply.

"So... How will I know when to repossess the boy?"

Michael only partially turned to Wrath.

"I will summon you through my sword. All you have to do is be ready." Michael returned himself to facing fully forward. "Everything will work out, under the presumption that the position of power you offered is still on the table."

"Sure, sure," Wrath replied casually. "If you help me out, you can have whatever you want in the Heavenrealm. Spare for the throne, of course."

Michael nodded.

"Of course," he repeated, his voice resonating out into the endless expanse of darkness. "What will you do with the boy?"

"Oh, him?" Wrath scoffed. "I will be sure to dispose of him accordingly. His measly artificial powers are no match for myself at full strength."

"And you are not currently at full strength?"

"Look at me," Wrath said, spreading his frail arms wide. "I'm a fraction as powerful as I once was. That's why I need this vessel. Despite being a human, he will work just fine for his intended purpose."

Michael turned to Wrath. He truly was a sight; He looked sickly in this form, as if he was an incomplete thought and not a standalone entity. Michael fully eyed him up and down for the first time since they had met.

"I imagine taking the throne will return you to your former glory," Michael told him with a forced air of optimism.

"Yeah, that's the idea," replied Wrath. He sat back down. "You know," he began, "It's almost comforting to know that things have gone downhill over there since I left. Maybe I *was* of some importance..."

Michael listened to the fallen celestial that now spoke so candidly to him. "The overall climate has shifted to that of a dictatorship."

"It's a wonder more people haven't done anything about it. Did you ever tell anyone of your ideals?"

"No," Michael replied. "It was not a safe situation to do so. Treason is punishable by death."

Wrath pondered this.

"You're compromising yourself pretty severely, then, aren't you? Being a high ranking Archangel."

"*The* highest ranking Archangel," Michael corrected.

"*Right, right.*"

Then, silence for a moment before Wrath started again.

"I wonder what has become of my sister."

Michael scoffed to himself. "I imagine, in her heart, that she is equally as perturbed as to her father's tyranny."

"That would be like her," Wrath said wistfully. "But, she's always been the 'good kid'. She always did as she was told. She wouldn't dare go against him."

"We will see what happens upon our arrival," Michael told Wrath.

"We certainly will," he replied.

· · · ·

CHAPTER 20

"**H**i, I'm Tav Segol. I'm in the tournament."

Tav stood in front of the desk at the Marks Arena Supercomplex. He had waited in line behind several other people, and it was finally his turn.

"Okay, great! Here's a copy of the bracket, as well as your uniform."

Tav took the paper and the folded uniform into his hands.

"You'll be in Locker Room 8," the lady at the desk told him, "Let us know if you have any questions."

"Great, thanks." He turned and headed back for where Rysha was standing some distance away.

"Got everything you need?" Rysha asked as Tav approached.

"I think so," Tav replied. "We're in Locker Room 8."

"Gotcha." Rysha looked around the crowd. There was quite the turnout this year, compared to the last tournament he had attended.

"Did you ever compete?" Tav had asked Rysha earlier that day.

"No, I did watch it once, though," Rysha had replied. "I didn't have time to compete back then." Which was true, Rysha was relatively tied up in the affairs of the force at the time. That was at least 5 years ago, if not more. Rysha wasn't entirely sure.

They headed down the long hallway to their locker room, which after being given directions by a bystander, they learned was the fourth one on the right. They passed each locker room numbered one through seven before arriving at theirs.

"I'm gonna change," Tav told Rysha before ducking into a stall. He took a glance at his fancy new uniform; It really was just a standard issue *gi*. It was nice, though; the material was comfortably heavy, but breathable enough that you could move around in it without feeling stiff. Tav tied the jacket over his t-shirt, then stepped out, holding his jeans and sweatshirt.

"Fancy," Rysha remarked at the sight of his pupil all decked out. Tav handed Rysha his clothes. Rysha was essentially acting as Tav's manager today; he even had a duffle bag to put everything in. Rysha unzipped it and looked at the crumpled heap of clothes he now held.

"Could've at least folded it," Rysha grumbled, trying his best to conceal a smirk.

Tav just shrugged.

"I don't care if they're wrinkly."

Rysha squinted his eyes playfully at Tav, then stuffed the clothes into the bag exactly as they had been handed to him.

"Suit yourself."

Now, to warm up. Tav stood in the center of the locker room and started stretching. Rysha was sitting on the bench, occasionally coaching him on stretches that would be beneficial.

"Arm circles," Rysha guided, doing the arm circles himself as he sat down.

"Right." Tav had totally forgotten about those. He began circling his arms, gradually increasing the size of the circle before dwindling it back down.

Rysha, meanwhile, was looking over the bracket paper.

"You're going third against Ashtonne Sinclair."

"Hmm," Tav said as he circled his head to stretch his neck. "Does it say anything else?"

"It lists their age, they're 19."

"Really?" Tav was genuinely surprised that he would be up against someone around his age.

"I guess with the participants being old enough to have had kids that are adults now, it makes sense," Rysha theorized out loud. He read through the rest of the beginner's bracket. "It seems like most of these people are around your age."

"Wow," Tav replied as he rolled his shoulders.

"The youngest I'm seeing is 15."

"That's only a year younger than me," Tav told Rysha.

"*Damn,* I'm old," Rysha remarked through a small laugh.

Tav laughed along with him, then sat down next to him on the bench.

"Let me see that."

Rysha handed Tav the bracket paper, and Tav looked it over himself. There were a total of 16 people in the bracket. Tav and Ashtonne were third on the list, so two groups of two would be competing before them. Tav wondered to himself what kind of powers Ashtonne had.

Guess I'll find out, Tav thought.

At the bottom of the paper, there were a set of instructions telling him where to sit during the matches that he was not a part of, how to get ready for his match, and the proceedings of the bracket system.

"There's also a digital bracket on a board out in the lobby," Rysha told Tav. "We'll check that as the tournament goes on, since it'll be updated after each match."

"Right." Tav's mind was quickly drifting elsewhere. He wondered if Carlina was actually going to show up. It'd be really nice if she did, but on the other hand, he would save himself from explaining everything if she decided not to come. Six in one, half a dozen in the other.

"Let's go look at that one, maybe it'll have more information on it," Tav said.

"Sure," replied Rysha.

The two walked out of the locker room, back down the hall, and out to the lobby. There were even *more* people now, standing in groups and talking amongst themselves. Some of them were dressed in the same uniform as Tav, others he assumed to be family or friends. They made their way over to the bracket board.

"This one has the expert's bracket, too," Rysha remarked. While Tav looked over the beginner's half, he looked at the expert's half. They stood in silence for a moment before Rysha noticed something.

"You said Michael had mentioned that he would be in the beginner's bracket, right?"

"Yeah," Tav replied. "But I don't see him over h-"

"That's because he's over here." Rysha pointed to Michael's name on his half of the board.

"Wait a minute," Tav stepped over to Rysha's half, "Really?"

"He's the only Michael on here."

At this moment, Tav finally understood Rysha's apprehension. Michael had straight-up *lied* to him about his powers.

"Oh..." Tav muttered.

Rysha looked over to Tav, who was maintaining eye contact with the board. He could tell that Tav was feeling guilty.

"Well hey, at least you won't have to fight him, since he's in the other bracket," Rysha told him reassuringly.

"Yeah, but..." Tav trailed off.

"Don't sweat it." Rysha patted Tav on the shoulder. "We all make mistakes. Today is about having fun, that's what's important."

Tav looked up at Rysha and smiled.

"I guess so."

"TAV!!"

Tav swung his head around to see Carlina barreling towards him. Before he could blink, he was entrapped in yet another big, squeezy hug.

"I'm so glad I found you before it starts," Carlina told Tav, muffled in his chest. Tav couldn't even move his arms.

"Hi, Carlina," he said, his voice cracking a little bit.

Carlina let him go, and the two turned to Rysha, who was smiling like a dweeb at this adorable encounter.

"Care to introduce me?" Rysha asked Tav.

Before Tav could, Carlina stuck out her hand to Rysha.

"Carlina Fuentes, president of the Video Games Club at Dalton High."

Rysha laughed and returned the handshake firmly.

"Rysha Barlett, president of the 'Bad At Video Games Club.'"

Tav put his hand up to his face and pinched the bridge of his nose in shame. Carlina let go of Rysha's hand and turned to Tav.

"I saw you're going third, that's exciting."

"Yeah," Tav replied, a dual tone of exasperation and optimism in his voice.

"You excited?" Carlina asked.

"Obviously," Tav replied with a newfound confident smile. "I'm gonna kick ass."

"That's the spirit," Carlina encouraged, putting her hand out for a fist bump. Tav quickly returned it.

"Carlina?" a voice from a distance away called out.

"Oh, gotta go, that's my dad," Carlina gave Tav one more hug before turning to walk away. "You're gonna do great today, Tav!"

"Thank you," Tav said to Carlina's back as she walked back over to her parents. Carlina's mom looked over to Tav and Rysha and waved. They waved back, Rysha flashing a big smile at the group.

"Well, she seems nice," Rysha told Tav.

Tav sighed dreamily. "Yeah..."

• • • •

The clash of swords echoed through the arena as the first two competitors of the tournament went at it. From what Tav had observed, one of them had water powers, and the other had electricity. It was an interesting pairing; The water wielder used their powers to redirect the energy currents, swinging their longsword and sending waves crashing around the sides of the ring. The electric wielder had a shorter sword, much more like a cutlass, that sent shocks of energy cascading towards his opponent.

The fight raged on, and Tav and Rysha were watching intently. This was the first time Tav had seen anyone besides himself, Rysha, or the Fallen, use powers. It was almost jarring to see two otherwise normal people able to create weapons and manipulate elements. With each hit, the crowd was going wild, much to the enjoyment of the two competitors. It hyped them up.

The electricity wielder sprinted towards the water wielder, closing the gap. The water wielder quickly summoned a water shield, completely encapsulating themself in a sphere of water. The electric wielder didn't hesitate in plunging his cutlass directly into the shield, sending a bright pulse of electricity resonating through the sphere. Tav swore he could hear the *zap* as the cutlass made contact. The shield dissipated as the water wielder collapsed, and with her remaining strength, tapped the floor of the arena to signal defeat. The crowd roared yet again, and medics ran out to the water wielder to check that she was okay. Even the electricity wielder was waiting with baited breath to see if he had done serious damage. But, after a moment, the water wielder gave the arena a thumbs up, and everyone felt a huge sense of relief.

To Tav, it seemed like the line between limiting your powers and going all-out was a line these competitors would frequently be toeing. He wondered to himself how his powers would shape up against his opponent. In all reality, his powers relied heavily on weapon creation, and not much else. He wasn't sure if he could still make an energy blast, as it only seemed to happen under extreme stress. He hadn't learned how to channel it into his weapon, either, so to him, his true powers were still very much a mystery. Tav internally hoped that his opponent would just take him down easy. He didn't care if he won the prize. Like Rysha had said, it was about having fun, and so far, getting shocked by electricity waves did *not* look fun.

After some cleanup, the next two competitors stepped out into the ring. These two bowed at each other before the referee signaled for them to start. With a wave of his hand, they were off. Immediately, the competitor on the left turned invisible, much to the confusion of the other person in the ring. He darted his eyes around, anticipating a strike, but nothing came. He put his palms together, and a wall of rock emerged from the ground, enclosing him in a circle. The other competitor became visible for a brief second, and began scaling the wall.

"Let's go," Rysha told Tav, interrupting his concentration. Right; he had to get down there and be ready for when it was his turn. They slipped out of their seats and down the bleacher stairs, then over to the gate that led to the arena. The security guard let them through, seeing that Tav was in uniform.

"You'll head over there," the security guard told them while pointing to a bench outside of the ring and out of view of the crowd. Rysha thanked him, and they headed that direction. He noticed that Tav was shaking a little bit.

"You okay?" Rysha asked.

"Yeah, just nervous," Tav admitted.

"You'll be fine, no need to stress," Rysha reassured him, putting a hand firmly on his shoulder.

Tav nodded, and looked up to the arena. The fight was much louder from here; Every rock pillar that shot up from the ground seemed to shake the ground. The invisibility user, however, struck silently, much to the confusion of the rock user. Barrages of quick strikes were happening all around him, one even nicking his cheek to the point of it bleeding. The rock user hadn't yet created a weapon, but at this moment, decided to create a mallet made of stone. It materialized in his hand, and he began swinging wildly, hoping to land a hit on the invisibility user. But, they were just too quick. The rock user suddenly went down to the ground, as if the invisibility user had tackled him. Sure enough, after a moment, the invisible person was now visible, and had the rock user in a wrestling hold. The rock user tapped the bottom of the arena, and the referee flagged the match as over.

"You ready for this?" Rysha asked Tav.

"I sure hope so."

"Remember, keep calm, keep your energy steady."

"Right..." With that, Tav stood up and prepared to enter the arena.

• • • •

CHAPTER 21

T av hadn't realized just how big the complex was until he was actually standing in the arena. There were over a thousand people, if not two thousand, if not three. Between the bright lights over the ring and his nerves, he couldn't make out a single face in the crowd.

"And next up, we have Tav Segol," the announcer boomed over the loudspeaker. Tav waved to the crowd, and their cheers soared up into the air.

"Versus, Ashtonne Sinclair."

Tav swore that the crowd cheered louder for Ashtonne. Maybe he was just hearing things. From across the ring, he got a first look at his opponent; They were marginally shorter than him, with short, bright blonde hair and green eyes. As they both stepped towards the middle of the ring, Ashtonne nodded at Tav, and he politely returned it.

"Three, two, one, fight!" With three swooshes of his arm, the referee signaled for the fight to begin. Immediately, Ashtonne stepped backwards, and put their hands out in front of them. Vines shot from their palms directly towards Tav. Tav quickly ducked and rolled out of the way to avoid the hit.

Plants? he thought to himself incredulously. *That's actually kinda cool.* Tav stood up from the roll and began to create a weapon. He made the split-second decision to make a machete, as it would be ideal for cutting through vegetation.

Ashtonne once again sent a barrage of vines swirling towards Tav. This time, instead of dodging, Tav sliced through the vines before they could hit him. He ran towards Ashtonne, weapon at the ready, with no intent of actually cutting them, but to disarm any shield they would create.

Before Tav could get close enough, Ashtonne shot vines at a lower angle, entrapping Tav at the ankles. Tav toppled over.

Shit, he thought. Now his guard was down. He flipped himself over and began sawing away at the vines. Ashtonne closed the gap between them, and with a quick fist, punched Tav right in the jaw. At the exact same time, Tav freed himself of the vines, and rolled with the flow of the punch out of the way. It certainly hurt, that's for sure. Tav stood up and prepared himself for whatever Ashtonne was planning next. They ran to the other side of the arena, away from Tav, and began creating a shield of thick vegetation around themself. Thinking fast, Tav sprinted towards Ashtonne once again, getting his machete ready to cut a hole through the plants. However, before he got there, he had another idea.

The top of the shield is open, Tav thought. *That way, they can't make more vines to protect themself.* Once Tav got close enough, he plunged the machete into the vine shield and began climbing. He stepped onto the machete and vaulted himself upwards, and sure enough, there was not a roof to the shield. Tav straightened himself as he dove down within the column of vines.

Ashtonne was completely shocked and totally unprepared. Tav began throwing punches left and right, hoping to knock them down. They took them, but in a moment of pause between Tav's hits, they retracted the vine shield, giving them the chance to escape. Ashtonne grabbed Tav's left fist as he went in for the next hit, and created a bundle of vines around his hand. With that, he escaped to the other side of the arena.

Tav now stood with vines around his hand. He couldn't even flex his fist, that's how tight they were. Tav used his free hand to create a new weapon, since the machete had dissipated: A short sword. To counter this, Ashtonne summoned a bow staff, with vines tangled around it. They ran at each other, and with one hand, Tav deflected every hit that Ashtonne went for. Ashtonne was very quick with the staff, pelting Tav with attacks from every conceivable angle. In a moment of lapsed concentration, Tav missed a block, and he felt the staff make contact with his side, knocking the air out of him. Tav dropped to his knees; He literally couldn't breathe for a second. His vision started to blur, and through the haze, Tav watched Ashtonne stand over top of him, staff at the ready.

"Give up yet?" Ashtonne asked, their tone stern.

Tav's vision slowly cleared. He could feel a rush of energy coursing through his core. This time, it wasn't panic that caused it; it was adrenaline. Tav closed his eyes and stood up. He channeled the energy through himself and to his sword, which was now being circled by a muddled black cloud. He opened his eyes, and jumped up in the air to get in an overhead strike. Ashtonne made a vine shield, but it wasn't enough; Tav's sword cut right through it, and the blade was now headed directly for Ashtonne's neck. Ashtonne dodged out of the way just in time, landing in a heap on the other side of the arena. Tav landed, sword pointed down, then looked up at Ashtonne. In his moment of rush, he had almost decapitated them. His eyes and Ashtonne's met, and for the first time since the match had started, Tav saw true fear. Without breaking eye contact, Ashtonne slammed their hand onto the arena floor three times, effectively tapping out.

The crowd cheered, as though watching Roman gladiators fight to the death. The referee ran out between them and put his hands out, rendering the match over. The ref grabbed Tav's hand, and raised it in the air triumphantly. The cheers got even wilder; Tav blinked a few times in an attempt to comprehend what was happening. He won. Now, he would have to compete against the winner of the next bracket. Then, if he won that match, he'd compete with the winner of *that* bracket. Was he really ready for this?

• • • •

"Let's go to this restaurant, their menu looks great and it's right around the corner."

Tav looked over to Rysha in the car. The beginner's bracket was over, and Rysha figured they would get back in time to watch the last few matches of the expert's bracket.

"Yeah, that looks good," Tav told Rysha as Rysha showed him the menu on his phone.

"Cool." Rysha started the car. After doing so, he dug a cigarette and lighter out of his pocket, and lit it up. He let out a puff of smoke, and rolled down his window.

Tav sighed deeply, almost happy to be breathing in the smoke as opposed to the air of the arena. He was tired, genuinely, and was having trouble keeping himself upright.

"I'm very proud of you, Tav," Rysha began. "You won the beginner's bracket."

Tav smiled weakly.

"Thanks."

"Are you happy?" Rysha asked.

"I'm tired, really tired," Tav admitted.

Rysha turned the corner and parked on the street, in front of the restaurant. It was a Mediterranean restaurant, which Rysha already knew he would love and hoped Tav would too.

"That's understandable. You'll feel better after you eat something."

"Definitely," replied Tav. He found the strength to open his door and get out, his legs wobbling a bit as he stood. They shut their doors in unison.

"Have you ever had Mediterranean food?" Rysha asked Tav as he held the door open for him.

"Nope," Tav replied shortly as he stepped inside. He was immediately met with the wonderful smell of unfamiliar cuisine. Rysha followed him in, and they stood at the host's podium.

"Hello, how many today?"

"Two," Rysha replied, holding up two fingers.

"Right this way," the host guided. Tav noticed the host eyeballing his outfit, and he remembered that he was still in his uniform. Oh well, it would be better to still be in uniform when he went back for the presentation of the prize.

They arrived at the booth, thanked the host, and took their seats on opposite sides. Rysha adjusted his glasses down to take a better look at the menu, now that it was real, laminated paper and not the tiny print on his phone screen.

"Hmm," Rysha hummed as he looked over the menu. Tav was also looking it over, studying the largely unfamiliar choices that lay before him.

"Hi! What can I get you guys to drink today?"

Rysha and Tav looked up at the waitress. Then, they looked at each other.

"Water is fine," Rysha began.

"Same here," Tav concurred.

"I'll be right back with those," the waitress told them before speeding off towards the kitchen.

"You should've gotten electrolytes," Rysha told Tav.

"You're right," Tav replied.

"I've got an electrolyte drink mix in the car. I'll go get it and you can put it in your water."

"Really? That would be awesome."

Rysha smiled. "Yeah, not a problem. I'll be right back." With that, he scooted out of the booth seat, and headed for the door. Tav was now alone for the first time since that morning. He heaved a heavy sigh, and looked around the restaurant. The interior design was amazing, and the lighting wasn't bright and aggressive like some restaurants. It was really peaceful; Tav felt like he could relax a bit.

"Here."

Tav was startled by Rysha's sudden presence. His hand was out-stretched with a small packet in it. Tav picked it up, and studied it a moment before setting it down.

"Thanks," he told Rysha.

"Of course."

They continued studying the menu.

"I think I'm going to get the Cranberry Walnut Salad," Rysha said, "What about you?"

"This Chicken Dijon Pita Roll looks good," Tav replied.

Rysha searched the menu for it.

"Yeah, it does," he remarked.

The waitress returned with their waters, and set them down in front of them.

"Are we ready to order?" She cheerfully asked. The two put in their orders, handed her the menus, and thanked her. Tav began dumping the drink mix into his water, and it became cloudy. He squinted.

"It's supposed to do that," Rysha told Tav when he noticed the odd expression on his face.

"Gotcha," said Tav. He unwrapped his straw and stuck it in the glass, swirling the contents around a bit. He took a sip, then looked at Rysha.

"Wow."

"Right? I think that one's cherry, that's what I usually get."

"Tastes like it," Tav replied. He took another sip.

Rysha smiled.

"You'll be feeling better shortly."

Rysha was right. Even after a few sips, Tav was starting to get a bit of energy back. He didn't feel like his entire body was being held up by sheer willpower anymore.

After what Tav estimated to be about 15 minutes, their food arrived at the table. Tav eyeballed the pita roll on his plate, taking in

the complex aroma of chicken and spices. Rysha looked over his salad, and rubbed his hands together.

"Yum, lettuce," he said jokingly. Tav laughed.

The two ate for a moment, then Tav asked,

"So, how does this awards presentation thing work?"

"As far as I know, we'll go back around 4:00, and they'll call you
up to the arena to get the trophy. I think." Rysha took another bite
of salad. "Truthfully, that's more of a guess than anything."

"It makes sense, though," Tav said. "And I assume they'll send a
check in the mail?"

"Probably," replied Rysha. "How much was it? 1K?"

Tav nodded.

"That's quite a lot, isn't it?" Tav remarked candidly.

Rysha nodded in return.

"Perfect to put in savings."

"Exactly."

Just then, Rysha's phone began to vibrate. He dug it out of his
pocket and looked at the number. He didn't recognize it.

"Detective Barlett," he answered in his typical fashion. Tav
watched as Rysha concentrated on the wall behind him.

"Early?"

A pause.

"Exhibition match?"

Another pause.

"Okay, we will be back in time."

A few more words on the other end that Tav couldn't hear, then
Rysha hung up after saying goodbye. He looked at Tav.

"Alright, so," he began, "The coordinator for the tournament just
called me. They're about to be finishing up the expert bracket, and
they would like you to participate in an exhibition match."

Tav's eyes went wide.

"Exhibition match?"

"A match between you and the winner of the expert's bracket," Rysha explained.

"Oh..." Tav was nervous now. "Won't I get obliterated by them if they won the expert's bracket?"

"No, no," Rysha assured. "It's entirely for show, they will go easy on you. If they didn't for some reason, they would be in quite a lot of trouble." Rysha caught the waitress' attention and motioned for her to come over. When she did, he asked, "Can we get boxes for these?"

Tav was suddenly far more concerned with the concept of the exhibition match than the delicious meal in front of him. He had not been there for the expert's bracket, and subsequently had no idea who won or what he would be up against. He started to panic a little bit, and Rysha could tell.

"Don't worry, everything will be fine. This match is purely for show and inconsequential."

Tav nodded, taking in a shuttering deep breath as he did.

The waitress returned with styrofoam containers, and the duo quickly boxed up their meals.

"They should be fine in the car, it's not that hot today, right?" Rysha asked, hoping to lighten Tav's mood.

"Right," Tav replied quietly.

• • • •

CHAPTER 22

B y the time Rysha and Tav got back into the complex, they could
hear the announcer speaking to the crowd.

"In just a moment, you will witness the special exhibition match between our two tournaments' winners."

Tav and Rysha had taken a glance at the bracket board when they got back. Many names were in red, except for Tav's, and one other: Michael. Michael was already in the ring at this point, hyping up the crowd and throwing some flashy moves around to keep up the energy. Tav didn't even have the *time* to be stressed about fighting Michael again. He had to get back in the ring.

Tav ran past the guard and over to the ring, climbing up into it and under the ropes.

"And here he is, back in the ring and ready for the match, Tav Segol!" the announcer boomed at the sight of the red haired boy.

Tav looked to the other side of the ring. This wasn't the same man that he had fought back at the gym; No, this guy in front of him now exuded confidence, and clearly, he had the skills to back it up, considering that he had won the expert's bracket. Michael looked away from the crowd and over to Tav. His eyes were bright, and he looked like he was more than ready to throw down.

Tav walked to the center of the ring, Michael following suit. The referee between them waved his hand.

"Three, two, one, fight!"

Tav had a newfound energy within him. He couldn't help but feel the rush, between the surprise of the match itself and the fact that he would once again be going toe to toe with this mysterious man. Immediately, Tav created two short swords, just as he had wielded against Michael back at the gym, except now, these were razor sharp blades instead of kendo sticks. The cool metal of his

swords' hilts felt reassuring in his palms, even despite only feeling the
phantom sensation in his right hand.

Michael, meanwhile, was taking a different approach. He levitated himself up in the air, hovering about six feet above the floor
of the ring, and darted to the other half, behind Tav. In his hand, a
longsword, and a huge one at that. It was glowing slightly, a white aura entrapping the inlaid metal in a cloud.

Tav, not to be caught off guard, quickly spun on his heel and prepared for the attacks. He watched as Michael raised his sword in the
air, a salute of sorts, to prepare Tav for what was coming next. Tav
crossed his swords in front of himself and narrowed his eyes.

Michael struck first, closing the gap with blinding speed. His
long sword sliced through the air, aimed directly at Tav's torso. Tav
parried the blow with one of his own swords, the clash of metal echoing through the arena. The crowd erupted at the skillful attack and
its subsequent parry. Tav knew he had to keep his focus; One wrong
move, and that beautiful longsword would be a little too close for
comfort.

A barrage of hits from both parties. Michael was at an advantage
due to his levitation, enabling him to strike from unusual angles. Tav,
however, was also at an advantage, with twice as much coverage to
parry attacks. Michael was clearly on the offensive. Tav could feel his
muscles working with every movement; he wouldn't admit it, but
he was still beat from the previous matches he had fought, and they
were of paling importance to the current fight.

Rysha was carefully watching the match from the sidelines. The
force and intent behind Michael's attacks were making him quite
nervous. This match was supposed to be for show, and Michael was
definitely putting on a spectacle. Luckily, Tav seemed to be strongly
holding his ground.

Then, in a crucial moment, Michael executed a remarkable spin
technique, his blade whirling toward Tav. Tav's instincts kicked in,

and he raised both short swords to deflect the attack. But Michael's momentum was too much, and the force of the blow sent Tav staggering backwards. There was something behind that hit that was different from the rest, an invisible force of energy that knocked the wind out of Tav. He felt his eyes beginning to blur, his knees wobbling beneath the weight of simply standing. Before Tav could react, he was on the ground, lying face up.

Through his confusion, Tav could just barely hear the silence hush over the crowd. His vision was ducking in and out of darkness. Should he tap? Was this the end?

"You went down easy, what's the matter with you?"

Tav felt the voice of Michael radiate through his body. He strained his eyes to look up, and saw that his opponent was now standing directly over top of him, the arena lights illuminating his sword. Tav was truly helpless.

"Where's the talented child that I fought at the gym?"

More swiftly than perceivable to the human eye, Michael plunged his sword into Tav's chest. Tav gasped, feeling the cold metal of the sword exactly where his heart should be. He blinked, holding his breath, as he watched as blood began to seep around the blade. He watched as a darkened muddle emerged from the sword, swirling around then entering his chest. His hold on his consciousness was dwindling as the taste of iron rolled over his tongue.

Michael removed the sword and stepped back. Soon enough, the familiar insignia of Wrath crawled across Tav's chest. It was finished. Before the referee could even get close to him, Michael disappeared into a cloud of smoke.

Tav, now entirely unconscious and quite possibly dead, lay in the arena. Rysha was the first on scene. It had all happened so fast; he hadn't even processed what was happening until after it was over. Rysha ran to Tav and dropped to his knees, pressing his suit jacket to his chest to stop the bleeding.

"I need a medic!" Rysha ordered.

Tav's face was white as a sheet, his eyes closed. He was losing blood, and fast. Shortly after, the medics arrived and took over. They returned Rysha's now blood-soaked jacket to him, and replaced it with copious amounts of medical gauze. They quickly discovered, however, that the wound was no longer bleeding. In fact, it looked as though it had already closed itself up.

When Tav's body opened its eyes, they were black with white pupils.

• • • •

PART III

A^{SCENDING}

CHAPTER 23

V watched the vision in the lake intently as Tav's body rose up from the floor of the arena. She had been watching the entire match carefully, waiting with baited breath for the exact moment that everything would go south. She saw it coming a mile away, having observed as Tav first met the mysterious man and sparred with him, right up to the moment that same man plunged his sword into Tav's chest.

He must work for Wrath, V had deduced. She withdrew her hand from the lake and stood. She needed to find Elias, and quickly.

V ran through the streets, panting as her feet hit the pavement with a newfound fervor. She had to do something about this, and ideally, her compatriots would feel similarly, now that Wrath was once again an imminent threat.

When V found the rest of the Fallen, they were standing on either side of an open portal, weapons drawn and ready. She sighed with relief.

"You knew."

• • • •

Wrath spread his arms wide, taking in the spectacle of the crowded arena. He *finally* had his vessel back, and what could be better than retaking the reins in front of a live audience. Wrath loved the attention, truthfully, not to mention that this would make for a perfect opportunity to kill off anyone that stood in his way.

Rysha now stood on the opposite end of the arena. He readied his sword with anger burning through his bones. He had been right, and despite his best efforts, there was nothing he could have done about it.

"You fool," the voice of Wrath cooed through Tav's mouth. "You really think you can stop me now?"

Rysha swung his sword in a confident display of power. In truth, he was conflicted; he couldn't remove Wrath's crest, as Tav had done previously, with it now being on his chest. But he couldn't kill him, either, because Tav was still in there. Somewhere.

Isn't he?

Just then, a low grumble shook the building. As if on cue, a portal opened up in the ceiling, and from it came the four Fallen. They each landed in the arena, surrounding Rysha and facing Wrath, weapons at the ready.

Wrath, seeing the Fallen before him once again, laughed from his core.

"Oh wow, this is getting *interesting,*" he said. "I didn't realize the boy was of such importance to you. If I had known that, I would have killed him off sooner and saved you all the trouble." Wrath flicked his wrist, and his sword appeared in his hand. "Let's dance."

The Fallen sprung from their positions and took stance around the arena. V was to Rysha's left, Azriel to his right. Elias was staggered in front of V, and Rukii was off to the side, bow at the ready.

Rysha was the first to strike, sending a column of flames forward from his sword. When the flames approached Wrath, he put up his free hand, the flames instantly dissipating. Elias and Azriel ran towards Wrath, hoping to catch him off guard while he was preoccupied. Azriel struck first, slicing the dagger across Wrath's neck. In their mind, if they killed Wrath by harming the body, Tav could regain consciousness and heal himself. Little did Azriel know that that was, indeed, the common consensus amongst the Fallen. Wrath, however, deflected Azriel's strike effortlessly, sending them staggering backwards.

Elias went in for the hit, swinging his scythe that was quickly met with the damascus steel of Wrath's sword. Wrath bared his teeth in a twisted smile as he swindled the scythe clean out of Elias' hands, sending it to the other end of the arena where it dissipated on the ground. Elias decided to get ballsy; he tackled Wrath and wrestled him to the ground, an arm across Wrath's chest and the other hand wringing his neck.

Rysha, seeing this, ran towards the duo. He crouched down and put his sword to Wrath's neck, narrowly missing Elias' hand.

"What do we need to do to kill you off?" Rysha asked through gritted teeth.

Wrath smiled.

"You'd have to kill the body, and the boy along with it."

Rysha pressed the sword closer to his throat, right up against Elias' hand.

"Bring him back, or you're going to regret it."

"Regret it?" Wrath asked. "If *anyone* is going to regret *anything,* it'll be you assholes regretting standing in my way."

Before anyone could react, Wrath released a bomb of energy, sending Elias and Rysha flying backwards. V took this as a great time to go in for an attack, while Wrath was still on the ground. Before her staff could make contact, Wrath was already on his feet. He met the staff with his sword.

"Change your mind yet?" he asked V. She gritted her teeth and pushed the staff forwards.

• • • •

Tav blinked awake in the throne room that was now a critical part of his mind. A few torches were lit this time, casting waves of yellow on the stone walls.

Tav stood on the other end of the throne room. Before him, Wrath sat in the throne, eyes closed as if engrossed in deep thought. Tav hatched a plan: If he could sneak up on Wrath while his guard was down, he had a pretty good shot at getting his consciousness back. At least, that's what he theorized.

Wrath's eyes quickly opened to meet Tav's own.

"I'm quite surprised you're even awake," Wrath said nonchalantly. "I thought for sure I had completely taken over the body."

Tav shook his head.

"It's going to take more than that."

Wrath chuckled at the newfound tenacity of the boy that now stood before him.

"That tournament must have lit a fire under your ass."

Tav put his hand out to summon his weapon, but nothing happened.

"Have you noticed yet that you can't have weapons here?" Wrath asked sarcastically.

Tav looked up to the throne, the torches' flames dancing in his irises. He took a few steps closer. Wrath sighed and stood from the throne; this is the first time Tav ever really got a good look at him.

"If your plan is to kill me, I bid you good luck," Wrath told Tav as he walked down the stairs to meet him at the throne room's conference table. "I'd sooner just talk about it."

Tav took a seat at the table.

"Okay, then. Talk."

Wrath sat down as well, placing his elbows squarely on the table.

"Once I possess a human, I am bound to that human until its soul leaves the mortal plane. That means that you are effectively stuck with me until you die. If you help me get back into the Heavenrealm, I will separate from you and you can live in the Heavenrealm unrestricted." Wrath picked up a cloth napkin and began fidgeting with it. "However, as long as you resist, I'm going to make your life a living hell."

"Do whatever you want. I'm not helping you."

Wrath raised his eyebrows.

"You do realize that I could just kill you myself and completely take over the body?"

"If you can, why haven't you?" Tav was now standing, palms pressed firmly on the table beneath them.

"Because, I made a promise, and I don't go back on promises."

Tav was starting to get frustrated. He jumped up onto the large table and began running straight towards Wrath. With one swift swoop, Wrath knocked Tav's legs out from under him, sending him flying sideways to the other end of the throne room where he landed with a *thud*. Wrath walked over to him, and Tav looked up.

"That promise being, that you would be my right hand man. I can't in good conscience kill my right hand man."

Tav lunged once again at Wrath, now that he was in close range. He knocked him down, and the two began to grapple on the floor of the throne room. Tav had a size advantage against Wrath, but unfortunately for Tav, Wrath still had more hand-to-hand combat skills than he did. After a few minutes of holding him off, Tav was fully pinned under Wrath.

"Give up yet?"

Tav could feel the anger rising in his chest.

"I never asked for this. I never asked for you to possess me, to take over my *body*." He struggled against Wrath, but it was no use. "All I wanted was a normal life. Just once, for something terrible not to happen."

Wrath shook his head.

"How do you think I feel? We share a commonality, Tav; a burning hatred deep within. *That* is why I possessed you."

Tav could feel tears running down his cheeks.

"Don't you get it?" Wrath asked in a heightened tone. "You and I can both leave our old lives behind. Get revenge, start over."

"NO!"

Tav's energy finally hit its breaking point, causing an explosion both inside and outside of the body.

• • • •

Rysha could feel his heart beating. So, he wasn't dead, that was good at least. After slowly blinking his eyes open, he was looking directly at Tav, who was face down at the other end of the arena. Rysha looked to his left; the silver haired man that had attacked them the other day was propped up against the cornerpost of the arena, and the shorter blonde was tending to him. To his right, the tall man with one eye looked to be slowly waking up, and the woman was on the other side of him. Her eyes opened and met Rysha's.

Just then, a team of medics arrived. Rysha watched as a few of them stopped at Tav, and the rest headed towards everyone else. Curious, Rysha looked up into the arena seating; every single member of the audience had been evacuated. Rysha closed his eyes again.

"Sir? Sir, can you hear me?"

Rysha looked up to the medic standing over him and nodded. His wits were slowly coming about him.

"Tav-"

Rysha went to stand up, but the medic stopped him.

"I need to ensure you don't have any injuries before you stand."

"I'm fine, I need to see if he's okay." Rysha stood up fully, his head spinning a little bit as he did. He blinked, then turned to the medic. "Excuse me."

Rysha ran over to Tav, who was now flipped over on his back. V was already there, looking rapidly between the statistics screen and Tav himself. One of the medics was in the process of performing chest compressions.

"What's going on?" Rysha quickly asked as he approached.

"Can't get a pulse on him," another medic calmly replied.

Rysha's eyes widened. He dropped to his knees over Tav, whose own eyes were peacefully shut.

"Come on, buddy..." Rysha told him, watching the medics work away. Soon enough, their efforts paid off, and quick successions of beeps began to emit from the machine.

"Yes!" V cheered, throwing her hands in the air. Rysha watched as his once-enemy celebrated openly, and smiled.

• • • •

CHAPTER 24

When Tav awoke, he could tell by the ceiling lights that he was back in a hospital room once again. This time, however, he was *not* handcuffed to the bed, which was nice. Tav sighed and closed his eyes.

"Hey!"

Tav opened his eyes again and turned to his left to see Carlina sitting across from him. He blinked a few times, then slowly brought his hand up to wave. That's when he realized he didn't have his prosthetic on; it was over on a nearby table, charging. But, it was too late now, so he fully committed to waving with his stump.

"How are you feeling?" Carlina asked, scooting her chair closer to Tav's bed.

"Okay, I guess," replied Tav. He looked down to see that he was wearing a hospital gown instead of regular clothes. He pulled the neck out to look at his chest, and sure enough, Wrath's crest was still sprawled across it. He looked over to Carlina. "How long was I out?"

Carlina pulled out her phone, and checked the time.

"Three days?"

Tav's eyes went wide.

"Three *days?*"

Carlina nodded.

"It's Tuesday now. I came as soon as I got out of school."

Tav sighed once again. School. He had totally forgotten about that.

"Have I missed anything important?" Tav asked.

"Nothing crazy, but I can only speak for Art class," Carlina replied. "I'm sure your other teachers will understand. They won't put you too far behind."

"Yeah..." Tav looked over to Carlina. Her hair was back in a ponytail, a few loose strands perfectly framing her face. Her eyes stared at him softly, with a certain concern that made Tav's stomach jump a bit.

Just then, a knock on the wall next to the curtain. Rysha stepped through the curtain, holding various snacks and drinks. He immediately noticed that Tav was awake, and smiled.

"Morning, bud," he said casually as he set the snacks down on the table. "How are you doing?"

"Fine, I think," Tav replied. "Carlina said I was out for three days."

Rysha nodded.

"Sure were. You woke up a few times, but for the most part you've been doing some serious snoozing."

Tav and Carlina both laughed. Rysha unplugged Tav's prosthetic and handed it to him, along with the sleeve. Tav got himself situated and flexed his hand a few times.

"It's been on the charger this whole time, so you should be good," Rysha told Tav.

"Awesome," Tav remarked. He still couldn't shake the fact that Carlina now had at least a vague idea of the whole situation. He decided to ask about it.

"So..." He turned to Carlina. "How much... do you, like..." Tav gestured vaguely with his hands. "... know?"

"Well," Carlina started, "Rysha filled me in on some stuff, but the gist is that some evil dude possessed you, celestial beings came to fight him, and this is the second time this has happened. So..." Carlina smiled awkwardly. "Yeah."

Tav looked over to Rysha, expecting some clarification. Rysha adjusted his glasses.

"She's not wrong."

"Don't worry," Carlina reassured Tav, "I don't think you're crazy. I literally *watched* everything go down. And I won't tell anyone at school."

Tav nodded.

"Good. Thanks for that."

"Of course," replied Carlina.

"Hopefully, you'll be out of here by tomorrow," Rysha told Tav. "It depends on how your bloodwork and such comes back. Good news is, it's been fine so far, they've just been letting you sleep because of how much energy that blast took out of you."

"Right," replied Tav.

"Oh yeah, I almost forgot!" Carlina suddenly reached down into her backpack and rustled some papers around, eventually pulling out a slightly crinkled sheet. She handed it to Tav. "We're having an art show in December. I brought you a flyer so you could look it over."

"Art show?" Tav asked as he took the paper.

"Yeah! The flyer doesn't say much, but I'm sure Ed-Boss will talk to you more about it once you get back."

"Wow," Tav said as he looked over the sheet. She was right; it really didn't say much, but it did have a date, time, and location. It would be at Dalton High, in the auditorium, near the middle of December.

"I really hope you can be a part of it," Carlina told Tav. "I think you'd enjoy it."

"For sure," replied Tav. He smiled at Carlina. "Don't worry, I'm gonna get out of here as soon as I can."

Carlina smiled back.

"You better!"

• • • •

Luckily for Tav, Rysha had been right: All of his bloodwork came back perfect, and the next morning, he was released from the hospital. Now, he and Rysha were on the way home.

Tav's mind was very much still preoccupied with the art show. He had never been a part of something like that.

Is it like a convention? he wondered to himself. From what he *did* know, or at least assumed, he would be submitting some of his own pieces to be displayed. What sort of art should he do? He'd have to do something more than sketches on notebook paper. This was, like, *fancy.*

Rysha turned the music down.

"So..." he began, breaking Tav of his thoughts.

"Hm?"

"I wanted to update you on something, once you were feeling better."

"Alright," Tav replied. "What is it?"

Rysha looked over to Tav for a brief moment, then back to the road.

"I've withdrawn both you and myself from Aim is Up."

"Really?" Tav asked, looking over at Rysha. This was the first time he noticed how tired he looked; his eyes seemed to have more bags and lines than usual, with stubble dotting his normally clean-shaven jawline.

"Yes, and for various reasons. The obvious of which being what happened at the tournament, but..." Rysha sighed more to himself than Tav. "There were a lot of things happening that I was not okay with."

"Like?" Tav asked.

"The fact that you and I had different employment contracts was a huge red flag. Not to mention, you being pulled out of school on your second day."

That all made sense to Tav.

"I guess I didn't see it the same way you did."

Rysha shut off the car.

"There's a reason I've always kept my distance from the organization. Everything that happened just further reinforced that sentiment."

Tav looked over to Rysha once again, the silence of the car hanging carefully over both of their heads.

"Did something happen before?"

Rysha looked at Tav, then back at the windshield. He seemed to be staring off into a distant place that Tav couldn't see. After a moment, Rysha exhaled.

"Yes. A situation that could have easily been prevented."

Tav hesitated, hearing the drop in Rysha's tone resonate long after his words had already been said.

"Well... Can I ask about it?"

Rysha closed his eyes, then his mouth curled into a small smile.

"I suppose he wouldn't want me to be weird about it." He turned his body in the driver's seat so he was facing Tav. Tav did likewise, and waited with cluelessness as to what Rysha was about to say next.

"Many years ago, there was another member of the New York chapter of the organization that I knew," Rysha began. "He was a good friend, a very good friend. After I graduated from the Academy, we kind of drifted apart, you know? It happens sometimes. But..." Rysha paused, gathering his thoughts.. "Living with powers is not an easy thing to do. It does things to you, affecting your health, your social life. Ronan was..."

Tav watched as Rysha turned away for a moment, then sighed. Tav found it heartbreaking that the man who always knew what to say was coming up short.

"Ronan was affected, just like the rest of us. He was strong, just like the rest of us. But, being strong doesn't mean you're invincible. At the end of the day..."

Rysha's eyes met Tav's.

"... We've all got battles. Does that make sense?"

Tav nodded.

"It does."

Rysha smiled, then opened his car door and stepped out, lighting up a cigarette in the process. Tav opened his own door and shut it behind him.

"Don't worry about it too much," Rysha told Tav. "We'll be fine. We've handled ourselves before, this'll be no problem, right?" He gave Tav a thumbs up from the other side of the car.

Tav smiled wide.

"Got that right!"

• • • •

CHAPTER 25

The return to school on Thursday was exactly as Tav had anticipated: A *lot*. He had missed three days, which didn't initially
sound like a very long time, but once Tav saw all the assignments he
missed, he realized that it actually kind of was.

"Have this to me by this time next week," his Math teacher had
said as he handed him a stack that had at least 5 separate assignments
in it. Tav looked down at the diminutive teacher sitting behind the
desk.

"Will do," he replied quietly.

As he walked to art class, his backpack felt seven times heavier
than usual. Once he reached the door, though, the weight of his
backpack felt lighter than a feather upon seeing Carlina. She was currently talking to a classmate, too preoccupied to notice him sit down
across from her. Which was fine; he needed a second to think about
what he was going to say, anyways.

Speaking of, what *was* he supposed to say if anyone asked why he
was gone? He looked fine, so he could really say whatever he wanted.
Vacation, he decided. *Five days is reasonable for a vacation.*

Art class commenced, and Mrs. Edwards notified the class that it
was a free day to work on their projects for the art show. Perfect. Tav
could ask her about it now. He walked up to her desk.

"Hey, Mrs. Edwards."

"Tav!" She exclaimed. "Good to see you're back."

Tav smiled awkwardly.

"Thanks. Um, I was going to ask about the art show."

"Yes, yes," Mrs. Edwards replied. "Did Carlina give you the paper?"

"Yep."

"Good. Did you have any questions?"

Tav nodded.

"Quite a few, actually. I've never done an art show, so I don't really know what it's like."

"Alright." Mrs. Edwards put her hands on her desk, preparing to explain the layout. "How it works: We set up the auditorium to look pretty much like an art museum would, right? Specific sections for specific students. You guys will have class time as well as whatever you want to do outside of school to work on it. And, you can have partners, if you want to collaborate on a piece. Does that make sense?"

Tav watched as Mrs. Edwards' hands stopped moving and she looked up at him. He nodded.

"For sure."

"Great! So, you can use class today to either start planning what you're going to do, or jump right into making something. However you want to do it. You'll have until the beginning of December to finish up your projects."

Tav looked over to the other side of the classroom, where Carlina was sitting at a table with some friends.

I wonder if she would want to work with me? Tav wondered silently. Mrs. Edwards noticed this.

"Oh, and I'm pretty sure Carlina said something about asking you to work on a piece together, so you might want to talk to her about that."

Tav was snapped from his thoughts. He nervously looked back at Mrs. Edwards.

"Thank you," he told her, then quickly scuttled off over to Carlina's table. This time, upon his arrival, Carlina's face lit up with a smile.

"Tav!" she exclaimed. "Wanna work on a piece together?"

Tav was genuinely surprised that she came right out and asked, in front of her friends.

"Totally," Tav replied simply, masking his own enthusiasm, hopefully to a level deemed appropriate.

"Yes!" Carlina pumped her fist to herself. "I have a couple ideas, if you want to hear them."

Tav sat down next to Carlina as she pulled out her notebook. "Absolutely."

· · · ·

Later that night, Tav was back at home, catching up on his schoolwork. He was all the way through Math, about halfway through English, and hadn't even started Science. That was his least favourite subject, and what was worse was that it was Chemistry. He didn't really understand that stuff yet.

As he quietly worked away at his desk, his thoughts began to drift. What should he do for the art show? Carlina had a couple great ideas for their collaboration, his favourite among them being a diorama of a fight stage from *Brawler 7*. It was a game they both knew incredibly well, so they would have no problem recreating any of the numerous stages available to them. They would also more than likely make models of their characters, which Tav was less than excited for; he struggled heavily with anatomy, and couldn't draw even a simple person to save his life. Luckily, anatomy was Carlina's specialty, Tav being most impressed with the fact that she could draw hands without a reference.

But, he thought, *what about* my *projects?* Tav still had to do something independently of the collaboration. Tav looked up at the art on his wall. Not only was the piece that Rysha had put there originally still above the desk, but now, the piece he had bought at Aim is Up's summit was underneath it. Rysha had bought a frame for it that gave it a black backdrop, and the gold contrast popped with the greyscale of the rest of the wall. Tav studied the form of the person in the painting.

Then, it dawned on him. Tav shuffled his papers to the side of the desk, and opened the drawer to get his sketchbook. He flipped through a couple pages until he had a blank sheet. Then, he began to sketch rough outlines of a person standing on the left, and a person standing on the right. The one on the right would eventually have his hand pointed as a finger gun, and the one on the left's chest would explode into butterflies.

Cool, Tav thought to himself. This was achievable. He sketched and sketched, the hours ticking on as though they were minutes.

Suddenly, a knock on the door.

"Tav?"

Crap, Rysha's home. Wait...

"Rysha?"

Rysha cracked the door to see Tav hunched over the desk, his head turned to the door.

"Tav... It's 3:00 AM. Why are you awake?"

"What?" Tav pulled out his phone to check the time, and sure enough, it was a few minutes after 3:00 AM. *That's* why Rysha was home.

"I saw your light was on and came to check on you," Rysha explained. "Don't you have school tomorrow?"

"Y...Yeah..." Tav stammered, looking down at the sketch on his desk before looking back up at Rysha. He had definitely gotten a lot done, but at what cost?

"Well, not trying to tell you what to do or anything," Rysha smiled at Tav. "You should probably get some sleep while you have the chance."

"You're right," Tav replied, flipping his sketchbook shut.

"Can I see what you were working on, though?" Rysha asked, now fully stepping into the room.

"Yeah, of course," Tav replied, reflipping the sketchbook open to the page he had been on. Rysha walked over to the desk and picked up the book, putting his glasses down to the end of his nose to get a better look.

"This is really nice. Is this a sketch for the art show?"

"Yeah, I'm eventually going to do it on a bigger sheet, with acrylics."

"Nice," said Rysha, handing back the sketchbook. "Well, it's almost the weekend, so you'll have plenty of time to work on it then."

"Right," Tav agreed, shutting off his desk light and putting the sketchbook down into the drawer.

"I'll be up a little while, so let me know if you need anything, okay?" Rysha walked back over to the door and stood in the doorway, awaiting Tav's response.

"Will do," Tav replied, finally feeling the sleepiness of the night hitting him all at once.

• • • •

CHAPTER 26

"Rysha!" Tav hurriedly huffed as soon as he got in the door Friday afternoon. *"Carlinawantstoknowifwewanttogo-toMarinarealmtomorrow."*

Rysha looked up from the kitchen table, where he was doing paperwork. He shook his head in confusion.

"What?"

Tav took a couple deep breaths. Rysha could tell he had run up the stairs to the apartment.

"Carlina wants to know if we want to go to Marinarealm tomorrow," Tav said, more slowly now. "Her parents are taking her and they invited us to come along."

Rysha adjusted his glasses back to the top of his nose.

"Marinarealm, as in the amusement park?"

Tav nodded.

"Hmmm..." Rysha put a finger to his chin, rubbing a small line of his goatee. Then, he smiled. "I don't see why not."

"YES!" Tav threw his arms around Rysha. Before Rysha could respond, Tav retracted himself. "Ahem," Tav cleared his throat. "Thanks."

Rysha was amused; Tav was clearly excited about this outing. He must *really* like this girl.

"What time tomorrow?" he asked.

"I think she said noon, but I'll ask."

"Good idea," replied Rysha.

Tav retreated to his room, threw on his regular clothes, and flopped onto his bed. He had gotten the rest of his work from when he missed school done during study hall, so once again, he had the whole weekend to himself. Well, now it would be spent with Carlina, which was even better.

"What time tomorrow?" Tav texted her. He set his phone down on the bed beside him and sighed. He hadn't been to an amusement park since he was too short to ride the cool rides, so tomorrow was about to be awesome. His phone vibrated, and he opened it.

"Noon, does that work?"

"Perfect, that's what I told Rysha," he replied. He then opened the chat conversation for Rysha and texted him simply, "Noon." He switched back to Carlina's chat.

"Great! Meet us at the front gate :)" Carlina wrote.

"Sounds good to meeeeee," Tav replied. Was that too many "E's"? He didn't even care at this point, *that's* how excited he was.

• • • •

The night dragged on and on, but eventually, Saturday morning came. Tav sprung out of bed, and before he even put on his prosthetic, was fully dressed. Today, he chose his nicest jeans and a red and black flannel, as it was finally starting to get cool outside. He also decided on his black high-tops, to match Carlina's red ones that she always wore. He realized that he couldn't tie his shoes without his hand, so he hobbled over to the nightstand to grab it.

After tying his shoes, Tav went out to the living room to wake Rysha.

"Rysha," he said, "Get up."

Rysha grumbled.

"What time is it?"

"Nine something," Tav replied.

Rysha rolled over to his other side, and muttered,

"We don't have to leave until 11:00. My alarm is set for 10:00."

Tav knew that Rysha was capable of getting ready quickly, but wasn't 10:00 cutting it a little close? Coffee and a cigarette could take up to half an hour all by itself.

"I guess."

With that, Tav headed for the kitchen. He might as well get some breakfast, since he had time. He opened the fridge and took a look; he was so used to having breakfast at school that he had almost forgotten what it was like to have something at home. He found a carton of eggs, and decided that he'd make himself some scrambled eggs.

"Hmmm," Tav hummed aloud as he opened the cupboard, searching for the perfect frying pan. Rysha had just about every pan imaginable, and even duplicates of some. It made sense, though, Rysha *did* cook a lot, when he had the time. This, however, would be the first time Tav had cooked for himself at this house. He found what he assumed to be the right pan, and set it on the stove. It was a glass-top stove, which Tav still found to be strange, as he had dealt with a gas stove his entire life up until this point. He got into the fridge once again and grabbed a stick of butter, as well as a few slices of American cheese. He'd specifically requested them last time Rysha went to the store, as he put American cheese on, well, pretty much everything that every other kind of cheese normally goes on.

Tav shut the fridge and looked over to the living room. From here, he could just barely see the top of Rysha's head, so he'd be able to tell if he accidentally woke him up, which he sincerely hoped wouldn't happen. Tav turned the stove on low and situated the pan overtop the burner.

Now, the eggs. Tav went to the cupboard and got out a metal mixing bowl, and cracked a couple eggs into it.

Crap.

Tav had to carefully fish out a piece of eggshell from the rest of the egg goo. He *hated* touching egg goo.

After carefully throwing away the eggshell, and washing his hands, Operation: Scrambled Eggs once again commenced. He beat the eggs with a fork until they were a perfectly fluffy consistency. Then, he dropped a small slice of butter into the pan, waiting for it to melt and sizzle slightly. It looked to be about ready, so he dumped the eggs in. Perfect. Despite not having cooked for himself in a few months, Tav was proud of the fact that so far, he had correctly remembered how to make eggs.

Oh yeah, he thought to himself, *salt and pepper.* Rysha was fancy and had salt and pepper grinders, both with what Tav assumed to be the expensive stuff in them. He turned the salt grinder a few times over the eggs, then the pepper. Everything looked to be going to plan.

After the eggs had cooked a moment, Tav carefully unwrapped the two pieces of cheese and set them in the middle. This way, they'd get evenly mixed through all of the eggs. He poked it with the spatula a couple of times, stirring it around so every side was cooked evenly. And, eventually, Tav had a pan of perfectly cooked scrambled eggs.

"Eggs, huh?"

Tav jumped about a foot in the air at the sound of Rysha's voice. He had completely forgotten to keep an eye on him.

"Y-yeah," Tav stammered, gathering himself. He shut off the stove. "Did you want some?"

"No, no, that's okay. Thank you, though," Rysha replied with a smile. "Coffee time."

Tav smiled back.

"I didn't wake you, right?"

"Nah," Rysha reassured him, getting a plate out of the cabinet. "Here."

Tav took the plate.

"Thanks." He served up his eggs, and set himself down at the kitchen table. Rysha, meanwhile, began preparations for coffee.

"Have you ever been to Marinarealm?" Rysha asked after a moment, grabbing a mug off of the dish drainer.

"I think so," Tav replied. "When I was little."

"Ah, okay." Rysha set the mug beneath the coffee maker. "I haven't actually, so I'm interested to see what it's like."

"I think it's aquatic themed," Tav theorized out loud, "But instead of just being like a zoo, there's rides and stuff."

"Right. Huh," Rysha remarked before sitting down with his coffee, across from Tav. "Well, I think today will be a great experience for all of us."

"Agreed," Tav replied in between bites. "I hope you and Carlina's parents get along."

Rysha chuckled.

"I don't see why not. If they can handle seeing you kind-of-almost-die..." Rysha paused to take a sip of coffee. "... a day at the amusement park should be no problem."

"Do you think they'll say anything about it?" Tav asked.

Rysha shook his head.

"I don't anticipate it, but if they do bring it up, just be honest. There's no point in hiding what happened if they clearly saw it."

"Right..."

The two sat in silence, Tav working away at his scrambled eggs, and Rysha contemplating the definition of "wakefulness" over his coffee.

• • • •

"Hey!"

Carlina waved Tav and Rysha over to where she and her parents were standing by the entrance to the park. They walked over, and after some handshakes between parents, Tav and Carlina set off on their own.

"Meet us at 4 at the Italian restaurant," Carlina's dad had told the duo as they left.

"We will," Carlina had replied.

The two walked around the park, eventually ending up at the information building to acquire a map. Even though Carlina had been here before, the park was big enough that a map was necessary.

"I wanna do this one," Carlina told Tav as she pointed to a spot on the other end of the park. "It looks scary, cuz of the sharks."

Tav looked over at Carlina. Today, she was wearing a yellow Dalton High sweatshirt, with jeans and her usual high-tops. She smiled wide, and Tav couldn't help but reciprocate.

"Okay, let's head over there," Tav replied. He was now noticing just how fast Carlina walks; Even with his long legs, he was having to quicken his pace to keep up with her. Occasionally, they'd walk close enough to where their hands would brush up against each other, and every time it happened, Tav felt invisible sparks emit from his fingertips.

Once to the ride, Tav took in the sheer complexity of the piece of machinery that stood before them; this coaster was huge, bigger than anything he had ever seen. It had a couple loops, which wouldn't be too bad. Tav looked over to Carlina, who was basically vibrating with excitement.

"Let's get in line," she told Tav.

"Right." Tav couldn't help but feel a mix of excitement and nervousness as they waited their turn. He glanced at Carlina, who still wore an ear-to-ear grin that was both infectious and reassuring. She always seemed to be up for an adventure, and today was no exception. All things considered, Tav was quite appreciative of that sense of adventure.

As they reached the front of the line, the ride attendant gestured for them to climb into one of the shark-shaped cars. Tav and Carlina settled into their seats, the safety harnesses locking securely into place. The sensation of anticipation built as the coaster slowly began its ascent up the initial hill. The coaster reached its peak, affording them a breathtaking view of the entire park. From this height, they could see the colorful chaos of rides and attractions sprawling in all directions, and the shimmering waters of the nearby lake. Then, they plummeted. The coaster raced along the steep descent, the rush of wind and the screams of passengers adding to the adrenaline-fu-eled frenzy. Tav felt like he was flying as they tore through the loops and corkscrews, the shark-themed cars snapping and diving as if in pursuit of prey. Carlina's infectious laughter filled his ears, and he couldn't help but join in. His initial nervousness gave way to exhila-ration, and he threw his arms up into the air, letting out a triumphant yell.

The coaster roared through a tunnel, and for a brief moment, they were plunged into darkness. Then, with a sudden burst of light, they shot out of the tunnel and into the open air, rocketing toward the final stretch of the ride.

After the coaster slowed to a stop, Tav and Carlina stumbled out of their seats, legs wobbly from the adrenaline rush. They were both breathless, their faces flushed with excitement.

"That was sick!" Carlina exclaimed, her eyes sparkling with ener-gy.

Tav nodded, still trying to catch his breath. "Couldn't agree more."

• • • •

Meanwhile, Rysha and Carlina's parents had made their way to the aquariums, which the park was well known for aside from the rides and attractions. Aquatic life danced around them in every direction, illuminating the otherwise dim building. Rysha felt that he was really hitting it off with these two; conversation hadn't stopped between them since Tav and Carlina wandered off.

At the front of the group, Carlina's father, who Rysha had learned was named John, stopped in front of a group of neon tetras. He stared at them for a moment, captivated by their bright beauty.

"Carlina could paint these, Lisa."

"Oh, for sure." Lisa stood beside her husband and took up his arm. Rysha stood a little ways down, noticing a bottomfeeder fish that was cleaning the bottom of the tank. He watched as it carefully hovered over a rock, undulating its weird lips to remove the algae.

"So, does Tav have any plans for college?" John asked Rysha.

Rysha looked over to the couple, who were now looking at him expectantly.

"Oh, we've talked about it lightly," Rysha replied, "But he is thinking about taking a gap year before he jumps into anything."

"That's understandable," Lisa replied. "Carlina is thinking about doing the same. She wants to have a year to figure out how to be a 'real adult' first."

John nodded.

"I think it makes sense, in the current world we live in. Well, good for him, he seems like a great kid with his head on straight. Oh hey," John pointed to Rysha, "Has anyone ever told you how much you two look alike? You and Tav, I mean."

Rysha, genuinely surprised, laughed.

"Really? That's interesting."

"Yeah, like in the cheekbones and eyes," Lisa chimed in. "And he's so *tall*. You can definitely tell he's yours."

Rysha stifled another bout of laughter. He really didn't have the heart to tell them that they weren't biologically related, but he couldn't just play along forever.

"Actually, believe it or not, he's adopted."

Carlina's parents' eyes went wide in perfect unison.

"Really?" Lisa asked.

Rysha nodded.

"Oh man, sorry about that, Rysha," John started, "We could have sworn from what Carlina told us that you were... Y'know..."

"Not a problem," Rysha told them with a wave of his hand. "I'm sure Tav will get a kick out of it as well."

Lisa chuckled nervously.

"Well, that's good," she said.

The trio walked around the aquarium in silence for a few moments.

Maybe they think that offended me, Rysha thought to himself.

"Which colleges has Carlina looked at?" Rysha asked, attempting to pick the conversation back up.

"Quite a few, actually," replied John. "Naturally, we would want her to go to Alda..." John removed his cap and showed it off. It was for Alda College. "... but in truth, we'll support her wherever she goes."

"Right," Rysha replied, then spoke to Lisa, "Didn't you say you're a professor there?"

Lisa nodded humbly.

"She knows that we want her to do her best, and while Alda has phenomenal sciences, I honestly can't say as much for the art program."

"Right. She seems to really have a knack for art. I'm glad Tav has someone to talk about those things with, because I don't know the first thing about any of it."

"Neither do we," John replied. The trio laughed as the sun of the outdoors filtered through the entrance they were approaching. Through the glare of his glasses, Rysha saw a flash of yellow booking it in their direction, followed by a bobbing head of red hair.

"Ah, there they are," he said. "Guess we'll hit the restaurant later."

"*Guysguysguys,*" Carlina panted. "You gotta see these, check it out."

Tav shuffled up behind Carlina, looking worn out. He gave the group a wave. Carlina, meanwhile, had started showing off her prizes: A photo from each of the roller coasters they had been on.

"Look at his face in this one," Carlina said to her mom, pointing at Tav in one particular photo. In it, his mouth was open, and his eyes were half closed. Carlina laughed at the sight of it again, and her mom joined in.

"Was that from Bog Adventure?" Tav asked, trying his best to conceal the tiredness strewn through his voice. Carlina turned to him and nodded, then returned her attention to showing her mom the photos. They flipped through them, Carlina kicking up in laughter at every new photo.

Rysha walked over to Tav.

"Having fun?"

"So much," Tav replied, giving Rysha a thumbs up. "I'm ready for food, though."

"What do you guys think? Ready to call it quits for dinner?" Rysha asked the other three members of the group.

"Totally!" Carlina replied.

• • • •

Evening came quickly, and the group headed for the park exit. The lights had just kicked on, adding a whole new level of ambiance to the various attractions and displays. The parents were walking ahead of Tav and Carlina, and whether intentionally or not, giving them some alone time before the night ended.

"I had a lot of fun today. Thank you for inviting us," Tav began.

"Oh of course, I did, too." Carlina looked up to Tav and gave him a big smile. Once again, their hands brushed together, and this time, Tav made his move. He carefully took Carlna's hand into his own, trying his best to not shake while he did it.

"Are you okay? You're shaking," Carlina asked. Apparently, it hadn't worked.

"Yeah!" Tav told her, dropping their hands down to their sides. "Just... Happy."

"Me, too, this was seriously the best. We should do it again."

Tav could feel the heat rising in his chest. He *definitely* wanted to do this again, and sooner rather than later.

As the group approached the parking lot, the parents' walks slowed. Eventually, Tav and Carlina caught up to them. They let go of each other's hands.

"Well," Carlina's father started, "Ready to head out?"

"I guess," Carlina replied with a playful huff.

"Thank you guys again," Rysha said, turning to Carlina's parents.

"No, no, thank *you*," Lisa replied. "She would have been bored just hanging out with us all day, right, girlie?"

Carlina scoffed.

"Well, when you put it like that..." The group busted out in laughter, and after a moment, they said their goodbyes and parted ways.

Now that Tav was away from the group, he realized just how exhausted he was. Riding rides all day seemed easy, in comparison to training or something, but somehow it ended up being more tiring than training could ever imagine to be. Tav could feel the weight of his legs with every step as he approached the car. He was *so* ready to go to bed.

• • • •

CHAPTER 27

If there was any time to strike, it was now; Wrath found that Tav was in a deep enough sleep that he could take control of the body without issue. If he was careful, he could sneak off to Heavenrealm before Tav could do anything about it. He had a promise to keep: He couldn't kill his right hand man.

Wrath opened his eyes, which were met with the dull grey of Tav's bedroom ceiling. He blinked a few times. Then, he sat up. He looked over to the bedside table, where Tav's prosthetic hand was plugged in. He wouldn't be needing that, so he decided to get dressed without it. He was already wearing a t-shirt, all he needed was pants; After all, he didn't want to stroll into the Heavenrealm with no pants on. He selected a pair of jeans, as well as slide-on sandals. This was good enough.

Shit, Wrath thought through Tav's brain. *What if the other man is awake?* He had jumped the gun at the opportunity to take over the body uninhibited, but had sincerely lacked forethought in every other aspect of planning his escape. But, no matter. He looked at the door in front of him, where mere feet away the man could be sleeping on his couch. He pressed his ear to it, and heard nothing. So, he decided to carefully crack the door. No one was on the couch.

"Ah," Wrath said to himself aloud, now aware that no one was home. "Probably at work." With that, he shut Tav's bedroom door behind him, and headed for the balcony. He decided to take one last look at the city; It was truly a work of art, unlike anything he had ever seen before. In the night, the lights of the skyscrapers looked like stars. He closed his eyes, and after carefully summoning and unfurling his wings, set off into the night.

• • • •

"Okay, I'm ready when you are," Wrath yelled up to the clouds. Michael was supposed to meet him here, "here" being wherever Wrath could get to in order to open the portal, which happened to currently be a large grass field.

Supposedly, Michael was able to keep consistent surveillance on Wrath, so he would know when he was ready to go. Sure enough, he was right; within moments, a large cloud of dust kicked up in the center of the field, and from it emerged Michael in his archangel form. He had no reason to disguise himself, this time, as the only other person who would see him was Wrath.

"I must ask," Michael began as he approached Wrath, "How you managed to take over the body without a fight."

"Easy," Wrath replied, pointing at his head. "The knucklehead is asleep, deeper than usual."

"Ah," Michael remarked nonchalantly. "And if he wakes?"

Wrath shook his head. "Shouldn't happen. Let's be quick, just in case."

"As you wish." Michael turned around and faced the expanse of the field. Opening a portal in which other beings can traverse to the Heavenrealm was no easy feat; it required careful consideration and-

"Hurry it up," Wrath urged as Michael prepared to open the portal. Cross, now, Michael looked back at him.

"This is a delicate matter," Michael replied, "It is not instantaneous. Now, if you'll excuse me..." Michael materialized a staff, very similar to the one he fought with in the ring. He struck the ground with it, and the earth beneath their feet began to quiver. Within a few seconds, the grass of the field was replaced with a large, circular opening. The portal was complete.

From where he was standing, Wrath couldn't see into the portal. He took a few steps forward and peered into it; Millions of stars lay on the other side.

Michael looked to Wrath.

"This is the moment of change."

With that, he plunged into the portal, disappearing into the seemingly infinite space.

Wrath, however, began to have his doubts. Would it really be as easy as walking in and taking the throne? As much time as he had had to plan, he really hadn't utilized it to its full potential. His plan really did boil down to walking in, killing everyone in his way, killing *God*, then, voila. It would be over, and plans of reform would begin to take shape.

"Hey."

Wrath looked around before realizing that the voice came from within himself. It was Tav. He was...

Awake? How?

"What do you want, brat?" Wrath asked Tav aloud. "You were supposed to be asleep."

"I was." This time, when Tav spoke, it was aloud through his own mouth. He used every ounce of energy he could control to fling the body backwards, landing belly up on the ground in front of the portal. Wrath and Tav shared control of the eyes now, and they watched together as the portal disappeared just as quickly as it had appeared.

Tav could feel his face manipulating into a grimace. His eyebrows furrowed, his eyes narrowed, and he now bared his teeth. Wrath was *pissed*.

"You insolent fuck," Wrath hissed.

"I never agreed to do this in the first place," Tav replied to Wrath internally. "Did you just assume I would go along with it if you caught me while I was asleep?"

Wrath hesitated.

"... You know what? You are entirely right."

Tav could feel the wings retracting into his back.

"I was entirely stupid about this, wasn't I?" Wrath asked, malice laced through every word. "I *really* should have taken a different approach. Here, let's try this..."

WHAM. Tav felt as though he had been kicked in the face. He turned to his side, still on the ground, and held his good hand at his temple. He screamed in agony while Wrath retreated further into the subconscious. Tav was in full control of his body now. Or, so he thought. When Tav opened his eyes, they were met with complete darkness.

"If you *really* don't want to help me," Wrath began, now speaking internally to Tav, "I will remind you of my promise to make your life a living hell until you cooperate."

Tav began to panic now. He couldn't see. He couldn't see *anything.* He sat up and felt the ground beneath him to be sure that it was still there. It was.

"What did you do to me?" Tav demanded. "Why can't I see?"

Tav could hear Wrath's laughter between his ears. "Since we share this body again, I can shut things off at will. Your eyes, your ears, your bladder control; I'll take it all, until you change your mind."

"NO!" Tav stood now, completely disoriented as to where he was. He would have no way of getting home, no way of contacting anyone. He would more than likely *die* out here. He crumpled into a puddle and began to sob uncontrollably.

• • • •

Rysha awoke to the sun filtering through the balcony door. He sat up and stretched, feeling his dress shirt come slightly untucked as he reached up towards the ceiling. He had fallen asleep in uniform again. Rough night at work. He stood up, grabbed his glasses, and fixed his attire as well as he could. It was Sunday, so he could change into regular clothes after his shower, since he didn't work that night.

He picked up his phone off the side table and read it: 1:42 PM. *Wow, it's pretty late,* Rysha remarked internally. Usually, he would try to at least be up by noon, even on days where he had worked the night previous. Something about today felt off already, and he couldn't quite put a finger on it.

Driven by instinct, Rysha went to Tav's door and knocked. No response. He knocked again. Nothing.

"Tav?" Rysha called out, his voice still groggy. Rysha cleared his throat. "You up, buddy?"

That was strange. He's usually say something even if he *was* still asleep, as he was a light sleeper.

"Tav?" He called once again. He jiggled the doorknob, and it was unlocked. Very carefully, he opened the door, unsure as to what would meet him on the other side of it. He looked at Tav's bed, then over to the desk. He wasn't there. He wasn't anywhere.

Knock knock knock. Rysha realized that that was coming from the front door. *Tav?* No, he wouldn't knock, he'd just walk in. He hurriedly walked over to the door and swung it open. On the other side of it stood V, panting from having run up the stairs.

"Yeah?" Rysha asked, skipping formalities with her.

"Tav is missing," V began breathlessly. "I know where he is, but I need your help to get there."

"Missing?" Rysha repeated. "What do you mean *missing?*"

V gestured wildly as she spoke. "I had a vision. Tav was in the middle of a field, and he was freaking out. I think Wrath fully took over his body at some point and... I don't know, but we need to hurry."

"Okay," Rysha told her, already on his way to grab his keys. "Let's go."

• • • •

"Down that road."

Rysha and V were already relatively far away from the city. They had been driving for at least half an hour now. Every once in a while, V would press her palms together and send out a sort of "sonic pulse."

"That's how I can track him," V had replied when Rysha had initially asked what she was doing.

"There! I see him!"

"Where?" Rysha asked, his eyes darting and hoping to lock onto the sight of him.

"Up there, in the field."

"I see him now."

Rysha pulled the car to the side of the road and shut it off. V got out even faster than he did, and the two began running towards Tav. He was laying on the ground.

"Tav!" Rysha called out. At this point, he didn't know if Tav was dead or alive. Considering the circumstances, he would hope that he was alive, even if it was due to Wrath's possession. Regardless, it would mean he was still breathing.

"Tav!" V called out in tandem. As the two approached, Tav's eyes blinked open. He still couldn't see, but he could hear pounding footsteps coming right for him.

"Tav!"

"Rysha!" Tav now recognized one of the voices that approached him. But, it sounded like there were two sets of footsteps. Who was the other person?

"Thank goodness you're alive."

"V?" Tav questioned at the sound of her voice. "Where are you guys? I can't see."

Rysha stopped in front of Tav. "Are you hurt anywhere? What do you mean you can't see?"

Tav waved his left hand in front of his eyes, just to be sure. Nothing.

"Wrath shut off my eyes, I think," Tav explained hurriedly, "He tried to go to the Heavenrealm, but I stopped him."

V crouched down on the other side of Tav. "Tried to go to the Heavenrealm? What do you mean?"

"I-I'm not sure," Tav stammered. "When I came to, there was a huge portal in front of me. So I threw myself backwards so he couldn't get in."

"We need to get you to a doctor," Rysha interjected.

"What are they going to do?" Tav asked, a twinge of anger lingering in his voice. "It's not like they can remove Wrath's possession. I'm stuck with him until I change my mind, he told me himself."

Rysha reached out and gently took Tav's hand. "Take a couple deep breaths for me, okay?"

Tav turned to where he believed Rysha was. His once brilliant silver irises were now dull, staring off into a distant void.

"I'm sorry, I'm just... Really upset, and confused, and..." Tav trailed off.

"For now, let's get you back to the car," said V. "It beats being out in a field."

Tav turned towards V and smiled just a little bit.

"True that."

With that, Rysha helped Tav stand, and guided him back towards the car. Tav's steps were shaky, unsure of the ground beneath his feet. As they approached the car, Tav said,

"I really should have just let him go through with it."

"No, you did the right thing," V insisted. "For the fate of both Earth and the Heavenrealm, it's better that we keep him away from his dad for as long as possible."

"But, how long am I going to be able to keep this up?" Tav asked as Rysha opened the passenger door for him. Tav made an attempt to sit in the car, and ended up hitting his head on the way down. "Ouch," he remarked quietly.

"Do you happen to remember if he was with anyone?" V asked as she settled into the backseat. "Last I knew, Wrath couldn't travel between dimensions by himself."

"I'm not sure," Tav replied. He felt Rysha get into the driver's seat and start the car. For the first time, Tav noticed the low rumble of the engine as the car set into motion. The world seemed so much louder, now that he couldn't see what was happening at any given moment.

"Well, I think our first step is to check in with Dr. Todd," Rysha told Tav. "She may know as much as we do, but she has more resources."

"Yeah... What do you think, V?" Tav asked.

Silence. Rysha glanced back to the backseat, and when he did, he saw that V was completely gone.

"She isn't back there," Rysha relayed to Tav.

"Oh." Tav turned to the backseat, and upon remembering that he wouldn't be able to see anything anyways, turned back around. "She must have gone back to her realm."

Silence for a moment as Rysha drove down the country road. Then, Tav thought out loud.

"I really hope that Dr. Todd can help me. I feel so lost. I can't be trapped with Wrath forever, not to mention not being able to see. This can't be my new normal."

Rysha sighed sympathetically. "We will get through this, one way or another. You have a support system that has your back, Dr. Todd being a part of it. Even if she can't fix it, she can offer support while you figure out what you're going to do."

"Right..."

• • • •

V felt herself getting yanked back into her dimension. The pressure from the atmosphere was almost too much to handle. But, she persevered, and landed face down on the ground in front of Elias.

"Care to tell me what you were doing on Earth again?" he asked.

"You already know why," V grumbled as she stood.

"I do. However, I wanted to hear it from you."

V sighed. "Wrath cursed Tav's sight and left him in a field. I knew Rysha wouldn't be able to find him by himself, so I decided to help."

V watched as Elias' eye darted to the right, then back onto her. "And, risked getting killed by being within Wrath's vessel's vicinity, am I correct?"

"Tav was in full control, at that point," V countered. "Aside from his eyes. Wrath is probably just waiting for Tav to cave and help him, so he'll more than likely remain dormant for a while."

Elias nodded.

"Keep an eye on him."

V's eyes went wide.

"What?"

"I said, keep an eye on him. I know you already have been, but now, I would like for you to pay special attention to his surveillance. If anything happens, we need to be the first ones to do something about it."

"So," V began to ask, "What should we do if he *does* cave and ends up helping Wrath?"

Elias chuckled slightly, which was unusual.

"Well, I guess we'll just have to follow him, won't we?"

V furrowed her brow.

"And how are we supposed to do that? Aren't you - actually, aren't we *all* barred from travelling to the Heavenrealm?"

Elias' expression softened in a strange and off-putting way.

"I don't think you fully understand the power that I hold."

• • • •

CHAPTER 28

Since it was Sunday, Dr. Todd would have to make a special trip to the office to see Tav. Luckily, Rysha had made the phone call to arrange that, and Dr. Todd was more than willing. Now, Tav was situated up on the exam table, and Dr. Todd was shining a light into his eyes.

"Can you see this at all?" she asked. Tav stared forward as the light wand moved across his eyes.

"No," he replied. He couldn't even tell where the light was. All he could see was darkness.

"Okay..."

Tav could hear as Dr. Todd walked away from him, then sat down on the stool.

"It seems as though the connection between the optic nerves and the brain may have been severed in some fashion," Dr. Todd began. "I'm not an eye doctor, so I can't say much beyond that, but... This is certainly strange. What did you say happened?"

Tav recounted the events as well as he could remember, between coming-to in the field last night, to his sight getting cursed. He could hear Dr. Todd typing away on her laptop now, occasionally giving him an affirmative "Yeah", "Mmhm", or "Right" as he spoke.

"Well," Dr. Todd started once Tav was through his explanation, "I can refer you to an eye specialist, but it's looking like they wouldn't be available until next week."

"Next week?" Rysha asked, speaking for the first time since they had entered the office. "What should we do until then?"

"My recommendation? Stay at home and try to relax until your appointment."

Tav's shoulders slumped. Stuck at home for a whole week? What was he supposed to do? He couldn't draw, he couldn't play video games, he couldn't even *go to school.*

"I know it's going to be hard, but there is a chance the situation will resolve on its own," Dr. Todd continued. "If it's anything like the temporary blindness people can experience with powers and the genetic abnormality, it'll be a couple days and then it will resolve itself."

"Right..." Tav attempted to conceal the disappointment in his tone, but it proved difficult. This next week was going to *drag*.

· · · ·

Tav was sitting in his room, cross-legged in what he assumed to be the center of the bed. He assumed it was night, from how much time had passed. Rysha had come to check on him a few times, offering him dinner, asking if he needed anything. Tav wasn't hungry, and he couldn't think of anything he needed.

In through the nose, out through the mouth. That's what Rysha had taught him for times where he was feeling particularly stressed out. Repeat this process a couple of times, and he would start to feel his center of gravity again. *In, out.* Thankfully, it worked. Despite not being able to see his surroundings, Tav felt grounded. Now he could actually think.

Tav was currently presented with two options: He could either wait it out and see if, for some odd reason, Wrath's curse on his eyes would dissipate on its own. Or, he could give in and help Wrath. If he did that, Wrath said something about being separated from him once he took over the Heavenrealm. Didn't that mean that, hypothetically, Wrath would let him go once he was done with whatever it was he needed to do? In truth, upon really thinking about it, he wouldn't even have to do anything except sit back and watch as Wrath seized the Heavenrealm.

It was boggling to Tav that helping the enemy was beginning to be the more reasonable of the two options. After everything that had happened, bargaining with Wrath seemed to be an unlikely solution.

It almost seemed wrong. How could doing what felt wrong end up potentially being right?

Tav sighed. He now presented himself with two new options: He could either sit there and think himself to death, or *do* something about the whole situation. His first course of action would be to discuss it with Rysha, who he assumed was still awake. Tav swung his legs over the side of the bed and stood up. Despite not being able to see, his room was familiar enough now that he was confident that he could navigate it. Rysha's floors were all laminated hardwood, with a lip around the doorframe to mark the transition from one room to another. Tav carefully shuffled towards the door, putting his hand out to feel for landmarks, such as the dresser.

"Rysha?" Tav called through the door once he found it.

"Yeah, bud, what's up?"

"I want to talk to you about something."

"I'm in the kitchen." Tav heard Rysha stand from his place at the table. "Do you need help?"

"No, I should be fine," Tav replied, stepping fully into the living room. The kitchen was on the right, and if Tav followed the wall, he would make it to the kitchen table. He carefully walked across the floor.

"You're almost there," Rysha guided, unsure as to whether he should help him or let him figure it out on his own. Tav got it, though, and found the chair on the opposite end of the table. He sat.

"What did you want to talk to me about?" Rysha asked.

"Well..." Tav started as he put his arms down on the table. "I think... I think I know what I'm going to do."

"What are you going to do?"

"I think..." Tav huffed before he continued. To him, it felt like he was about to admit defeat. "... I'm going to work with Wrath."

"What?" Tav could hear Rysha's tone harden.

"Listen, like... I've thought about it. He wants to use me as a vessel, right? So really, that's all I have to do. Be a vessel. He said once that he would separate from me once he took over the Heavenrealm, so that means there is a chance I could escape and come back."

"A 'chance.' That's not guaranteed."

"I know, but..." Tav's voice began to waver. "It's between him shutting off my body until I cooperate, or cooperating with the chance of having a normal life again. I don't have much of a choice, but it is a choice I can make myself."

Rysha carefully contemplated Tav's words. He was entirely right in that it was a decision that only he could make, but a protective part of him didn't want him to risk it. Then again, Tav was also right in saying that it was between Wrath making his life miserable, or the chance of freedom. Once again, he was in limbo, between a place of normalcy and a place of unpredictability. He looked over to the young man now sitting in front of him. His eyes were looking right at him, despite not actually looking at anything at all. His red hair was disheveled, his clothes were on sideways. He looked run ragged.

"You're right," Rysha began after a moment. "You are the only one who can make that choice. And, from what you've told me, it sounds like your head is in the right place. I will support you however I can." In truth, Rysha had no idea what he, himself, could do to remedy this situation, except instill confidence in Tav that he would succeed.

"So, I guess I'll tell Wrath I'll help him," Tav planned aloud. "Then, go to the Heavenrealm, and..."

"And what?"

"Maybe he'll be nice enough to transport me back here. Or at least, *someone* up there should be."

"Not to mention, the Fallen would help you, yes? Maybe you can get in contact with them somehow."

"That's where it gets tricky. Wrath is their sworn enemy, I'm just the guy who happens to be attached to him right now."

"Yes, but they seem to care about your well-being separate from Wrath. Otherwise, they wouldn't have shown up at the tournament to fight."

Rysha was right. Out of everyone, the Fallen had the best chance of helping him. But, as far as he knew, they were all barred from entering the Heavenrealm.

After a moment, Tav spoke again.

"I don't know when I'll be back."

"Alright," Rysha replied. "And you won't have any way of contacting me until you're done?"

Tav nodded, certain that Rysha was looking right at him.

"I won't let you down."

Rysha could feel a tear welling up in his eye. But, he kept his tone steady, so as to not alert Tav of his insurmountable concern.

"I have full faith in you, Tav. You know what needs to be done, and you know what you need to do to achieve it." Rysha stood up, and walked over to Tav. "Come here."

Tav did, and Rysha engulfed him in a hug. Tav was happy to feel the warmth of someone caring about him in a situation that most people would find extraordinary. He wrapped his arms around Rysha in return.

· · · ·

When Tav awoke within his sleep, he was once again in Wrath's throne room. He walked quickly now, his internal sight not hindered by Wrath's curse. When he approached the throne, Wrath leaned forward.

"I've been waiting for you," Wrath nearly sang to Tav. "Have you finally changed your mind? Was the curse too much for you to handle?"

"Let's get this over with," Tav bit back.

Wrath smiled.

"Good. Let's carry on, then."

. . . .

Wrath awoke Tav's body. He was in full control, and his eyes were fully changed over to his own. He stood up and headed for the door.

Wait, Wrath thought to himself. *That man is a witness, I can't let him live.* He exited the room and stepped into the kitchen, where his eyes were met with those of Rysha, staring back hard. Rysha knew that the Tav in front of him was not the real Tav, and was a mere entity within a vessel. They stared at each other for a moment before Wrath spoke.

"Strange to see you again," he said. Rysha stayed silent, quietly migrating his hand to his holster.

"Likewise."

"Look," Wrath said as he began to materialize a dagger. "Don't take it personally. The kid is just collateral. It had to be done."

Rysha didn't flinch. He stared back into Wrath's cold, black eyes, maintaining eye contact as Wrath began to slowly approach him.

"Unfortunately, though..." Wrath stopped at the other end of the table. "You are, as well." The dagger went flying through the kitchen, nearly landing in Rysha's throat, had he not dodged it with lightning speed. It stayed stuck in the cabinet for a moment before it dissipated.

Wrath lunged for Rysha, getting ready to create another dagger that *wouldn't* miss this time. Before he could, Rysha had him in a hold, his hands behind his back and Rysha's knee planted squarely on his shoulders. Wrath, at this point, just laughed.

"You really put up a fight for a human, y'know? Most of your species are weak, fragile. You? You would make a great minion of mine, if you're interested."

Rysha tightened his hold.

"Never."

"Suit yourself," Wrath replied, the air being squeezed out of him by the second.

"Complete your mission, and send Tav back unharmed," Rysha ordered. "Promise me."

"Okay, okay," Wrath said, squirming, "I won't hurt the kid, geez."

"Promise me."

"Okay, alright, I promise." With that, Rysha let him go, and the two quickly stood up. They were eye to eye, Rysha startled by the difference between Wrath and Tav, yet both of their beings being contained in the same body.

"Go," Rysha directed.

Wrath turned and walked towards the balcony. When he reached the door, he turned to Rysha.

"Don't wait up for him."

Rysha watched as Wrath unfurled his wings and set off into the night.

• • • •

"Okay, for real this time."

Wrath was back in the same field as before, arms outstretched.

"I'm ready. The brat finally agreed to help me."

Within a moment, Wrath watched as a cloud of smoke once again engulfed the center of the field. Before he even saw him, he heard Michael say,

"You failed me last time."

"I know, I know," Wrath replied indignantly. "It's not my fault the kid was being difficult."

Michael approached Wrath.

"And you say that he has agreed to work with you?"

"Yup, and without a fight, too. Just made the decision himself."

"Hm." Michael turned away from Wrath and out to the field. "Remind me of your plan for infiltration."

"Right. So basically, I'm going to walk in there like I own the place, talk to God for a few, then, *WHAM*. He'll just think his prodigal son returned to say hello or something."

"Didn't he deliberately seal you away the first time?"

"Well, yeah, kind of," Wrath replied, choosing his next words carefully. "That was more due to a misunderstanding, than anything."

"You will be met with heavy opposition," Michael continued, seemingly glossing over Wrath's explanation.

"Oh, I know. Nothing I can't handle. Not to make you feel special or anything, but you are the strongest Archangel, and what's more is that you're on *my* side. It won't be a problem."

Michael nodded.

"And God himself?"

"He's a pushover, when it comes to his kids. Like I said, he'll be happy to see me."

Michael began to open the portal once again.

"I trust your intuition," Michael told him, lying only a little bit. "Regardless, I can just kill you if you defect from the plan."

Wrath chuckled. "Suit yourself."

The portal was fully realized now. Michael took the leap, and Wrath followed closely behind.

• • • •

CHAPTER 29

The sight of the current state of the Heavenrealm instilled feelings within Wrath that he didn't know he was capable of feeling. Firstly, the ornate street lamps that would normally cast their glow onto the streets, now lay mostly in ruin. Secondly, well, the streets themselves; parts of them were cracked and raised, as if roots had pushed the stones out of the way. The buildings were not in a much better state. Wrath could see windows that were broken, as well as pieces of decorative architecture that had crumbled and landed on the ground, yet to be cleaned up. It was a sight to behold; to see the once great realm that he had inhabited as a child, once wondrous and full of life, now dilapidated.

Michael and Wrath walked silently down the road, Michael walking slightly ahead of Wrath. Right now, this was more Michael's realm than it was his, in terms of authority. Michael was well-respected as an Archangel in the Heavenrealm until recently; the downfall of the realm had led to a near collapse of the holy hierarchy, including God, the Archangels, and higher-ranking Angels. The only thing preventing a full collapse was Mercy. Mercy, being the only daughter of God, was an important figure in the grand scheme of the Heavenrealm. At this point, it was questionable whether she herself or her father was the stronger member of the Trifecta Sanctus. Wrath, of course, was not even considered as an option.

Much to their ruination, Wrath thought to himself. Despite having been banished, he was still a formidable force. Well, *now* he was, now that he had a body to control. He thought inwardly for a moment to see if Tav was present in the conscience, only to be met with silence. Good. Hopefully, he would stay quiet and not cause any problems.

As they approached the castle, both Wrath and Michael took note of the two guard Angels posted at the wide castle doors. In the

total darkness, their footsteps were undetectable, weaving now between the trees that surrounded the outskirts of the castle. Michael
broke into a run, his sword materializing in his hand. Wrath followed
suit, increasing his speed and getting his own sword at the ready.
It was as though Michael was telepathically sharing his plan with
Wrath. That, or their fighting styles were so similar that they merely
mirrored each other. Wrath himself wasn't sure of what powers he
could access within the Heavenrealm. He knew now that he could
still create a weapon, but what else was he capable of?

Wrath, in a split-second moment of thought, strategized to hit
the rightmost guard head on with an energy blast from his sword. He
wasn't entirely sure what Michael was going to do, so he readied himself for the possibility that an attack would also come from the left.
Michael *had* to know what he was doing, though; Clearly, he had
been plotting this takedown for a while. Then again, he hadn't employed the help of Wrath until recently, so perhaps it really was just a
flying-by-the-seat-of-the-pants operation. Regardless, Wrath considered himself ready.

In a blitz, Michael skillfully decapitated the first angel. Wrath
was second to strike, stabbing his sword straight through the chest of
the second guard before he even had a chance to see his now-head-
less comrade. Wrath retracted his sword and turned to Michael, who
nodded for the duo to head inside. Together, they pushed the huge
doors open, each of the doors creaking at a slight variant pitch.

"Fall behind me. Can you obscure yourself?" Michael whispered.
Wrath just shook his head.

"There's no need for that," he whispered back, slightly louder
than Michael had been. While Michael was hidden in the shadows,
Wrath was standing under the light of a torch.

"Hey!"

The two swiveled their heads to see where the voice had come from. It was one of two guards who had just happened to be patrolling the entrance area.

Without hesitation, Michael went for the kill. The other guard shrieked in horror, freezing up at the sight of Wrath slowly approaching him. Michael looked at Wrath, confused.

"Why aren't you-"

"*Shhhh*," said Wrath. He sauntered up to the second guard, who was now quivering, his sword as ready as he could get it. Wrath carefully tipped the guard's blade down with his metallic right index finger, drawing a semicircle as he guided the sword down to the ground.

"Do you know who I am?" Wrath asked.

The guard quickly shook his head. Wrath rolled his eyes.

"Of course not."

With that, Wrath sliced the guard clean in half, right through the center of his abdomen. Michael watched as the puddle of blood beneath the guard exploded, his torso landing on the other side of his legs. It was gruesome; nothing he wasn't already familiar with, however.

As they walked down the winding hallways, they encountered a few more guards that were quickly taken care of. It was night, so not many Angels would be out and about the castle. God, however, would be awake. He always was at this hour.

In front of the door to the throne room were 12 Angel guards, spears and shields in hand as they held post. Surely, they had heard the chaos of the slaughter of their brothers in the halls leading to the throne room. Yet, they held their stances, unwavering. Michael readied himself for combat, and Wrath waved his hand dismissively.

"Do any of you fine soldiers of God happen to know who I am?" Wrath asked, sword down at his side. His head was down, so the guards couldn't see his face. They exchanged confused glances amongst each other before the six guards on the outskirts of the doors went in for a takedown.

Just then, Wrath raised his head, revealing his eyes. A look of fear washed over each of the guards as Wrath became a whirlwind of steel amongst them. Michael supported from the back, Taking out the soldiers that had somehow made it past Wrath's onslaught. By the time they were done, the floors and walls approaching the throne room were bathed in blood.

"You will go in by yourself first," Michael directed. "Then, I will assist when I feel it is necessary."

"Fair enough," said Wrath, wiping some residual blood from his cheek. He approached the door, then carefully cracked it open, like a child entering their parents' bedroom in the wee hours of the night. He was met with mostly darkness, spare for two torches lighting either side of the three thrones. Wrath took note of the leftmost throne, which was empty. In the other two, Mercy sat on the right, and God himself in the center.

They had clearly anticipated his arrival.

· · · ·

CHAPTER 30

"**D**id you miss me?"

Wrath watched and waited for his father's response. God was an imposing figure; at least seven feet tall, with a white robe that only added to his dramatic aura. His hair was long and grey, his eyes a brilliant, nearly blinding white.

Mercy, on the other hand, seemed miniscule compared to her father. She was about five foot seven, maybe over, maybe under. Her rose pink hair was flowing neatly on her shoulders and dress, barely obscuring the dangling eye earring in each of her ears. Her own eyes were a brilliant blue, perfectly matching the earrings.

God didn't even twitch at the question.

"You decided to come back."

"*Decided?*" Wrath asked indignantly. "It's not as though I ever had the option. Can I at least hear that you're happy to see me?"

"I'm indifferent."

The terse words of God, Wrath's own father, stung like daggers in his chest. But, he had at least half expected it. Wrath turned to Mercy now.

"And, my dear sister, how have you been?" Wrath asked in a sickeningly sweet diction. Mercy didn't move, her gaze to the other end of the throne room unwavering, not even bothering to acknowledge her brother.

Suddenly, Wrath felt the floor beneath his feet shake. Before he knew it, he was surrounded by at least 50 guards, specifically Archangel guards. There was no chance for escape, even with his specialized skill set. A grin crept across his face.

"You all should have stayed home."

With that, the show began. Wrath went for the frontmost guards first, the ones now guarding the thrones themselves. He began slicing them down one by one, his speed and brilliant battlesense shining in comparison to that of even the most skilled of Archangels.

Meanwhile, Wrath heard as the throne room door flew open. Michael now stood in the center of the doorway. He immediately charged for the guards in the rear, fighting and killing some of his once-closest compatriots without hesitation. It was, after all, for the greater good.

The fight raged on, Wrath and Michael effortlessly taking down every guard that dared enter their field of range.

"Is this not enough?" Wrath asked, his tone crazed as he plunged his sword into the skull of the last guard. "Is this not enough for you?"

"Run," God told Mercy quietly, ignoring Wrath's plea. Mercy got up and headed for a back room. Then, in the eerie silence that now filled the throne room, God spoke in a calm, booming voice.

"You took the form of a mere human. Pathetic."

Wrath looked up to his father, who was now standing. He watched as he put out his hand, expecting a sword to be summoned at any minute. Sure enough, a sword nearly as long as Wrath's entire body was now in the hand of God. It shone a brilliant white, as if the sun itself was trapped within the blade. God swung the sword, and a wave of wind blew over the throne room, vaporizing the bodies of his now-deceased guards, and leaving Wrath and alone in the center. Wrath was on one knee, as if kneeling for the great entity that stood before him. But, he wasn't kneeling for him; he, personally, didn't even feel as though the battle had truly begun. After all, he hadn't landed a single hit on his father yet.

"I know your intentions," God began, his sword at the ready. He looked behind Wrath at Michael, who was about to transform into a cloud of smoke in order to make his escape. Before he could, God had him in an invisible chokehold, effortlessly clearing the distance between them. As God brought him forward, Wrath heard Michael struggling to breathe as he was dragged towards the throne.

"As for you," God began, Michael's throat now firmly in his hand. "How does it feel to be a traitor to the throne that you've worked so hard to protect?" Michael struggled against the hand of God, but got nowhere. God clenched his hand, and Michael's crushed head landed in a puddle of blood on the floor. His body crumpled, and God now saw Wrath standing, watching.

"You know, I expected better of him," said God to his astonished son. "His techniques were fashioned after yours, after all."

Wrath furrowed his brow and bared his teeth, unsure of his father's next move. God walked forward from the throne and down the stairs.

"A human with powers," God began cryptically. "I *knew* of humans having artificial powers, however they appeared to me to be useless. To you..." God was now standing directly in front of Wrath, having moved at a speed incomprehensible to the eye. God's eyes met Wrath's. "... It seems to have been quite advantageous."

Despite Wrath truthfully feeling that Michael was nothing more than a tool to aid in his endeavours, the brutality of his death was nothing short of humbling. God was a force to be reckoned with, even despite the now-weakened state of his army. God, himself, clearly still held a significant amount of power. God's hand, still curled, extended out to Wrath.

"Do you want the same treatment, my son?"

Wrath let out a war cry and lunged forward, aiming the tip of his blade straight for God's heart.

"Your tyranny ends here!" Wrath yelled. Before the blade could make contact, God's own blade was against Wrath's.

"You've changed," God remarked simply as Wrath struggled to keep his blade steady. Wrath smirked.

"This body's powers aren't *entirely* useless."

The two blades clashed as God and his son performed their deadly dance around the throne room. It was truly an art; Wrath finally met the only form of opposition that he knew full well he couldn't immediately slaughter.

"You have trespassed on holy grounds," God's voice boomed as he fended off Wrath's onslaught of swordsmanship. "You will answer for your deeds."

Wrath pressed on, even quicker than before. His eyes had a certain glow about them, as if the souls of the dead Angels now inspired him to take what they all knew was rightfully his.

"This throne is no longer holy, and neither is your reign," Wrath replied, using his wings to propel himself backwards. Now, for some range attacks. Wrath swung his sword and sent a field of energy flying forth from it. God, seeing the attack coming from a mile away, summoned a shield that protected him from all sides. The energy blast fizzled away when it made contact, and Wrath huffed.

"You're not even going to let me have fun with this?" He asked his father. Without hesitation, God once again closed the gap between the two, and the close-quarters sword fighting began once again.

As the battle raged on, Wrath's malevolence grew. His desire to unseat God, to become the ruler of the Heavenrealm, burned infernaciously within him. He fought with unparalleled ferocity, his strikes and maneuvers pushing even God to his limits.

But God, eternal and omniscient, knew every single one of Wrath's weaknesses, even despite him having taken on a human form. He could see that Wrath was losing steam. He was biding his time, waiting for the right moment.

And then, it came.

Wrath, fueled by anger and arrogance, made a reckless move, leaving himself momentarily exposed. In that fraction of a second, God seized his opportunity; his sword found its mark and pierced through Wrath's defenses, striking his body with a blinding burst of divine energy.

Wrath cried out in pain as the celestial power coursed through him, and as his body convulsed, he sank to the ground. Just as God raised his sword for the finishing blow, a piercing voice echoed through the throne room.

"STOP!"

It was Mercy, who now stood in front of her throne, her outstretched wings quivering with emotion, her own holy sword at the ready. Her sword was made of rose gold damascus steel, in contrast to the gunmetal of her brother's. The hilt was inlaid with flowers, the handle tipped with rose gold to match the blade.

"Regardless of what you think he has done," Mercy yelled, her voice trembling as tears formed in her eyes, "He's still my brother. He's still your *son*. How can you kill your own son in cold blood?"

God looked down at the battered face of Wrath. His eyes were barely open, now barely holding onto the consciousness that had once coursed through that body effortlessly.

"The prophecy," God replied, turning his head only halfway towards his daughter. "He was destined for this from the start."

"Forget the prophecy!" Mercy pleaded. "You are going to kill your child, is that not reason enough to go against it?"

Just then, a whirlwind of energy exploded from the center of the throne room. When the dust settled down, the Fallen stood ready in perfect formation, Elias at the front.

"Separate Wrath from the boy," Elias firmly demanded.

· · · ·

CHAPTER 31

"Surprised to see you again," God told Elias as he removed the sword from Wrath's chest. Somehow, Wrath was not yet dead, the combination of his own consciousness and that of Tav's fighting to keep the body alive. "Do you really care that much about him?"

V now stepped forward. "He is an innocent human, he doesn't deserve the punishment that Wrath has incurred."

God chuckled to himself, amused at the sight of his once-subjects returning to his realm solely in order to protect a measly human.

"Well, if you truly care so much..." God brought up his hand once again, and put his palm against Wrath's forehead. Within seconds, darkness began to emit from the body of Tav, and collected in a vaguely person-shaped form to Tav's left. Out of the darkness now stood Wrath himself, entirely separate from Tav.

Tav blinked open his eyes. This time, he saw through his own eyes, *not* Wrath's. He swiftly stood up and took mental note of everyone who was currently standing in the throne room: The Fallen, consisting of Elias, Rukii, V, and Azriel, who were behind him; Wrath, who was beside him; God, who was standing over him; and Mercy, who was standing behind God and slightly to the left, near Wrath.

Despite having just been stabbed through the chest, he didn't feel any pain. In fact, when he looked down, there was no blood. His clothes were clean and undamaged.

"Cheap move," Wrath huffed with what little breath he had left. It seemed to Tav by the sight of him that despite having been separated, Wrath retained the damage that God had done while he was still within Tav's body. He was battered and bloody, the essence of his life ruining the impeccable shine of the throne room floors.

Tav jumped backwards as Wrath summoned his sword once again.

"What..."

"This fight doesn't concern you anymore," Wrath told Tav quietly. Despite everything, it seemed as though this fight wasn't over. A wound in the chest wasn't enough to stop him. *Nothing* was enough.

"Over here!" the familiar voice of V echoed through the room. Tav ran towards the Fallen, and took up a spot behind Elias, dual swords drawn. He was entirely uncertain what would happen next, and it looked to him as though the Fallen were right there with him.

As Wrath readied himself to attack God once again, Mercy now stood by her brother's side, sword drawn. God couldn't help but laugh at the sight of it; Mercy, a formidable force in her own right, standing beside her weak and pathetic brother.

"How can you, the holiest of children, defend such a vile creature?" God asked her. "You dare challenge me in *my* realm?"

Mercy didn't waver.

"I challenge you not out of defiance, but out of love."

"*Love?*" God hissed. "You speak of love after he turned his back on holy reign? After he sought to seize the throne?"

Mercy's eyes brimmed with tears, but her resolve remained unshaken.

"He is my brother, and despite whatever you may think, I will not abandon him."

With a mighty yell, Wrath once again lunged at his father. Their swords clashed, sending sparks flying. Wrath was fueled now not just by hatred and passion, but by desperation. He couldn't lose; there was no *way* he could lose. Not like last time.

Their swords continued to clash with ferocity, and Mercy watched as her brother put up what little fight he had left. God clearly had the advantage here, between his irrefutable strength and the weakened state of his son. And yet, Wrath pushed on, defending the barrage of attacks from his father.

But, it didn't last forever. Mercy watched as God sent Wrath's sword flying across the room, and since Wrath didn't have the strength to summon an energy blast, was left effectively disarmed. Wrath began to back up, the far wall of the throne room getting closer with every backwards step.

"Now, Wrath," said God, inching ever closer to his son, "You will pay for what you've done. For your attempts on the throne, for defying the Holy Order, and for *corrupting your own sister.*"

Wrath was not about to take this lying down. He realized, however, that there really was no getting out of it this time. God was fully ready to kill him, and if that's what God wants...

"BROTHER!"

Mercy put her hand out and summoned a portal beneath Wrath's feet. She hoped that this would offer him some escape before their father had the chance to kill him. God's deadly blow of his sword was met with air, and Wrath was gone..

God lowered his head. Despite not being able to see his face, Mercy could tell that he was beyond angry. He had transcended anger; his rage now knew no bounds.

· · · ·

"I have to do something."

Elias turned back to Tav.

"What?"

Tav raised his head.

"I can't just sit back and watch while she fights by herself." The battle shifted focus from Wrath to Mercy, and all of God's pent up anger was now directed at her. She was putting up a pretty good fight, but Tav could tell that God was still pushing the advantage.

"Let it happen. This does not concern us."

"But I feel like it does, though," Tav countered, walking forward. He and Elias were side by side now. "If she's this place's last line of defense, then the least we can do is help."

Tav walked forward, then broke out into a sprint. He readied his swords, and went in for a strike to God's side. God, all-knowing, parried the strike, and sent Tav flying backwards. But, Tav wasn't about to give up that easily. He stood up and went again, attempting to get a hit in while Mercy was fighting for her life.

"What are you doing?" Mercy asked Tav hurriedly.

"Helping you," Tav said between strikes of his swords.

"You shouldn't get involved," she cautioned him in between strikes. "He's more powerful than you could ever imagine."

"All the more reason that I should help."

Mercy looked at Tav, and Tav looked at Mercy. In a fleeting moment, they exchanged a smile.

"Well shit," Rukii started, "We can't just let them have all the fun. Let's get in on this."

Elias looked around to his compatriots, all of which looked like they were itching to fight, especially now that Tav was involved.

"So be it."

With that, the Fallen took off. Rukii was the first to get a hit in, his tracking arrow flying straight into God's shoulder. That wasn't enough to take him down, however, as God just pulled the arrow out without so much as a drop of blood. V was next to strike, getting up close and personal with the opposition, her staff landing each counter perfectly.

Azriel went for a risky move and threw their daggers from a distance, hoping they would behave similarly to throwing stars or kunai knives. Fortunately, both of them landed, but God's defense was just too strong, and the daggers soon dissipated into nothingness.

Mercy was at the head of the fight now. Her swordsmanship was better than any of the Fallen, so she had the best shot at taking him down. The Fallen were aware of this, and chose to only go for hits when Mercy's defenses were open.

"Did you not learn your lesson the first time?" God asked as he defended himself against enemies that were once loyal subjects. "I would have thought one instance of getting banished would have been enough for you."

Another arrow from Rukii that God had to remove. He was starting to get frustrated.

"I am all-powerful, you can't possibly hope to kill me!"

In his moment of pride, God had left himself wide open. Mercy plunged her holy sword straight through God's heart, his true weak point. They all watched as God, the once almighty, dropped to his knees, gasping for air. He dropped his sword, and it slowly ceased to exist.

Mercy gritted her teeth, shoving the sword even deeper into her father's chest.

"This. Ends. Here."

God looked up to his daughter's eyes, which burned bright blue with the ferocity of a thousand suns. He took in a breath to speak.

"Mercy..." He sputtered blood. "You know I will always love you." Another struggling breath. Then, like stardust, the body of God began to disintegrate.

"You will regret this."

• • • •

CHAPTER 32

In the moments after the battle, Tav took note of the state of things. He hadn't even realized how the fight had affected the architecture of the throne room; stone pillars were toppled over, dust littered the ground, and the shine of the blades that once cast light across the room were now dormant.

Mercy was now on her knees, feeling the ground with her hands for the dusty remains of her father. Her tears intermingled with the dust.

Tav approached Mercy, desiring with every bit of himself to comfort her somehow. He put a hand on her shoulder, and she flinched.

"Oh," she whispered, no longer startled. "It's you."

Tav crouched down next to Mercy, watching as she retracted her hand from the ground.

"I'm sorry," said Tav gently.

Mercy shook her head.

"No, it's..." She sighed heavily, then looked up. All of the Fallen were now surrounding her, V and Rukii crouched down at her level. Elias and Azriel remained standing, ever at attention.

"I... I know now... what I must do..." Mercy stammered with every last ounce of strength that she could muster. She stood, legs shaky, and walked towards the three thrones at the front of the room. Very carefully, she sat down in the largest of the three thrones.. Her tone then took on an air of royalty.

"Tav Segol, of Earth," Mercy began. "Come forward."

Tav stood and walked over to the throne. He kneeled, looking up to Mercy expectantly.

"I sincerely thank you for your efforts. You may now return to Earth. I will return you to the state in which you left, however the curse of Wrath will no longer be effective."

Tav nodded. "Thank you, Mercy."

Mercy smiled weakly at Tav, then directed her attention to the fallen. "Azriel, Elias, Rukii, V. The Fallen Angels of the Heaven-realm."

The Fallen came to the throne, each of them dropping to a kneel in respect.

"You are faced now with two realities," said Mercy. "You can live the rest of your days on Earth, and one day return to the Heaven-realm. Or, you can remain in the Heavenrealm as of this moment. It is up to you individually to decide."

The Fallen looked amongst themselves, certain that they all knew what they would prefer to do.

"We will serve you on Earth, your majesty," Elias uttered quietly, ever with a sense of diplomacy. "We will return to you when the time comes."

"Very well," said Mercy. "I thank you all once again for your services. May you live your days in peace and prosperity."

• • • •

Knock, knock, knock. Tav stood in front of the door, unsure as to why he decided to knock instead of just walking in. It was his house, after all.

Within a moment, Rysha answered the door. His eyes lit up with a dual sense of relief and pride.

"You're back," he said quietly.

Tav nodded, and before he could think of anything else to say, flung himself into Rysha for a hug. Rysha returned it, happy that his son returned in one piece.

"What happened?" Rysha asked.

Tav stood back, and a smirk crept across his face.

"It would take longer for me to explain than I probably have left."

Rysha laughed.

"Hey, that's my thing." He motioned for Tav to come inside, and Tav stepped into his home. He was finally free.

Meanwhile, the members of the Fallen walked in tandem on the streets of New York City. They were each fully human now, dressed to the nines as they approached the restaurant, *Le Bistro Avenue*.

"I've been dying to check this place out," said V, adjusting her sunglasses against the September sun's rays.

"I can't believe I put on a suit for this," said Rukii, tugging at the hem of his shirt.

"Oh, quit," replied V. "It could be worse."

"That's for sure," Azriel muttered.

They all stopped as they approached the doors.

"Well," said Elias, "I think this is all worth celebrating."

"To new beginnings!" V cheered.

• • • •

"Thank you," Tav beamed as he stood adjacent to his art exhibit. December could not have come soon enough; he and Carlina had had their pieces ready since the middle of November, so the rest of school before winter break had been nothing but one big waiting game.

Now, in this moment, Tav wanted the show to last forever. Everything, from the high-class people, to the smells of fancy perfumes, all the way down to the snacks at the snack table; Everything was perfect.

"Of course, my boy," The man replied as he adjusted his glasses to get a better look at the art on the wall behind Tav. Tav had ended up with a total of five pieces, each different but similarly styled from each other.

"I particularly like this one, what did you draw inspiration from?" the man asked, pointing at a specific piece on the wall behind him.

"Oh, this one?" Tav looked behind himself to see which one the man was referring to. It was the one that depicted the fight with God and the Fallen. In it, white beams of light emitted from a center point in the ground, with a sword, specifically Mercy's, stabbing through it.

"Personal experience," Tav replied. He had been practicing that response ever since Mrs. Edwards had asked him about his inspiration.

"Interesting," she had said.

The man stepped closer to get an even better look, and Tav sidestepped out of the way.

"The details on this sword are immaculate," the man remarked, studying every detail of Mercy's blade. He then stepped back and looked around himself, then to Tav. He stepped very close to him, and handed him a card.

"I'm the Fine Arts professor at Timber Creek Conservatory in Ohio. I'd really love to see you in my class once you graduate high school."

Tav took the card in his hands, then looked up. Richard Foxx, was his name. "Really?"

"Absolutely. Your art is not only passionate, but *detailed* in a way that I'm not used to seeing. I think you would fit in well at the Conservatory."

"W-wow," Tav stammered, not sure exactly what to say. "Thank you... Ohio?"

"Yes, it's not as bad of a drive as you'd think. Mostly corn fields and highways." The man chuckled to himself, and Tav followed along. "But, regardless, when you get around to deciding what to do after college, give me a ring."

"Thank you," Tav replied once again. He and the man shook hands, and the man started to walk away.

"Oh, one more thing," the man said as he turned around, then stood fully in front of Tav. "I think I can help you get scholarships, perhaps full ride. I've only offered that to one other student here, so do with that what you will."

Tav nodded. "Right." Then, the man walked away. Tav once again looked at the card in his hands. *Full ride?* he thought. *Isn't that like, everything getting paid for?* Tav looked off into the distance as he thought. *In Ohio? That's kind of far away.*

"Tav!" His thoughts were interrupted by the sound of Carlina's voice. "Come look!"

Tav turned to where Carlina was yelling from, which was over by their joint-exhibit, the *Brawler 7* diorama. It had ended up being a lot bigger than either Tav or Carlina could have ever anticipated, taking up nearly an entire card table. Tav approached the table and looked at Carlina, who was holding up a ribbon.

"We got first in the 3-Dimensional category," Carlina proudly declared, yet at a lower volume now that Tav was standing right beside her.

"No way, really?" Tav asked, motioning for Carlina to hand him the ribbon. She did, and sure enough, they had been awarded first place by the New York City Art Society.

"Damn," Tav muttered as he looked over the badge. "This is awesome!"

"I know, right?" Carlina replied. "Oh, and something else cool happened, but I'll tell you later."

"Oh?"

"Yeah..." Carlina looked at Tav, and Tav looked at Carlina. He was certain he knew what she was talking about. Entirely on a hunch, Tav took out the card the art professor had given him. Carlina gasped.

"You too?" She asked, shuffling her own card out of her own pocket. Tav nodded. Carlina shook her head playfully, then smiled at Tav. "Sheesh."

Tav smiled back, then put his hand out, asking Carlina for her own. Once their fingers were interlocked, Tav felt the weight of the world lift off his shoulders. He couldn't wait to tell Rysha.

• • • •

END

Milton Keynes UK
Ingram Content Group UK Ltd.
UKHW010838220224
438295UK00004B/190